"Think *Angela's Ashes* magnified. . . . To read a writer as skilled as Aitken is a pleasure and the sincere hope is that she has more novels in her."
— *The Free Lance-Star*

"From the very beginning, I was mesmerized by how the story was written. . . . A complex and multilayered story that is beautiful, magical and sad, *The Island Child* is a book that you will want to consume in one sitting."
—Dunja Bonacci Skenderović, Bookreporter.com

"A confident tale. . . . Inspired in part by Irish folklore and in part by Persephone . . . this is a story steeped in fable, but also inescapably rooted in the real world."
— *The Irish News*

"Aitken's evocative prose immerses us in island life. . . . [The novel] excel[s] at depicting [these] hermetic communities and liminal landscapes. . . . Oona is a wonderful creation, alive on the page. . . . The success of the book is the vibrancy of its writing and narrative voice. Readers will be carried along by Oona."
— *The Irish Times*

"Haunting. . . . Aitken's prose is by turns placidly lyrical, humorous, and sharply pointed. . . . Bold and perceptive, Aitken's self-assured storytelling and understanding of classic themes stand out in contemporary Irish fiction."
— *Publishers Weekly* (starred review)

"A dreamy fairy tale winds its way through this moody story of loss and redemption." —*Library Journal*

"A fevered intensity drives British writer Aitken's debut. . . . Aitken's lyrical voice evokes the perilous fishing community and the harsh beauty of the island." —*Kirkus Reviews*

"I read *The Island Child* in a day, and I know I'll be coming back to it. It reads like a dream. Written in quietly sorcerous prose, this novel combines the uncluttered abstraction of a fable with the odd calamitous detail. Like the casts of fairy stories, Aitken's characters can stand for as much as you want them to—but they're also fully realized individuals who come to you through peeks and glances, so that without being able to pinpoint how it happened, you know them, and feel you always have. This is a thrillingly original debut, and I can't wait to see what Aitken does next." —Naoise Dolan, author of *Exciting Times*

Molly Aitken

The Island Child

Molly Aitken was born in Scotland in 1991 and brought up in Ireland. She has an MFA in creative writing from Bath Spa University, where she was awarded the Janklow & Nesbit Prize for her novel. She was shortlisted for *Writing Magazine*'s adult fairy tale competition in 2016 and has a story in the *Irish Imbas: Celtic Mythology Collection 2017*. She lives in Sheffield, England.

The Island Child

The Island Child

A NOVEL

Molly Aitken

VINTAGE BOOKS

A Division of Penguin Random House LLC

New York

FIRST VINTAGE BOOKS EDITION, JUNE 2021

Grateful acknowledgment is made to Carcanet Press Limited and W. W. Norton
& Company, Inc. for permission to reprint "The Pomegranate" from *In a Time
of Violence* by Eavan Boland. Copyright © 1994 by Eavan Boland. Subsequently
published in *New Collected Poems* by Eavan Boland. Copyright © 2005 by Eavan
Boland. All rights reserved. International copyright secured. Reprinted by
permission of Carcanet Press Limited and W. W. Norton & Company, Inc.

The Library of Congress has cataloged the Knopf edition as follows:
Name: Aitken, Molly, author.
Title: The island child : a novel / Molly Aitken.
Description: First edition. | New York : Alfred A. Knopf, 2020.
Identifiers: LCCN 2019044205
Classification: LCC PR 6101.A84 185 2020 | DDC 823/.92—dc23
LC record available at https://lccn.loc.gov/2019044205

Vintage Books Trade Paperback ISBN: 978-0-593-08091-7
eBook ISBN: 978-0-525-65838-2

Book design by Soonyoung Kwon

www.vintagebooks.com

Printed in the United States of America
10 9 8 7 6 5 4 3 2 1

For my mother, Maureen,
and for all the other mothers

The only legend I have ever loved is
the story of a daughter lost in hell.

—EAVAN BOLAND, "THE POMEGRANATE"

The Island Child

The Virgin in the Storm

I began with my mam, just like my daughter began with me.

My mam whispered the story of my birth to hook the fear in me, to keep me shut up at home with her, but as a child I loved to hear how I came to the island, because it linked me to him, the other baby born during the storm.

Mam told it like so: she was stood by the wall in front of our cottage, waiting. No one was about on the road or in the fields, but below her the bay was busy with boats. Purple clouds climbed the blue; thin and wispy at first and building to heavy stacks that spread like flames in the gorse. A storm prickled in the air. Mam scanned about for Dad's currach but didn't know his from any other. She thanked God my brother Kieran and the baby Enda were too young to be out and were safely playing in front of the neighbour Bridget's hearth so Mam could arrange the house before I came. Already the fishermen were struggling back towards the pier against the sharp-toothed waves. The fear had lit the men.

On the island, the sea was what separated women from men. Women weren't taken by the water. Instead, mothers were drained by dropping tears over the bodies of their dead sons. Grandmothers vanished into old age early, almost as quick as waning moons, and girls were drowned in the tides of birthing blood. Men fought death on the sea, women in the home.

Mam pushed away these thoughts and turned her focus inwards. For weeks I'd been beating against her belly like a bird trapped in a chimney. She couldn't wait to be rid of me and not a drip of terror had entered her about it. She'd already had my two brothers without a bother. What could go wrong with the third?

Thunder rumbled as far off as the mainland, rolling in across the waves to shake the stones, waking the giant, sleeping whale beneath, the mother of the island. Mam had never heard the tale—and it was Bridget who told me—but still, Mam felt the whale's shudder and unease build in her as she watched two currachs skip further out across the swell. She could picture the laughter on Dad as he and the other rowers pushed on into the wild waves. If the sea stole him, Mam would be left to fend for herself with three children and she knew if she was alone the island would kill her. She told me all this on one of our many drawn-out days of sighs and work in the kitchen, but still I must have sensed her weakness. With my new fingernails I scratched at a thread inside her and snapped it. Water splashed her bare feet—I couldn't say why she wore no shoes on that day but before she had me she must've lived in a wilder, happier woman.

Pain ripped through her then and she sank to her knees as if to pray but it was curses that appeared on her tongue—I know because I shouted those words myself when I was having my own daughter—but, unlike me, my mam swallowed them down, leaving them to rot in her chest.

Mam hauled herself through the doorway and forgot to look back to see if Dad's boat was coming home.

A square of light shifted across the floor and was extinguished with rain slashing through the wide-open door. Mam sat on the floor, lips bleeding from biting back the shouts inside her while the Virgin watched her from the dresser, a string of prayer beads wrapped around her saintly neck and a wilting meadow flower at her porcelain feet. For the first time since Mam had landed on the island, she didn't pray to the mother of Himself. She never told me why, but it might have been because she felt she couldn't live up to the Mother of Mercy with whom she shared a name or she believed a mortal woman was no good in a case as bad as me.

With Mary's painted blue eyes burning her back, Mam braced herself against the wall and pleaded with God—she only ever made the big requests to Him—to cut the agonies of me, her child, away, but like most men, He wasn't one to involve himself with women's matters.

Somehow Mam got herself into the big room. Lightning flashed in the matchbox window and was swallowed by the dark clutch of the storm. The pains tearing through Mam went on and on and on but I gave her no urge to push. She wouldn't let herself think this was different from the times before but somewhere at the back of her mind she knew I would be the difficult child.

She prayed again to God and listened for His answer, but all she heard was the tormented roar of the storm. Where was Ardàn? Why didn't Bridget return the boys to her? Through the open bedroom door the kitchen stared its blank emptiness at her. She laid herself on the bed and gave in to the moans and shouts.

*

On the ragged sea, Dad, Old Daithi and Young Liam rowed back, their laughter plucked from their throats by the wind. They weren't far, almost in the shallows, when Dad's hat was whipped from his head and, looking back, he saw the tiny boat belonging to Colm, the pretty man with wicked eyes who was loved by all the women, even Mam. As Dad watched, the sickle of boat vanished into the tar-painted fingers of cloud and rain.

*

Over the sound of her broken breaths Mam heard the groan of a door and the drip drip of water on the floor.

The sheets scratched rough against her damp and heaving body. She panted, waiting for the next wave, and as it rolled through her she looked up and a blue vision of the Virgin stood before her. Mam knew in her soul, even though she'd ignored the figurine on the dresser, that the cold ceramic had transformed into blood and flesh and come to save her.

"Holy," Mam said. It was the only word she could think of for the beautiful, saintly face hovering over her.

The room flickered with shadows cast by one sputtering lamp. Somewhere, far off, she heard a whisper: *Your child will die.*

"Did you hear that?" Mam mumbled.

No one answered. She looked about, but all she saw was dark and light swirling into each other. Fear gripped her throat and she wanted to weep. Had it been one of the little folk or the words of our Lord? She knew in her bones what she had heard was true.

Soft hands smoothed across her stomach and, above her, hair stuck out like moon rays.

"The baby hasn't turned. She's stuck," the Virgin said in English, and to Mam it seemed right that a holy woman would speak with education. "I need to cut her out."

"No!" Mam cried in Irish.

"You'll die if I don't." There was something familiar about that shimmering hair, but Mam couldn't grasp it, even when she reached out and clutched a straw strand, it slipped away. She's fat herself, Mam thought, with Himself no doubt, but then a hand reached inside her and all thoughts, except of fish hooks, vanished.

*

Outside the storm swelled the sea.

Dad, Liam and Daithi dragged the currach up the rocks. When the boat was far beyond the shoreline Dad swung the basket of fish over his shoulder, waving to the others, and pushed through the rain towards home. When he banged open the cottage door Mam's shouts cut through the wailing of the sky. It was many nudges of the clock's finger before Dad moved, and when he did he didn't go to her. Instead he poured a whiskey and drank it from the tumbler in one gulp and filled another. The big room was no place for a man.

Someone had caught wind that Mam was having me and a shoal of fishermen trudged into the kitchen, brave enough to come into Mam's sacred space now they had the reason: to wet my head. They perched on stools, passed pipes and swigged from bottles they'd carried with them through the lashing rain. Old Daithi appeared with my brothers on each hip, delivered back from the warmth of his wife Bridget's hearth, and laid them down in the nook.

"Did any of yous see Colm go out in his boat?" Dad croaked.

The men shook their heads and Dad wondered if the storm had tricked his eyes.

Young Liam called for a song from Dad, who was well-known for his voice, but he had no fire in him for it. There was a fearful hush among them. Mam or I might die in the cold bedroom while they sat warmed by the tongue burn of poitín and the lit turf. Dad watched the clock by the light of every candle.

Kieran stood up from where he'd been sat in the nook and began to sing. While he sang that tune, bringing mist to wrinkled eyes, my brother was probably the sweetest he'd ever be, still wearing a dress to scare the little people away as everyone was sure it was boys they wanted and not a girl.

No one thought to boil the water for tea.

*

Mam woke to a searing red pain. She pulled up her dress and across her belly a wobbly line of stitches grinned up at her. The Virgin's sewing was neat.

She bit her arm to stifle the scream.

*

In the kitchen, there was a hum of snores and the quiet talk of those who'd woken for another glass. The air was blue with smoke, but as the door of the big room burst open red seeped in and the men still sleeping woke. Stained feet poked from under a splattered nightie and against Mam's chest she clutched a baby dipped in dye. Red; not like the stacks of kelp that lined the beaches, or the flash of a grandmother's skirts, or the lips of a child. It was the red of death.

The men pulled away like waves parting from the shore.

"Where's the Virgin?" Mam said.

They shifted and stared at their soft cowhide shoes. Not one of them said a word, but a few glanced fearfully at the figurine tenderly smiling at them from the dresser.

"Am I all alone now?" Mam moaned, somehow forgetting the whole new person in her hands.

"You're all right," said Old Daithi, the only one able to find a good use for his tongue. "Will I take the child from you there?"

"No." Her fingers gripped me. No man would take her only girl from her.

"I'll get my Bridget to be with you," he said. "A woman's touch is what you need, Mary, and you shouldn't be alone in there." He pointed at the birth room. No one thought to ask why he'd not gone for his wife earlier. "Amn't I right, Ardàn?" he said.

Dad stood, blinking at these two strangers who were his wife and child. He was halfway across the kitchen, arms opening, when she turned and trod back into the other room, leaving him looking down at a dark wet patch sinking into the earth-packed floor.

"Well," Daithi said. "Shall we welcome the child to our island?"

Dad nodded slowly. "I've a terrible thirst on me."

*

The lamp had sputtered out in the big bedroom; only the scent of burnt fat still hung in the air. Mam lay cold, bare-legged on the bed. She lifted her dress again to run a finger along the grinning line of stitches on her stomach. She shuddered and let the dress drop. Forget, she told herself, forget the Mary with the knife. Forget the voice that whispered to her of death. Forget.

Beside her was a small, mewling thing. She parted its legs and smiled. This girl wouldn't be like the boys. A daughter needs her mother. A daughter never drowns, never leaves.

She didn't feed me but I stayed quiet and she thought it a good sign for our future together.

*

Far from our cottage, on a rocky shore, a woman sat trembling in her blue dress waiting to see if her man would return from the sea. There was blood on her hands and her prayers were not to God or any pure woman, they were to the sea-people, the ones with spined fingers that dragged fishermen down to their deaths.

She begged and sang to the waters, calling to them, to her people, and on a bed of fish skeletons and shell coffins she pushed out a boy. The crash of waves was his arrival choir. The howl of the storm his midwife.

The woman named him Felim.

Once, a woman gave birth to a daughter. The girl was beautiful and unspoiled and the new mother loved her. With her baby in her arms, the new mother felt whole and perfect too. Her daughter at her breast, she knew the circular nature of the world. Life flowed through her.

But time passed, and her child grew and grew, and the new mother, no longer new, began to feel afraid.

———————————

The Woman

If I was to tell the story of my daughter, Joyce, I wouldn't start with her birth. I would begin with the first time I lost her. She was four or five, wearing an egg-yolk yellow dress I'd sewn for her, and we walked through town together. She skipped beside me, scorching away the last of the winter bitterness with her bright glow. We'd eaten our first ice creams of the year and there was chocolate on her chin when she turned her face up to me and laughed. We were hand in hand, her blood pulsing in my palm. We were joined, and suddenly she was gone.

*

Lake water nips my feet, stones drive up sharp between my toes, and I am walking in the shallows with too much time to think.

It's been six days since I saw Joyce, back from university, her fingernails gnawed, runners scuffed and a pink heat rising up her neck. Her breath was mint and tea as she asked me to tell her where she came from, and after years of stopping up the words I could say nothing except the one thing that would hurt her most. Words said cannot be taken back.

After she left me I stood there on the porch, alone for a long time, until the sun bled behind the black trees. Even though her shoulders now brush adulthood, the loss of her feels the same as when she was small; no, it's worse because now I know she will never come back to me.

When Pat drove up to the house, night had fully landed.

"Joyce inside?" he called, half out the car door, struggling with something on the passenger seat.

"No. She's gone."

"But there's no bus at this time. It's pitch-black on the road."

"She just wanted to leave."

"Did you fight?" He was walking up the path towards me, whatever it was on the seat abandoned, forgotten.

"No, not really." I found I could move again and I was running down the path and yanking my car's door open.

"Oona!"

I drove blind, away from the town, keeping off the roads Joyce might have taken, and somehow made my way to the lake.

Pat didn't follow me.

*

It's twenty years since I came to Canada, landing in a city of strange fogs, empty of the crash and shush of the sea. I stepped off a boat, and then a bus, and the further away I got the easier it was to numb that early part of my life, to try to forget, but now all I seem able to do is remember. Joyce opened up something in me and now it's all rushing back.

From this spot I can see the stretch of water where ten years ago she learned to swim with her dad and uncle Enda. She screeched every time Enda threw her, the sun hammering down and her and Enda getting progressively pinker, Pat browner, while I in the shade of an oak sank against the earth, watching. I wanted to run but I stayed to soak in her joy at the day and her new-found uncle.

Enda dazzled with the brilliance of a dying star and she gazed up at him, the only one of us not blinded. So many memories are grimy now, but I remember that afternoon with a pure clarity. Memories with him and with Joyce are colourful. I can still smell the fat sparking on Pat's barbecue and her laughter at the men's jokes, told just for her.

Joyce and my childhood are the clearest in me still. They are what I choose to remember.

I brought almost nothing with me here to the cabin. Only the clothes on my back and whatever was in the trunk. I passed the gas station and never thought to stop. The lack of anything useful has made the cabin like a place outside of time, a place where memory lives.

I wake when the dawn light brushes the fir trees on the other side of the lake, I fill the kettle from the stream for my tea and the mourning dove coos from a branch close by. Even when it's raining and the other birds are silently sheltering, she still blasts out her sadness.

*

It's cold at night here, even though it's May, and I lie awake. I remember that year I wasn't Joyce's mother but just a body trudging about the house, never once combing her hair as she cried into a pillow, I never once sang her to sleep but she still came to me while I was curled up by the stove. In a faltering voice she asked me if I was awake. There was a rustle and a sigh as she sank down close to me and her long body wrapped against mine and I was able to sleep. When I woke she was gone, but it was easier to breathe.

*

I lost her and she was only four years old and every piece of the past fell away and I realised none of it mattered, because my hand was empty. I ran about the streets shouting her name, for some unknown reason looking up instead of down. I told myself, I will be a good mother. I will love her, every part of her. And when I did find her squatting by a black cat, her head to one side, everything, every piece of the past, rushed back again and I was whole, but broken.

How quickly I ignored the promises I made myself while I searched for my child. When she left me standing on the porch six days ago, I didn't run after her to say I was sorry for what I had done.

*

I came here to the lake to plan the end of my story, but I can't stop thinking about the beginning and about Joyce.

Spinners of Tales

"Would you believe, I saw Aislinn naked on the shore?"

I sat up straight, all my body straining towards Pegeen's words. It was late in the afternoon and the rhythmic clack of the pedals had been lulling me to sleep where I was curled in the hearth nook but the hum of the wheels slowed. My heart bumped loud in my ears. No one spoke of Aislinn. I stayed still as a dead man, hoping they'd forgotten I was there. She was my forbidden fruit, the outsider, and like every child I wanted what was secret and denied.

"When did you see her?" Mam hissed.

"Last night. Bold as anything."

"Were you alone?"

"I know what you're meaning, Mary, but Liam wasn't with me. He'd have fallen down dead to see such a sight as that."

Bridget snorted.

A basket of wool concealed me from the three women. I was crouched, sticky in the warmth, by the hearth on the thin bed. I liked it when Mam had the neighbours over. She shouted at me less and I had not yet begun school, even though I was almost eight, so it was good to have faces and voices different from Mam's.

"Only a bad soul would be out when the little people are about," Pegeen said, sounding gleeful.

"And what were you doing out, so?" Bridget was quick, even though she was ancient, at least seventy. She was the one who told me Aislinn's son was born in the big storm like me. It meant we were destined to be friends so I watched through the back window, waiting for my first sight of him.

"Aislinn was standing there, nothing on her, calling down a storm on us," Pegeen continued. "You know she killed her husband with a storm. If anyone is a sea-fairy, it's her."

"God protect us." That was Mam.

"It's only a story," Bridget murmured.

"But it's a true one," Pegeen said.

On the island, what was true was loose; a truth was generally agreed by everyone to be a good story.

I peered out of the nook. Pegeen wore a fancy shawl that Mam was eyeing with the kind of fierceness I sometimes caught the men giving her scooped-out hips. There was a bleak hunger in those men's eyes. It made me wish Mam had the salty hair and wind-hardened faces of the other island women.

I stared hard at Bridget as the pile of wool like sea froth in her lap transformed into a smooth thread on the wheel, willing her to turn and see me. Last winter she had come only the odd time and never stayed long enough for me to soak up her gentle hands and rumbling voice. When I was small she had been with us most days as my birth had weakened Mam and, perched on Bridget's knees, I was fed milk and stories about the little people. I would push my nose against her to catch the tangy smell of black bread nestled in the folds of her skirts and skin. In the nights when Bridget was gone Mam whispered to me that my badness made me hard to love, hissing prayers to make me good. It was all in English, just for me. The islanders all spoke Irish for everyday, for fishing and farming and the hearth, and English was just for the tourists, but I knew it in a personal way, the language of what was bad in me. It was only later I learned the good in English, how it could set me free.

Once I heard Mam telling Bridget a voice of an angel told her I would die. She didn't sound all that sad about it. My death was a holy excitement to her. The old woman laughed, but I knew Mam had faith in angels' words.

Pegeen sneezed and her wheel faltered.

"I like Aislinn's teas and medicinals," Bridget said. "She kept my Daithi with me last winter with her healing."

Mam had never once visited Aislinn. I would know. She always kept me with her.

"I send Liam if we need a cure," Pegeen whispered.

My legs were aching from being bunched up to balance my chin. The women were quiet again, their wheels whirring. Talk of the strange woman had seeped away as if she was a creature they only dreamed of. Everyone was like that about Aislinn and her boy. They were forgotten until they had to be remembered.

I was about to climb down when I heard the door, a slight footfall and the smell of altar oil and rotten eel.

I sank back onto the mattress, gritting my teeth as the straw stuffing creaked.

"Afternoon." It was the priest.

I held my breath. He set everyone jumpy.

"We were just talking about Mrs. Kilbride, Father," Pegeen said. "I saw her dancing like a pagan on the seashore last night."

There was a long pause. I tried not to move, even though my underarm was itchy.

"I was thinking," the priest said—he was new to the island and got to thinking a lot. "We must bring Mrs. Kilbride and her son to the church. You could talk to her, Mrs. Coughlan. You two women have a lot in common. Both outsiders here with children the same age."

"I'm nothing like her, Father," Mam spat. He must have touched a private hurt in her because she usually would never be rude to a holy man.

"Aislinn's not a believer," Bridget said. "English," she added, as if this explained everything.

"Didn't you know she's a heathen, Father?" Pegeen asked. "And she's bringing that boy up pagan too."

"You can't blame a child for their parents' sins. The boy's an angel at heart."

Bridget believed it most, as she loved all children, but people were always saying Felim was an angel. Dad had told me that when God banished Satan, He threw out the bad angels too and they became the little people, the ones who lived in the sea and rocked the waves to swallow men's souls. The ones who wandered the land and led us down their hidden paths with blinking lanterns. No one ever returned when a fairy touched them. I thought and thought on it but couldn't get to knowing how he had become so precious the night we were born.

"I'd not want Aislinn in our church, Father," Mam said. "She's a bad influence."

"Aislinn's a beauty," Bridget said.

"Wouldn't all the men's mouths be hanging open," Pegeen said. "And not one of them would listen to a word of the Bible. But I'd not expect you to notice a woman in that way, Father."

"Well, now." He cleared his throat.

I tried not to giggle.

"You are a good Christian woman, Mary." The priest's voice was always raspy when he talked to the men, like he was dying of the thirst, but when he said Mam's name it came out gentle as a sigh. Maa-rryy. Maaarry. It was the same when he was reading in church and I was always near falling asleep. His words were so smooth and empty. "You could invite her in, Mar— Mrs. Cough-lan. Show her God's love."

Pegeen snorted and coughed to cover it. She thought, like me, that Mam had very little love of her own to share around, God's even less.

I couldn't see why they'd be wanting to force Aislinn and her boy to go to church too. They were the only people who were free on Sunday mornings.

"Aislinn thinks church is a pain in the arse," I said and stood up on the bed, my head scraping the roof of the nook. "And so do I."

The spinning wheel treadles clattered to a halt.

A beautiful freedom had come over my tongue and I wanted to run with it. I jumped over the basket of wool and stepped out of the spitting hearth—Mam never got the island way of keeping the fire low to save turf.

I wouldn't let myself look at Mam, although I felt her stare prickle across my cheeks. Pegeen and Father Finnegan looked at me like I was a fish that'd sprouted wings, but Bridget gave me a quick flash of her wondrous crooked smile and this made me bolder.

"I know Aislinn doesn't listen to God," I told them. "She's a fairy so He threw her out." It didn't matter that I'd never met her.

I knew she felt like me. "She's better things to be doing with herself than going to church anyway."

The priest pressed a manky square of cloth to his nose and I finally let my eyes rise to Mam. She was red-faced and her hands were clenched around a bobbin thick with string. The warmth in me began to seep away. I should've kept my mouth shut and stayed hidden. I should not have let her see me, not when the talk had been of God and the woman she hated.

"Oona," Mam hissed. "Where did you hear such language?"

"Dad."

She sucked in a breath. I should've kept my mouth shut and not let the neighbours know Dad didn't believe in God.

"Say you're sorry to Father Finnegan," she said.

"Why?" I couldn't stop my mouth.

"Oona!" Mam's black eyes were on me.

"I'm so very sorry, Father." I put my hand over my mouth and stuck out my tongue the way Kieran did to Mam when her back was turned.

Mam yanked me to her side, away from the priest as if I might soil him with my dirty words.

"I'm sorry, Father," she said, her grip on my arm tightening. "I'll see she's punished."

"I pray for you that you do."

Father Finnegan went outside where he shook himself off in the rain, getting rid of the taint of me no doubt. Mam stared after him, a look of fear on her face like she was worried he was wondering whether to send her to hell because of my evil ways.

"I'd like for you to go now," Mam told Pegeen and Bridget.

Pegeen sniffed and gathered up her spools of wool and eyed me as she went out the front. The whole village would know by evening what I'd said. Bridget lifted her wheel, planted a peck on my forehead and left too.

I was alone with Mam.

I began edging towards the back door but in two strides she was across the room, grabbing my hand again.

"I'm sorry, Mammy, but does Aislinn really bring storms and kill men?" The words fell from me before I could swallow them to save for a sunshine day.

She dragged me towards the dresser and pushed me onto the floor. My knees smashed into the packed earth and I bit down the sobs scratching at my throat.

"Don't mention that woman's name under my roof."

"But why?"

"Pray, Oona."

On the dresser, Mary in her blue cloak with bone-white hands pressed together gazed above my head, silently judging me, and I judged her back. She never did anything, only had a son. She was nothing, not like the magical naked woman, Aislinn. And she wasn't like me. I would never be like the Virgin.

"Pray," Mam hissed. "Pray He'll forgive your wickedness."

I looked up to heaven, at the sky through the window, and asked for another mam.

The Little Window

My knees were already purple in the firelight; the praying had worn through my flesh to the bones. While I'd knelt for the rest of the afternoon, I begged Mary, in my mind, to make Mam forgive me for what I said to the priest and let me get up and have a scone. Mary ignored me. I tried God. He ignored me too. I thought about asking Mam herself, but as it had gone so bad with the other two, and they were holy, I couldn't see Mam showing kindness.

It was evening and Dad sat smoking in the nook, Mam outside taking down the washing, and me on the floor, determined to bruise my arse as well as my knees just so I could doubly pity myself. I chewed my lip, swallowing back the weeps threatening.

"What's that on your legs, girleen?" Dad asked.

"Nothing." I dropped my skirt and stood up.

"Come here to me." He beckoned me with a scarred finger. I loved his hands. They were just like him: strength under the thick skin; gentleness in the cushioned palms; fire too in the quick fingers.

I ran to him and climbed onto his lap. He smelled of pipe smoke and tar.

"Mam had me praying."

"Did she?" His voice hummed low and tuneful, but I still caught the slice of his anger in it. He fled religion the way Mam chased after it, more at home out in the sharp wind of the weather than in the dry and godly air of the church. It was a cause of constant silent sparks between them. One day, before I was born, they agreed to never talk about it with each other, although Mam talked plenty to the kitchen about God's grace and Mary's goodness. Dad would leave whenever she was wearing the ears off the walls, which was often, and I'd miss him then. He never took me because I was a girl so I was Mam's.

"How did it happen?" he asked.

"The praying, you mean?"

"Aye, that."

I told him what Pegeen had been saying about Aislinn singing naked to the sea.

"Well, you know you shouldn't believe what that woman says."

I settled myself, legs up, head back against his shoulder.

"How did Aislinn come to live with us on the island? Why did she not stay in England?"

Everyone knew that tourists like Aislinn who'd stayed weren't quite right. They didn't know the island ways, like how you had to stop in on your neighbours in winter to check on them, or that you should throw the dirty feet-water out at night so the fairies wouldn't break in.

"Aislinn," Dad said slowly, like her name was an oyster he was chewing over. "Was there ever an English girl given an Irish name like Aislinn?" He shook his head.

"Where did you meet her?"

"It was on Éag I first saw her."

A shudder went through me. Éag was the dead island where

we took the drowned after the wake to bury them before night came. Clouds and fogs and rains and shafts of blinding sunlight kept Éag hidden but when Éag appeared there was sure to be a death. Éag was showing Aislinn's husband the way to the shore, Kieran said, but Colm never made it. Kieran crowed with joy when I gasped and I didn't think how he couldn't have seen it because during that storm he was at Bridget's hearth.

"Not long before your brother Enda was born and Kieran was just below my knee, we were all over on Éag for a funeral. Aislinn was there to listen to the keener, she said, and I believe it, as a tourist likes to hear a funeral song, but people thought up all kinds of other reasons for her going. They said she was out fishing for a man and, well, there were a lot of whispers about her after. She had a queer kind of beauty that caught you like a spell and many of the men proposed to her right there at the funeral."

I laughed. "Did you ask her, Dad?"

"No. I was already wed to your mam." There was a sadness in his eyes as he watched the fire. I understood. I'd be sad if I married Mam myself. "Aislinn chose Colm," he said. "But it's good for her he drowned, even if it wasn't so good for himself. Colm was a hard man to get to know or like, and Aislinn—well, everyone was suspicious of her. She laughed a lot and was awful enthusiastic about everything. You couldn't walk into a house without hearing whispers about her. Although no one really had anything to go on, but Colm started to listen to them." He rubbed his forehead and I stayed quiet, letting him think. "Your mam was from the mainland, you know," he said. "And people didn't trust her at first, but she worked hard to be like us. Aislinn never tried to fit in and it brought out the worst in Colm in the end. I once saw her with a black eye."

"Pegeen said Aislinn killed Colm."

"Ah, no. Sure how could she have? He rowed himself out into that storm. The sea does what it will. Aislinn had nothing to do with it. Aislinn's—"

"What're you telling her?" Mam was stood in the doorway, her black hair yanked back in a knot, pulling her face tight like skin over a drum.

"Just a story," Dad said, as sweet as a sparrow, although anyone who knew Dad would know there was nothing birdlike about him. He was a water creature, slippery as anything. He was a seal.

Mam crossed her arms and went back outside.

Dad winked at me and put me back on the floor. It seemed like a good place to make a request. "Can I go to school after summer, Dad? I'm older than some of the children who already go."

"I'll speak to your mam about it. Now, I'd better be getting to gutting the catch or you'll go hungry."

He went out the front and I searched the bottom shelf for a bit of bread, but Mam had put all the food out of my reach. I knew he'd not say a word to her about school. Dad never rocked the boat of Mam's kitchen but I wished he would. I wished he would take me down to the water with him but he laughed whenever I asked.

My days were always the same, always with Mam. Up with the light to fetch the dried dung for the hearth and filling the teapot with two spoons—not three—of brown leaves. After breakfast, when Dad and the boys were gone, we cleaned the table; we sewed, mended, washed. We always stayed inside or close to the cottage. If I found the chance, I would gaze out the front window at the boats and imagine life was different. I imagined I went to school with my brothers, or lived on the mainland with my aunt Kate, or sometimes pretended the little people had stolen me away to Tír na nÓg to be their queen. In my dreams, I was free like Aislinn. In my dreams, Mam was dead.

Some days, when it was only Mam and me at home, she wept and wept and went back to bed. If a neighbour came to the door, I was to say Mam had gone to wash the clothes or to fetch my brothers or gather seaweed. I was never to mention it to Dad or the boys but I was sure they knew she cried, because at night I often heard her through the wall. But once, when I said to Enda that Mam had spent the day in bed and I'd made the dinner myself, his eyes grew so wide and his forehead so creased I never opened my mouth about Mam's sadnesses again. I'd seen that if you spoke your bitterness it spread and grew in others too.

The only days we were sure to leave the cottage were Sundays. Mam and I walked up the road, me on my toes trying to see the island, to drink in this place I called home, but I was too short so I waited to grow, and I did, but at seven, almost eight, I still wasn't tall enough to see beyond the grey stone walls.

Still sitting in the nook where Dad had left me, I blew on my knees to soothe them. The door banged and I jumped and turned but it was only Enda with a basket tied to his back and a frown on his wind-beaten face. Even though he was only a year and seven months older than me, he'd grown into the sleekness of a young crow while I still had the tufty hair of a pony, as he told me often.

Enda came and knelt near to me, his hands held out towards the fire and the basket still strapped to his back. He smelled of outside, of salt and air and sweat.

"I had to pray today," I said.

"And what did you talk to God about?"

"Nothing. He's never one for answering me."

"It might be that you're not talking to Him right. You have to be polite, Oona."

He was easily the best to look at in the family. Even without ever seeing myself I knew this, as everyone always smiled at the sight of him and never at me. Once Pegeen had said to me, "You're the picture of your brother," and I cried, "You don't mean Kieran, do you?," and she laughed so I knew she did. Enda was slim for his age, made for flying into the sky, but no good for heavy work. He still hadn't grown the muscles that had already pressed into the seams of Kieran's shirt at his age. Dad once growled to Daithi, "My youngest"—he meant Enda, not me—"was made for the schoolroom." And the old fisherman had grunted his sympathy. I knew this was true as Enda had a small frown line between his eyebrows from thinking and reading the Bible aloud for Mam some evenings. She would shut her eyes, her whole body rigid with listening. After he was done, she would sigh in a joyful way I never heard when I made her tea or helped with the scones or fetched the eggs without being asked.

Enda unhooked the basket from his back, set it on the floor and rubbed his shoulders. Kieran strode through the door in a haze of smoke; even though he was only twelve he had a lit pipe between his teeth almost as often as Dad. I never knew where he got the tobacco, as it wasn't cheap and had to be brought from the mainland. He was the spit of Dad. Short but with thick shoulders and a rounder, more boyish face than Enda. His lips were always busy either chewing, smoking, complaining or laughing.

"Food?" he cried to the room.

"Mam's at the washing," I said.

He strode across the kitchen and through the back door, calling out that he was starving in the pitiful, whining voice he used only for her. She could never resist him.

"Will you do us a play tonight, Enda?" I said.

Most nights Mam asked him to read from the Bible and he tickled all of us, except Mam, by doing the voices. The Old

Testament was best, although Mam wasn't as fond of it as she was of the New. Dad would make Enda do the stories he'd heard as a child at his mam's knee. They were the best of all. They were the ones Enda acted.

"Which story would you be having, littlie?" Enda asked me, as he climbed into the nook and rested his head against the warm hearthstone, staring up at nothing. He often was empty like this when he got back from a day's work.

"Saint Patrick is always a pleaser," I said. "Or—"

"I could act a new one," he whispered, as if he wasn't sure.

"That'd be nice for us."

"Don't sound so disappointed. I'll do the good man Saint Patrick for you, littlie." He held out his hand to me and I took it and squeezed. The light was coming back into him.

"What's it like out there today?" I asked.

"Well, Kieran and I went hunting. We climbed the cliffs and more than once I thought myself or him would fall to our deaths. In the end, all I got was a seagull."

I smacked my lips in appreciation.

"Kieran got more than me."

"Will you take me with yous next time, Enda?"

His smile fell away. I toed the floor.

"When I'm your age, do you think Mam will let me go off to hunt too?" Enda's nine years seemed so far away.

"Girls don't hunt, Oona."

Mam came in and laid the table with steaming potatoes, fried mackerel and two scones, which I knew she would split and butter for us. I hooked my leg over the bench to sit next to Enda, eager to hear more about the hunt. I reached out for a potato and Kieran pinched my arm, making me squeal. Mam's beady eyes darted towards me.

"Go to the little room, Oona, and think about what you've done."

"But, Mam—" Enda said.

"No, Enda. She'll learn this now. Saying filth to the priest, a man of God, there's no worse crime. My own daughter."

I could think of much worse crimes but I didn't say them. I marched into the bedroom I shared with my brothers, tears stinging my eyes. I stood on my mattress and peered through the tiny window. I could just make out the green fields behind. I watched and waited for a movement, the sign of someone I'd only heard stories about. Like in the legends Bridget told me, I pictured Aislinn as a child, with long hair running down her back like water, and lips as ripe as berries. The room darkened and on the bed I curled up around my empty belly. I wondered if Aislinn had told the waves to take her man away because she was a sea-fairy like Pegeen said. I wondered could she make the water take other people too.

Someone opened the door, piercing the black with light and voices from the kitchen. I turned away but felt the softness of a half scone pressed into my hand. It was warm. I turned and saw Enda's dark head lit up in the doorway.

Outside the sky moaned and I could see all of nothing out the window. My knees ached, but after the boys had come in and were snoring gently, I too fell away from thinking and into dreams.

I dreamed I was the daughter of a sea-fairy.

As the woman's daughter grew, she watched, forgetting to sleep in her fear that she would miss a moment of her beloved's life.

She sprinkled petals over the crib and watched. Five-pointed fat fists reached up to catch the falling blossom stars.

The mother wept because life is fleeting and one day her child would be gone.

The daughter had cheeks as ripe as fruit and a quick and easy smile. The mother's heart overflowed with a love that ran to the corners of the house, sealing up the windows and doors. The woman began to feed her child less and less to keep her small, to keep her young, but the girl kept growing, expanding, and started to look out the window, searching for what lay in the meadows.

———————

The Daughter

It's not yet dawn and I stand in the lake. It's 1987. As a child, I never knew the names people on the mainland gave to years. I noticed only the change in the weather, the bitter wet breath and dark of winter blowing gentler into the green and bird song of spring. I only came to know time when Joyce was born: Friday, 15 March 1968. That was the day I started counting forward, and counting back.

Joyce is now nineteen. Her birthday was two months ago. Pat drove down and fetched her from his mother's house. We took her out for a meal to the Italian in town and ordered three pizzas, which was a mistake as none of us were hungry. She was quiet; we all were, still in shock from Enda's death. Five months had passed but I still couldn't speak about him. I gave her my gift wrapped in old newspaper and tied with brown string. When she opened it and unfolded the quilt I'd made her, she chewed her lip and gave me a watery-eyed smile. I'd been making it for years, using pieces of the dresses she'd grown out of and some of mine. Her yellow dress took the form of a sun at its centre. I was stretching out my hand to her and she was reaching back. But three weeks later I had torn us apart again.

The water nips my toes and, above, the sky is paling but I can still make out a few frozen stars. Mayflies hum, wind plays scales through the trees and the lake whispers with the voices of the dead.

In the distance, I hear the hum of Pat's car—no one else would drive up here. A flame of fear lights in my belly. He must have some news of our daughter.

I picture the blue Ford climbing the road through the pines and him squinting into the dark. Like a fox, he uses his nose to find his way. I dab my feral hair and smooth my tatty jumper.

Yesterday I caught a glimpse of myself in the gas station window. I was a wild animal, a beggar in the Bible who is stoned to death because of her monstrousness. I was a white face with dark eyes gouged out and framed by dark, grease-wet seaweed for hair. The boy behind the counter looked kindly up at the ceiling. Lake washing had clearly not been enough.

Pat's car judders to a halt on the grass and he jumps out and looks about.

I balance unmoving on a stone and watch him waiting too. If I wait, I won't have to hear his news about her.

"Oona?" he calls. "I see you."

I slip; water drenches my rolled-up jeans. I trudge up the rocky shore. Under my damp feet the stones clack against each other. No quiet approach.

From a distance his still-fair hair is lit by the first glimmers of morning. He must see every straggled end of mine, and the blue stains I'm sure weigh under my eyes. We reach each other halfway between the lake and car. His hands lift and hover above my shoulders. I wait. It's been years, years of us living side by side, lives brushing, skin never touching.

When Pat first took me up here, he blindfolded me. By the time the car stopped I was fuming with him, but I let him lead me across the grass and whip the scarf off my eyes. Nestled beneath tall, mossy trees was a buttercup-yellow cabin. I ran but didn't step inside; there was no turf-stacked hearth, no rocking chair or spinning wheel, no fishing rods or baskets perched in the corner.

My fist was a stone against my chest.

"Do you like it?" he said. "I thought you might like to be close to the water."

The breath I had imprisoned in my throat rushed out and he reached out to touch me, but stopped.

"I like it," I told him.

A rush of air passes me. His hands fall to his sides. That stern and worried expression of his is so familiar.

I step backwards, widening the gap between us.

"What did Joyce say to you?" There's an infuriating rasp of fear in my voice. The cold night grates against my throat. All my subtlety is gone. I've become wild here. Unused to people. Unused to lovers.

He takes my hand. His skin is cool and smooth and I want to say thank you for touching me in spite of everything but I swallow the words. He's touching me, so Joyce has told him nothing. His glasses flash as he turns his head and his ice-blue eyes settle on me. I drink in the lines of his face, the slight turn up of his mouth on the left.

"Joyce is missing," he says.

Somewhere behind me, the lake slaps the shore. I strain for the song of my mourning dove but for once she is silent.

"How long?" My voice is coming from somewhere outside my body.

"My mother rang me, I dunno, two hours ago. I came straight here so it must be two hours. She said Joyce hasn't come home for three days."

"Three days? She got back to your mother's after . . . ?"

"Yes," he says. "I found her and drove her to the city. When I got back you weren't there."

"Three days. Why is your mother only ringing you now?"

"She must have thought Joyce was with a friend or—"

"A boyfriend?"

He pulls his hand from mine, shaking his fingers. I was crushing them.

"No," he says. "She doesn't have a boyfriend."

"You don't know."

"Joyce doesn't keep secrets."

The wind sighs at me on its way through the trees.

"Some of her things are gone, some clothes. She used to come to the lake so I thought . . ."

"She wouldn't come here. Not with me in the cabin."

When he first brought me here, the floor was swept and he had placed a few of my potted herbs in the window. He'd made the thin bed with clean sheets and when night fell he piled blankets on the floor. It was there Joyce curled up in his arms, her heavy child's head on his chest, and drifted off. I slept deep and woke to an unfamiliar bird calling in the morning.

If Joyce were like him, she wouldn't have hated me. But she is like me. Anger and resentment burn just below her surface.

The damp morning air laces across my shoulders and down my spine. I open my mouth to speak but nothing comes out.

"I have to go." He gives me a look that says, if you don't come with me, you will lose us both.

I stare out at the shimmering reflection of leaves and broken blue sky on the water. She left me on the porch without looking back over her shoulder. No regrets. Maybe she doesn't want me to find her.

My mouth is dry. I could stay here. The lake is deep. It would be easy to slip away beneath its weight.

You are not my mother.

Waves slap the shore.

"I'm coming with you, Pat," I say.

The Angel and the Whale

In my dreams I walked hand in hand with the child Aislinn, along the ragged cliffs that were said to cut off Éag from the sea. We ran so fast my heart soared.

When I woke I kept my eyes shut to stay with her but she drifted away and the morning light pressed through my closed lids.

It was a rare dry day for the island, a day for washing, and not a sound to be heard but the whisper of waves on the shore and the odd tread of men's boots down to the water. Mam and I sang as we did our work, the old songs Mam's mam had taught her, and we were shining with a lightness we passed between each other.

It was times like this, when I was all bubbling over and Mam smiling, I remembered she wasn't from the island and her foreignness made our life hard for her. Dad told it that he trapped her like a bird in a net in Ennis town, stealing her away from my grandmother's nest with its blue-and-white china, gas cooker and clean-cut marmalade. Mam'd never see such a fine kitchen again. It was Dad's shimmering black hair and soft words that charmed her away and she suffered the aching arms and legs and constant fear of death that every island woman wakes to.

We finished tidying up the breakfast and got to the two baskets' worth of catch Dad hadn't bothered to clean the night before. We gutted, salted and hung the fish all morning until my hands were bleeding and my eyes burning, but I sang until Mam snapped at me to stop deafening her.

I waited for her to remember that on this day I had turned eight.

She slammed the knife down to cut the head from a glistening mackerel and I knew it was Dad's head she was thinking of. She stood up and marched into the big room. I looked outside and saw the sky was darkening with a heavy pile of cloud.

The freckled, fair face of Jonjoe poked around the back door. He had the applest of cheeks, the kind you want to bite into, crisp and juicy. I knew him only to see at church and once, when Kieran saw Jonjoe hovering close to me after the Mass, he'd laughed and said I'd be wed in a year. I never made eyes at Jonjoe again.

"Oona," Jonjoe whispered, his muddy green eyes on me.

My skin grew hot and I dragged the bucket of fish bits closer. I was sat under the table gathering the guts Mam had dropped.

"We've found a monster on the point!" he said.

"A monster." Mam stood in the doorway of the big room, her hands tangled in her red skirts.

"Aye," Jonjoe said, standing straight at the sight of Mam. "Everyone's down at the shore out by that Aislinn's. You'd be missed if you didn't show yourselves." He flashed a smile at me and took off before Mam could shut the door in his face. I dropped the bucket and lunged to run after him but Mam grabbed the neck of my shirt.

"Mam, please."

She was looking at Mary on the dresser.

"We'll go together." Her teeth were gritted. It would be the first time I'd known her to go beyond church or out to our field to dig dinner.

In front of the small high mirror in the big room, Mam fixed her bun tighter and pinched her cheeks. I'd never seen myself in that mirror. I was too short to reach it but Dad had once said I looked just like Mam. The idea made me shudder like I'd eaten a mouldy potato. Mam's skin was white as a ghost's, her hair like threads of the night and her eyes were burned black.

Outside the cottage the air cut away the inside smell of rotting fish guts, leaving only grass and salt. As we walked along the road, Mam's hand gripping mine, a fire burned in me to run. Twice someone overtook us, waving and nodding their hellos, and I nearly chased after them, my feet hardly able to obey my repeated whispers to slow, slow, slow. If I rushed off she'd make me go back home without ever seeing the monster.

The sea was wild from the storm the night before and it was still high up the shores and crashing fiercely on the rocks. It had stopped the islanders taking the boats over to Éag for the Saint John's Eve fire, the only time anyone visited Éag without a death, and I had never been but a monster was sure to make up for the lost fun.

"I saw you looking at that boy," Mam said. "God is always watching. He knows your thoughts."

Sometimes, Mam spoke in ways I didn't understand. I'd learned not to listen and never ever to ask questions.

This road was new to my feet. Mam always took the sea way on the odd days we went visiting but this one ran along the top of the island's hill that rose behind our cottage. The castle stood at the highest point of the island up there and looked out at the four villages, ours being the biggest with over fifty people, and across the sea towards Éag as if it was watching out for the old people to know when the next deaths would come.

We were further away from home than I'd ever been. Starlings darted up in front of us into the freedom of the sky. I shut my eyes and I was with them, skimming the air, the green cut out by grey walls below and the wind to guide me wherever I chose.

"Oona, wake up. We're going back." Her face was as drained as leached earth and her hand shook in mine. I never thought to ask her how she knew the way to Aislinn's.

"If you're not there, they'll talk," I said. I was young but I knew Mam's fear of being the one that Pegeen whispered loudly over walls about.

"Stay beside me," she said.

I didn't answer. Sweat from her hand dampened mine.

Cries rose above the smash of waves and rushed up to meet me. We reached the end of the road where it fell into the sea. Below, on the grey shore, a crowd hung close to the water, gathered around a great black mound as high as the men's waists. I yanked free of Mam's grip, and even as she shouted after me I dropped down the overhang and slithered along the green-slicked rocks. Jonjoe waved at me and I looked down at the ground again, heat in my hand. The men's voices slapped like wet ropes against each other. Washed up in the storm, someone said. Another called that it was a bad sign. But most were laughing.

I pushed between their legs to get to the black creature that lay like a sleeper on the stones, the small waves rippling around her. I touched the cold, slippery skin and a sadness, deep as the water, washed into me and I wanted to cry. Inside the glassy eye, I saw myself reflected back: a small, wild-haired girl.

"She's dead," a smooth voice said behind me.

I turned and the sun shrank from the shine of a boy's hair. Even though I'd never seen an angel, I knew I was looking into the face of one. I looked at him and, as all children must with beautiful things, I loved him. Completely and unquestioningly, the way Mam loved the Virgin on the dresser.

"This morning, she was alive," he said, faltering, his Irish a little unsure of itself. "When she washed up she was alive." He gazed up at the tall figures all around us. "They've killed her." No one looked down. Like all adults, they were deaf to everything below the waist.

The feel of her cold skin still pressed into my hand.

"I saw her baby," he said.

"Did you really?"

"I did. Believe me or not. I don't care."

"I do believe you."

"I'll show you." He ducked away from the crowd and I scrambled after him.

There was no sign of Mam. No sharp fingers reaching out to grab me, but my heart leapt about. I'd never separated from her outside the cottage before.

"Let's run," I said, glancing about.

He ran and I chased after him, along the rocks, and pressed my hands over my ears in case Mam was shouting after me. We climbed the ridge and, panting, walked along the rim. Ahead, a huge white stalk grew from the rocks on the edge of the waves.

"What's that?" I called.

He glanced up. "The lighthouse. It stops men from drowning."

Enda once described it to me as like a fairy lantern to lead children down to Tír na nÓg.

We passed a small cottage clinging to the cliff edge, the old thatch sprouting grass and purple and blue flowers. As we walked by the high wall that surrounded it, a sweet smell drifted up.

"Do you know who lives in there?" I asked.

"Me and Mother."

"Your mam. Aislinn? Is she home?"

"Yes," he said.

"Let's go in and see her?"

"No." He turned and his eyes on me were bluer than the summer sea.

"She won't like you," he said.

Everywhere the rocks were sharper than I'd noticed. "Why wouldn't she like me?" I had dreamed of Aislinn and she was always my friend in my dreams.

"She doesn't like the islanders," he said. "But they hate her too, most of them."

"It's because she's English."

"I know," he said. "And they think I am too, but I'm not. I'm an island boy."

"Sure you are."

He said nothing, not hearing the tease in my words, and I realised he knew less Irish or less about people than I'd thought.

He sat on a bit of cliff that poked out over the water. A good ways off, I could still make out the crowd on the beach. I settled beside him, letting our shoulders touch, and the thrills fluttered up inside me like midnight moths.

"Are you an angel?" I asked.

"What's an angel?"

"Well," I said, happy I knew and he didn't. "They work for God. Deliver messages like the one that brought the news to Mary saying she would have God's son. I don't think she was all that happy about it. But anyway, my dad told me some angels were thrown out of heaven when they were bold and sided with the Devil and they became the fairies. That's what you'd be, a fairy."

"I don't know if I'm one," he said. "I never met God."

"No one's met God, especially the fairies, so you might well be one. People probably didn't want to upset you by telling you. Fairies aren't liked. They're dangerous, you know."

He rubbed his nose with a grubby hand. "No one talks to me much."

"Me either," I told him. "It's because we're children. But as you're a fairy they'll never talk to you. They'll be too afraid."

He began tugging grass from the stone cracks and letting it sail off on the wind.

"It's my birthday today," I said.

"I know. We're the same age."

"Do you always go about on your own?" I asked.

He nodded. Boys were all free while girls were tied to the hearth and kept sleepy inside like gentle calves in spring.

He stared at the water and so I did too, picturing him running along the beaches and hunting and fishing with no one to wear the ear off him if he stayed away all afternoon.

"If I was your sister we'd go wherever I wanted."

"I'd like a brother," he said.

I scuffed a rock with my foot. "Kieran pinches me and ignores me when I talk but Enda's my friend. He's not much older than me, only a year, well, a bit more than that but, you know, we're nearly the same."

"He's an angel too," Felim said, all thoughtful.

"No, he's not like you."

Felim shrugged and hummed to himself, staring out at the spiky grey sea. The silence was long and we kept watching the water, waiting for the baby monster to show itself.

"What'll it do now its mam's dead?" I asked, searching the jagged surface.

"He will die too."

I could only make out the side of Felim's face, but he wasn't unsmiling or smiling, just blank and smooth.

"No, he won't," I said. "And it could be a girl."

"It's a boy." His eyes were on me and they were fierce. "They die without their mothers."

"Even monsters?"

"It's a whale."

"Fish that breathe air. I heard of them before from Liam. He and his wife Pegeen are our neighbours."

"I know them."

"But why did the mother not breathe on the shore if she doesn't need water?"

He shrugged. "It killed her to be apart from her son."

"That doesn't sound right," I said. "My mam doesn't mind being away from my brothers at all. It's me she doesn't like going off. That whale's baby is a daughter."

"You don't know," he said. He scrunched his fists.

"We won't ever know for sure unless we see it."

It began to rain on us and I was starting to feel cold when he stood and pointed.

A small shoot of water spurted from the grey swell and a smooth black back curved up and under again. I jumped to my feet and opened my eyes wide, but we waited and waited and the baby didn't rise to see us again.

When I began to shudder and think of the praying Mam

would make me do for running off, I glanced at the shore where the villagers were gathered. The sea was red. It spilled from the beach and into the water like a gash in the side of the island.

Felim flashed from my side and again I chased after him, past the cottage with the sweet-smelling garden and along the cliff, watching my feet so I wouldn't fall on the sharp rocks below. Scraping my legs against the cliff edge, I slipped down the short drop to the shore. When I turned I saw her, his mam, running down the beach with hair flying behind her. She was even more beautiful than he was, distant, unreal, and in a breath I loved her more.

I halted on the seaweed line as she reached the crowd and began howling. The men had turned to her, glints like fish silver in their hands. My stomach twisted. They were cutting the mother whale to pieces. Aislinn wrenched a knife from a hand and hurled it into the waves. The men were still, in the grip of her shouts. She ripped another blade from another hand, but this woke them. Pegeen grabbed Aislinn's arms and forced them behind her back. Aislinn struggled, yelling, "You're murderers, all of you." The blood spilled onto the villagers' shoes. The priest was there, talking loudly, and she laughed at him, a cold, broken laugh. Pegeen's husband, Liam, wrapped his arms around Aislinn to hold her still and in his grip she wilted. Felim ran to her and gently, it seemed, pulled Liam's fingers from his mother's wrists and she sank to the blood-stained stones. Felim's lips moved with words only for her and I wished I could hear the magic of them because they changed her. Slowly, she folded around him, and all the time his mouth kept moving. As I got close, he led her away. They passed by me and her eyes shone on me with fury.

It was a good while before the men went back to their hacking.

Dad and Kieran, their faces spattered, and a saw between them crunched through the bones. Enda loosely held a knife, the tip dripping black drops. Behind them all, the sea turned redder.

I watched and watched. Mam took my hand and we walked home. I was shook with the sight of all that blood and the burning anger of the beautiful woman. Mam would never blaze like that and tell everyone what she thought of them, because she always kept her thoughts the same as everyone else's. She tucked her outsider self so deep inside everyone had forgotten she wasn't one of them. She was the most skilled liar.

I glanced up at her. Dark wisps of hair were escaping from her bun, but she hadn't tucked them back. She was quiet, thoughtful. Halfway along the road she stopped and hunkered down, gripping my shoulders. I tried to look away but her eyes were cold as winter, freezing me to her.

"You won't see that boy again, Oona."

"But—"

"He's the Devil's child."

"All right, Mammy."

Inside me a bird was hammering her wings against my bones, trying to escape.

Unholy People

"How do babies appear in their mams' stomachs?" I asked Mam.

She marched across the kitchen; four days of whale meat seemed to have given everyone more speed. I hadn't let a bite of the mother whale in me. For the first day Enda didn't eat it either, to support me, but he was thinner than me and hungrier and on the second day he was spading it into his mouth. My evening plate only had potatoes, but every time I saw the pink flesh I thought of her baby, alone in the sea.

"Mam?"

Once the baby whale swam inside its mother and in a scarier unnamed way I lived and swam in Mam.

She picked at the broken skin around her nails. "Did that boy put thoughts in your head?"

"No, but I was wondering about babies."

"Jesus was put into Mary by an angel."

"Did an angel deliver me?" Mam'd once said a golden-haired angel had cut me out with a silver knife.

"This is no talk for a Sunday, or any day, Oona." Mam said to

Mary on the dresser, "Children are sent by God to test and punish us, as everything is. You were a torment in your coming."

"Why did you let me in your stomach at all then?"

She spun to face me. "Do you think I had a choice, Oona? Do you?"

"I don't— I didn't."

"Brush your hair. It looks like you've been dragged through a bush backwards."

Mam went to the dresser and began arranging the cups. Her skin was blotchy, bun uncoiling at the top of her neck, but her skirt was smooth and neat. I often wondered what Mam was like when she was little. I wondered if my grandmother kept her tight at home. Did Mam long to escape? Was that why she said yes to Dad all those hundreds of years before?

Dad came out of the big room, whistling, fixed his hat at an angle and tousled my mess of hair. He called for Kieran, who strode in from the back, grabbed a dry hunk of bread and the two of them left without Enda, not that he was around as he'd already gone to church to talk to the priest before Mass. None of us knew why Enda was close to God. Dad only went in winter, as it was the best place to natter with the men from the other villages, and Kieran followed the old man everywhere, except into the big bedroom. We never went in there. It seemed a holier place than church. Not to be touched. At night, noises crawled out from under the door. Kieran said in the dark Dad turned into a sea monster and chased Mam around the room until she collapsed from tiredness. What happens then? I'd whisper. He eats her, Kieran would say. He laughed.

Late one night, when Kieran was snoring, Enda told me it was how Dad tried to make more babies. How? I asked. He was quiet for a while, and I thought he'd fallen asleep; then he said he didn't know.

Dad and Kieran's voices faded as they stalked down the road to the sea. Mam, still facing the dresser, raised her shoulders to her ears and dropped them with a sigh.

*

In church Mam's cheeks were still flushed. She looked up at the priest with that love of hers she gave only to him and the statue of the Virgin.

Enda, sat on the other side of her, was unchanged by Father Finnegan's words, but his head was cocked to one side, listening. The greasy God-man had only just begun but my legs were already bumpy with cold and the arse-ache of the hard bench had begun to bite. A rain-spattered light fell through the real glass windows, put in after the shutters were blown away during the storm that brought me and Felim to the island. Behind me, someone coughed and feet shuffled. A breeze rushed over my shoulders and I turned my head to see who'd opened the door.

The boy clung close to her side, a shadow. I hadn't noticed their clothes four days before but in this place, where everyone wore their good set, they stood out. Every stitch they wore seemed more patched than new. His were too small, the creamy jumper creeping halfway up his forearms, but she looked even stranger. She wore the same red skirt as many of the older island women, but somehow on her it looked smoother, skimming off her legs and falling away like water, while her hair seemed to glow brighter even than the white of the altar cloth.

It was the first time I ever saw them in church, and Mam and

I had never missed a Sunday. Them two standing there shattered the dullness of the church. Everyone seemed to hold their breath; even Father Finnegan had lost his voice. They all felt her swirling anger and sadness, even the few who didn't look at her, their hands clasped tight and white in prayer. The guilt for killing the whale seeped like rain under their doors. I was glad I hadn't eaten the whale.

Felim looked in our direction with his watery blue eyes and I smiled to show I remembered our baby whale, our secret, but his gaze fixed on someone else. I glanced about but there was no one near to me that might interest him. When I looked back he was staring hungrily at the priest, but he and Mam were the only ones. Everyone else was fixed on Aislinn or their own feet. Even Enda stared at Aislinn, his face partly hidden by Mam's hands smacked together in prayer but I could see how he was in love with them too.

When the priest fell silent Aislinn walked out, her head high, prouder and better than all of us, and dragging her son behind her as he gaped at me, Mam and Enda.

Before the woman had a daughter, she met a man in a field and lay down with him.

She lifted her skirt for him and let him shove his way inside her, releasing his salt spray into her fertile belly. When it was done, she smoothed down her dress and turned to go.

"Will you marry me?" he called after her.

"But we are already married," she said.

He looked down and saw the ring upon his finger.

"But will you come across a river to my home?" he asked. "It is beautiful there and we will be happy."

At these soft words she laughed at him. "I have all I need from you," she said.

He hovered around her, watching her belly grow, but she pretended not to know him and when the babe was born a girl he moved on, to pastures greener.

———————————

The Parents

Across the kitchen I see the cradle. The fire's been lit in the stove and I smell bread or is it wet pine? There is no sound, or just a gentle hum that vibrates against my left ear. My child is so close. I know they are asleep in their tiny bed, but I can't see inside. Just a few steps and I will clap my eyes on the downy head and hold the warm bundle again.

Oona. I don't turn to see who is calling. I must get to my child.

I take a step, another and another. I'm almost there; my hands reach out, but I know in my belly, my empty belly, the way I have always known, the baby's bed is bare. They are dead.

"Oona, wake up."

Grey-black rolls beneath me. My cheek is pressed against glass. It's grey out, morning, and we're speeding along a highway.

Pat's gaze is fixed on the road, his knuckles white on the wheel.

There's a metallic taste in my mouth. My knowing jolts back into me. It wasn't just a dream. Joyce *is* missing and we are driving to Ottawa to find her.

Pat's jaw is working but his eyes stay focused on the road. I don't know what he's thinking. If he was a normal husband he would be suspicious and ask me questions, ask me what I had done to send our daughter running. But he is not like other people. He has never pressed me for anything.

Green blurs outside the window. We need to get there, to question Pat's mother. I always see every judgement in her stony face, never able to keep anything hidden, but she'll have held some truth back. Mrs. Lightly knows everything that goes on in her house and Joyce wouldn't vanish without her knowing.

"I'll drive now," I say.

"You're still half-asleep."

"We're going so slow."

He nods and the car shoots forward, throwing me back against the seat. I only realised he will do anything someone asks when Joyce, she must've been four or five, begged him for another ride on his back, and even though he had done more than twenty trots around the kitchen that evening, he relented.

I should have come to see my child in the city but all those thousands of people are stifling, and then there was Mrs. Lightly. I never did manage to use that name for myself. It's always just been hers and I have always just been Oona. No last name. I missed Joyce sometimes but I didn't know how to talk to her after everything we lost. It's seven months now Enda has been dead but really it feels as if no time has passed at all. I remember him at the worst times, like when I'm arguing with the librarian about whether Yeats really is a genius, which he is of course, but it's fun to see her so affronted, I am laughing, and then mid-argument I see Enda by the fire, reading "The Second Coming," and I lose track of myself and lose the argument.

I glance at Pat without turning my head. He looks old. His shoulders are a little hunched and his eyes squint through his glasses. His hair is tangled at the back like a child's. I resist the urge to run my fingers through it. Pat was always beautiful, like a girl in a song, the kind you go to war for or would kill her husband just to have a chance with her.

He clears his throat. "You're staring at me."

"I know."

I wonder if he's noticed my dark hair is run through with ash-coloured strands now too. I avoid mirrors because the older I grow the more I start to look like Mam. She was in her early forties when I left the island and it will only be a few years before I am there too.

"Your arms are bruised," he says, eyes on the road.

The purple stains are bunched like irises across my skin. "I must've walked into a wall."

"Sleepwalking?"

"I locked the cabin door, so I was safe enough."

"God, Oona."

"I'm fine." I rub at them, then smooth my palms against my thighs and jumper.

While I knitted all through Joyce's childhood, she would sit in her nappy, and later on a stool, among the balls of wool, and carefully unravel each one then gaze up at me, waiting for me to re-roll them so she could begin her work all over again. Once I had finished Pat's jumper, I made a tiny one for her and she squealed with such glee I just couldn't stop knitting for her. As soon as she'd grown out of one, I'd have three more ready. It was then I started sewing the patchwork with the pieces of old clothes for her. I'd seen one in a shop in town and the little woman explained how her grandmother made them from clothes that no longer fit or were too torn to be worn. "It's a record of a history," the woman said. I didn't know how to tell Joyce about my past but I could stitch it together for her. No words, only patches of worn colour.

I unwind my window and stare out at the blur of green. Here the forest is like Inis's ocean. It hems me in, and if I were to go too deep I would lose myself. But the trees are not so haunted as the waves.

I shift closer to the door. We were once warm with Joyce between us on cold evenings by the fire, our fingers woven over her downy head. There were happy years then. She wasn't able to speak yet.

"Do you remember," he says, "when Joyce ran away and walked six kilometres to get to Ottawa?"

"She was about eight, wasn't she?"

He nods, smiling, the skin around his eyes all creased.

"It was because I wouldn't let her go live with your mother," I say.

"No. She wanted to see Enda."

"Oh."

The trees claw overhead, snatching at each other and throwing us into shadow.

"Listen," he says. "I'm glad you didn't let her leave us. I never could say no to her." He coughs, covering my silence. "Joyce took the road north instead of going to town. Must've been some natural instinct in her, like the duck she is. Drawn to water."

"You always knew where to find her," I say.

The air between us stills.

He chews his bottom lip. "She was usually at the lake. Like you."

I snap the glove compartment open, flipping through the maps, although he knows just where he's going and so do I.

His breathing is steady now. Too steady. "I brought a bag of things for you," he says. "Your clothes and toothbrush. Just what you'll need."

"How did you have time to pack if you drove straight to the lake after talking to your mother?"

"When you took off, I thought you'd need some warm things. I kept planning to drive over and give them to you. But then I thought you'd come back if you needed anything."

"Pat—"

"I have your mail as well. It's on the back seat."

I reach over and grab the bundle. I rip the first open.

"Library fine," I say.

"Nothing new." He smiles.

The second is an envelope with our address written in a spiky, childish hand. I drop it unopened in the glove compartment and flip it shut.

"I'm awake now," I say. "I can drive."

He glances at me but says nothing and pulls over.

I open the door and the wind rushes in.

"You're not going to drive off and leave me here, are you?" I ask.

He manages a smile, unbuckles his belt and gets out and so I do too. The forest darkens the road but just on the edge of the trees a dogwood is still in bloom. It's as if time has stopped here, like the last week never happened.

He presses a hand to his eyes and shakes his head like he's ridding himself of some thought. I want to reach out and pull him into the safe, leafy shade. He walks by me without a glance.

In the driving seat, I ease my foot off the clutch. The dogwood branches wave their goodbye. He pulls at his collar. The top two buttons of his cotton shirt are undone and a few greys have crept into the wispy hair there too. I stare at the tarmac vanishing ahead.

"I miss you," he says.

"I wasn't meant to be a mother."

"I'll find her," he says softly.

Joyce was only a child when she used to run away. Now she's nineteen with money and sense to hide somewhere we won't know to look. I open my mouth to tell him but he gives me his smile, fissures cutting from his eyes and mouth. He smiles and smiles because if he stops he'll cry.

Stolen Eggs

Is a gift that was stolen still a gift?

I found it, the blue-black wing on the windowsill, and knew Felim had left it for me. It set my heart battering and I decided one day he and I would fly away from the island and live in another country like England, and we would bring Enda too, as he couldn't be left behind. We would all be free and grow together.

The men were at home for my tenth birthday but Kieran moaned about it because he wanted to go to Éag for the yearly Saint John's Eve fire. It was the only day people ever went for a celebration rather than a death, although, as I understood it, death was celebrated on these occasions. I had never been, as Mam said it was a pagan fancy and not to be bothered with. A lot of years the sea was too rough anyway and the races were held on a beach on Inis instead, but Liam complained it just wasn't as wild, and Pegeen agreed, saying it was much better to have it at home where everyone, meaning the men, could be watched.

We sat around the table and everyone handed me a present. Dad gave me a tiny wood-carved haddock; Kieran: a kiss; Enda: a bunch of wildflowers that he stuck in my hair; and Mam: an extra scone. It was a generous offering from her because more and more I was catching her hunched by the dresser, shoving butter-lathered bread into her mouth and spraying crumbs on Mary. She was growing fat and wept and snapped at me and prayed more than ever.

Throughout the day and the ones that followed, I stuck my fingers in my pocket to stroke the wing Felim left for me until it started to smell and I had to throw it over the back wall. I kept one feather.

*

A few nights later, after he'd read and Mam had sent me to bed early, Enda crept into the room and lay down on my mattress beside me. He was warm and I held his hand to keep him with me longer.

"Littlie," he whispered. "Would you like to come with me tomorrow?"

I sat up. "What about Mam?"

"She's at the priest's tomorrow."

"Where will we go, Enda? The mainland?"

"I've an idea for us but I won't tell you now."

"I won't sleep with the nerves," I said.

He laughed. "Wait for Mam to leave in the morning and then come down to the shore to meet me."

He bounced up and left the room.

I lay back and began our adventure, visiting the lighthouse, hunting on the cliffs, walking the whole island until we came to Aislinn's and she had us in for biscuits.

The next morning I pushed open the little room shutters and the sky outside had paled to the colour of seagull dirt and a wetness hung in the air.

I rushed with the morning meal, spilled tea and Mam yelled at me, but her words slid off me like rain on bare skin. Enda smiled one of his magic ones, his snaggletooth pinching his bottom lip and his cheeks rolling up into roundness like moulded wet sand, and I grinned back.

"What's the matter with yous?" Dad said.

"Nothing," Enda said.

"Nothing," I said.

Mam's hand froze, gripping her teacup. I stared at my plate, feeling her eyes on me, but I didn't look up and soon I could hear her usual soft sipping.

Mam listed the day's tasks for me that I was to do without her and left before the table had even been cleaned up. I glanced at Enda but he was whistling at the cut hide hung drying from the line over the fire.

"I'm going down to the shore to fix up the currach," Enda said.

Kieran wiped his nose on his sleeve. "I'm coming with you."

Dad nodded at them. "I'll leave yous to it. I'm seeing Liam about his bull."

The Virgin Mary watched me from the dresser. She knew what I was planning but she didn't warn Mam as she left, running her fingers over the Virgin's skirts.

The boys were off right after and I cleaned up the breakfast, quick.

As I went out the front door, the sun darted out to warm me and even though it dipped away again I was free, for a while. I rushed away from the cottage, nose towards the sea.

The shore was just down the curve of road and when I got

there Enda and Kieran and two other boys were bent over the currach. One looked up and waved at me, and I recognised the straw-coloured hair and freckles of Jonjoe. He was smirking at me in a way that made me want to hit him.

The other boy straightened too, pulled off his hat and the light caught his hair so it gleamed. My fingers plunged into my pocket and found the feather, but Felim only glanced at me.

"Why's he here?" I snapped, stung.

"Felim's our friend now," Enda said, as if there hadn't been any judgement in my words.

Felim gazed at my brother, amazement on his moon face.

"How do yous even know each other?" Kieran said, dragging a damp length of rope out from under the plank seat of the currach.

"Father Finnegan," Felim said. "He tells us about God together."

Kieran groaned, the mention of the priest always enough to set him whinging.

Enda's cheeks were pink as he tried to lift the front of the boat on his own.

"What're you doing?" Kieran said.

"I thought your mam didn't like the priest or religion," I said to Felim.

He darted me a look from under his pale eyelashes. "I don't have to be like her."

"Have you been out on the water before, Oona?" Jonjoe said. "I don't know that I've ever seen a girl fishing."

"No." I stared at Enda, hoping he'd come to my defence, but he was distracted, talking in low tones to Felim. "I've not been in a boat."

He kicked at a rock, his head crooked down. "Do you like me, Oona?" he mumbled. "I know I'm your Kieran's age, but—"

"Jonjoe. I don't know what you're on about," I said.

"Did you ever think of coming to school?"

"Mam doesn't think I need it. She teaches me Bible and speaks English with me."

"Ah, but school is grand. We could sit together."

"Enda?" I yelled, turning away, but he, Felim and Kieran were already carrying the boat down to the waves.

"Come on." I lifted an oar, which was heavier than it looked. "Let's go down to them."

"I know you're younger than me. But when we're grown it'll not matter."

"Stop dancing around my sister, Jonjoe," Kieran roared over his shoulder. "Grab the oars."

Jonjoe jumped and grabbed the oar off me, balanced it on his shoulder and swaggered down to the water.

"I'm going home, Enda," I called as they ploughed through the shallows.

"Good," Kieran yelled. "Mam'll take the Bible to us for bringing you."

"You're coming, Oona," Enda said.

The boys jumped in. Jonjoe beamed at me and held out a hand for me to take. I paused, still on the dry.

"Come," Felim said.

I did, splashing in up to my knees, and reluctantly grabbed Jonjoe's hand. He dragged me in and I wiped his touch off my fingers as soon as I was safely seated in the middle beside Felim. The boat rocked as they took us over the low waves. My belly sucked up and down, rising and falling with the water.

I wanted to say thank you to Felim for giving me the wing, but it felt wrong in front of my brothers and especially Jonjoe. I brushed the feather and thought of taking it out to show him, a silent message, but the wind might steal it away. Our shoulders rubbed and Felim, keeping his body low, went to sit with Enda to balance the rowing, although he gritted his teeth to keep up with the other boys' strokes. I tried to be happy to be out and free, but I couldn't help the jealousy rising in me. I had so wanted to be alone with Enda, and have this day to ourselves.

I lay in the belly of the boat among the ropes and looked up at the sky. Seagulls spun above, calling sharply to each other, the wind snatching at the smaller, younger birds. I pressed my ear to the tarred bottom and listened for the silver fish slipping beneath. Enda whistled quietly. I sat up as we passed further out to sea. For long breaths everything seemed still, as if the island and the sea had quietened to match the peace that had washed over all of us in the boat.

"Row close to the cliff," Kieran yelled.

"What about Oona?" Jonjoe said. "It's not safe."

"I want to see," I shouted.

"That's you told." Kieran hooted at the sky. "Now! Left. Left."

The oars ducked and rose, ducked and rose, and we sculled closer to the scarred rock face.

"Get up," Kieran yelled at me.

I crawled over the seat and back towards Felim where he was perched with his knees drawn up to his chest. Kieran squatted in the middle of the boat. He was going to jump. The currach rocked, but Kieran was still beside a lobster pot. I looked up and Felim was slithering up the cliff, his bare toes finding cracks to wedge in and fingers hauling him up towards the top. The seagulls nesting above cawed in deep, gurgling voices, casually warning him off. He vanished behind the beating wings.

"Careful," I yelled and he glanced down, his hair blown up by the wind. He was smiling.

When he slid back into the currach his hat, clutched at his chest, was full of seagulls' eggs.

"You could've killed us," Enda bellowed. "You've never jumped before."

"None of you know what I've done," Felim said to the eggs.

Kieran licked his lips and tickled my stomach. "You hungry, littlie?"

I slapped his hand away. "I'm not a baby."

"Let's get this one back, lads," he roared.

As we rowed away, the curdling cries of the mother seagulls hit me. Felim stole their babies and they could do nothing to stop him.

We all jumped out in the shallows, Felim cradling his hat like it was a baby. As soon as the currach had been hauled up above the tideline, Kieran, dragging Jonjoe with him, trudged off, saying he needed to get some real work done.

Enda threw himself down on the grassy slope, tossing his legs out, and I felt his joy at the sky and the wind and the waves. He laughed at nothing and it caught in Felim and me, rang between us, tying us together.

"Show us the eggs," Enda said, pushing himself up on one hand to look at Felim.

The white-haired boy scattered rocks about him in his rush to get to my brother. Enda made everyone want to please him. It wasn't Felim's fault but he had said almost no words to me; it was like we'd not shared that moment with the baby whale at all, like he hadn't given me the wing.

I hovered a few steps away as Felim knelt at Enda's feet and placed the hat between my brother's knees. Felim's head was tilted up, still, gaze fixed, I thought, on my brother but I couldn't see their faces.

"Give me one," Enda said.

Felim reached into the hat and he lifted a grey speckled egg out. Their hands met around it and Felim startled backwards like he'd been stung. The egg smashed.

And then Felim was off, running through the long grass and up into the yellow rye, a pale smudge on its freshness. Above him, the clouds blew away and a watery sun crept out.

The egg's clear and yellow innards seeped into the pebbles, wasted.

"Do you think we'll see him again?" I asked.

"Oh, I do."

I lay down next to where Enda sat on the stones. "Felim gave me a birthday present, you know."

"Did he?" For a moment I thought I heard a scratch of jealousy in Enda's voice.

"It was a bird's wing. He left it on the windowsill."

"A dead bird's wing isn't a present, Oona."

"You could say the same for a bunch of flowers I could've picked myself."

"All I mean is it might not have been anyone meaning anything. Someone walking by saw the wing and put it there without thinking."

"It was meant for me."

"All right."

"Will Mam be home now, do you think?"

Enda was silent, looking down at Felim's hat of eggs by his feet.

"What is it?" I said.

His fists were clenched tight at his sides. He stood.

"Enda?"

"I'm going home."

He strode away, up the beach.

But when I got back he wasn't there and Mam was waiting for me, the Bible in her hands.

I never wondered how Felim got the wing, or whether there was a poor blackbird limping over the island unable to fly.

The Sea-Fairy

In the black, the need to escape again danced through my feet. I'd stayed awake since supper. Mam hadn't noticed me missing because I told her I was just round the side of the cottage fetching water. I watched her closely all evening. She poked at the small smile on her lips as if she was confused where it had come from. I knew it was the priest that gave it to her.

I waited until the night was so thick my hands in front of my face were imagined. I opened the shutter a crack and peered out into the air. The soft wind seemed laced with words in a foreign tongue. I pulled it closed again and the wind's voice was silenced and the only sound was the snores of Enda and Kieran. I flew to the door and crept across the kitchen panting, ready to run back to bed at the smallest sound, the briefest cry from Mam, but all was still and no one came.

Outside, the night opened up for me like a flower and I stretched out my arms to meet the cool sky. I wanted to yelp and cry out with my freedom but I kept my silence while I was still close to the cottage. I would not wake Mam from her dark dreams now I was finally escaping into the night.

It was bright and sweet-scented out but still the fear crept into me. At night the fairies walked in the lonely places, carrying lights to lead you into stone circles where you'd dance till morning but when you returned to your village a hundred years would've passed and your family would all be dead and buried on Éag. I let my eyes wander the high ground as I climbed, searching for their lights, but my skin went cold. Did the little folk have leering faces and fangs like Kieran always said? I searched the moonlit fields and— No. That's what they want. That's how they'll catch you. Look away. Look away.

My legs were stiff from the cold wind slicing up off the sea and getting under my thin nightie but no rain wet my face. The sky was pricked with winking stars, watching. I walked fast. Below me a rocky shore was crushed by waves. I had arrived at the place where the whale's blood was let. I pressed myself to the cliff edge and stared out at the flat sea. It was a short drop beneath me to the beach. The silver moonrays stroked the water, making it glitter like fish scales. On the beach black mounds of seaweed lay like sleeping sea-fairies, ready to catch me in their slippery grips and pull me down under the waves, but only if I was fool enough to go down to them. My breath caught in my chest. A shadow. She stood on the line where dark pebbles met the tide and moved with the smoothness of waves. Aislinn.

On the water a round and glistening shape floated towards her. My fingers clamped cold to the damp rock. She was calling her dead husband back. Bringing life to him again. The waves rushed up against the hard stones. Shhh. Shhh. *Shee*, the sea said as Aislinn pulled her dress over her head, tossed it. My stomach pooled and thrilled.

She ran screeching into the waves and, laughing, she called

out to him, a melodious sound without meaning. Her long fingers reached out for him but he sank and vanished.

There was a crunch of stones just along the cliff; from behind a large rock a dark, skirted figure flitted up and away. Aislinn looked up and captured me with her ocean eyes.

When the woman took her daughter outside into the sunlight, she was filled with hope. The girl laughed and strung daisy chains and in her small fists presented her mother with gifts of beetles, shells and fallen feathers.

The mother stopped up her fears for a time and didn't look into her child's future. She tried not to notice that her little girl was a tree stretching into the sky, reaching for something better, brighter.

The Mother-in-Law

When I drive us into Ottawa, it's ten past nine in the morning.

I pull onto the kerb of Pat's mother's street. All the clipped
yards look the same. Her house is just as clean. I can tell by the
way the windows glint coldly.

Pat jumps out and runs across the road.

I lean over from the driver's seat and fiddle with the handle
of the glove compartment. It flops open and the letter lies on
top of the maps. Small and threatening. The jagged writing cuts
me with its sharp familiarity and I remember blistered blue fingers scratching with chalk on my slate.

The letter is from Felim.

The back of the envelope is blank. There's no return address.
I flip it over. The handwriting is definitely Felim's. I would know.
I taught him to write.

It's covered in stamps. Perhaps he didn't know how many it
would take. But they're Irish. The last time I heard of him he was
in New York. But now he might be on the island. I pincer the letter
between finger and thumb and shove it into my jeans pocket. It
presses against my thigh.

The last time I saw Felim was that summer day at the lake with Joyce and Pat and Enda. He vanished before morning and I never heard from him again.

I lock the car, grab the bag Pat packed for me from the boot and stride across the road and up the trimmed path. Through the large window the overstuffed blue-and-grey sofa is still there. It's not even faded. I put my hand to the shiny metal door handle but it swings open before I can touch it. In the distance a siren screeches like a warning and there in front of me is Mrs. Lightly. She must've been watching me in the car through the door's glass panel.

"So you finally came," she says.

Her hair is dyed a severe dark brown and shaped like a mushroom on top of her head. A chemical smell of hairspray wafts towards me, tickling my nose. I sneeze and it's only half-intentional.

"Bless you," she says.

"How are you?" I ask. "You look different."

Despite a pink lipstick, her mouth is still so tight it looks zipped shut; if only it was.

"Oh, Joyce thought it would suit me." Her hand floats towards her hair but she drops it. "You haven't changed a bit." And she gives me that up and down, raking look as if searching for an ounce of style in my frayed jumper and mud-stained jeans.

She crosses her arms. "I've not heard anything about her."

"Really?" I prod. She doesn't flinch but I still don't trust her.

"Your daughter had to be missing for you to come here. That's the only way you'd leave your cave, isn't it?"

She turns and prowls down the hall towards the kitchen. I hate her habit of never letting me answer her accusations, especially when she's right.

In the sitting room there's nothing of Joyce. No abandoned

paperback on the sofa arm or forgotten bunch of keys. She made no impression on this house that I can see, but Mrs. Lightly always tidies any bit of life away. In our home Joyce always left her books and clothes and mugs of tea all over the place.

I go upstairs with my bag. The door to the room Pat and I shared when we were first married is open. It must be Joyce's now. There is still a ghost of her here, a small silver breath caught under the bed like a piece of her soul. Above the bed fish, women and birds swim and dance and fly in red, blue, gold. The painting's so bold. Mrs. Lightly must hate it.

There is a pair of small black knickers forgotten in the middle of the floor. She must have dropped them as she packed in haste.

I sink onto the bed's patchwork blanket. The stitched squares of my past are worn thin, like the fields of the island, leached by time. What a burden I sewed for my child. All my history and Joyce's in each piece of fabric and no words to explain the weight of each scrap or what it means. Stitched with the smell of Dad and Kieran's pipes, the sounds of Enda whistling and the pains I felt while kneeling in front of Mary.

Her shelves burst with books and I pick up the old thumbed copy of the Greek myths I read to her as a child. They always made more sense to me than the Bible tales. At age six or seven Joyce would carry its great weight into the kitchen and ask me to read. We both had our favourites and read them over and over, their truths tying us together. I never told Joyce the stories of hell and heaven. Despite her grandmother's Bible readings and gifts of trinity necklaces, she didn't suffer the pains of prayer at least. That's one of the reasons I stopped visiting old Mrs. Lightly. Her fervour was too familiar.

Pat stands in the doorway and his eyes are heavy as stones; his navy jumper droops from his shoulders.

"I'll go through her desk," I say. "She might've left something. A note or . . ."

I peel through essays, class notes, the birth certificate—I don't remember giving it to her. Born here, in Ottawa. Conceived on an island. I search for anything but there's nothing to say where my child has gone.

I drop beside him on the bed.

"What's your mother said?" I ask.

"She's not heard anything since I spoke to her on the phone."

"If Joyce packed clothes then she's chosen to go somewhere," I say.

"I don't know what to think," he says.

We sit for several minutes side by side.

"I lost her once," I blurt out. "I never told you. She was four. I was in town with her and she just wandered off."

"Where was she?"

"With a black cat."

Pat smiles weakly and so do I.

"I thought you'd worry if you knew."

"I would have."

I feel Felim's letter against my leg.

We go down to the kitchen together. Mrs. Lightly has made one of her breakfasts—God, do I remember those dry creations. I would lose my appetite just at the sickly smell rising up from downstairs.

"I don't want to eat anything," Pat says to her. "I'm heading over to the police station soon. I'll just grab a coffee."

"I already spoke to them," she snaps. "They've not heard anything. Eat something now or you'll be hungry later."

I swallow a smile. Not even her beloved son can escape her poisonous cooking.

He sits and I take the chair opposite. Mrs. Lightly delivers us each a horrifically high-stacked plate of fried bread and sloppy eggs.

"What would make her leave?" Mrs. Lightly stares at me as she delivers glasses of water.

I look right back at her. "I couldn't tell you, Mrs. Lightly." It's much easier lying to her than to Pat.

He clutches his coffee. "Maybe she had a study trip and forgot to tell us?"

"She would've told me. Joyce always told me everything."

"Why are you talking about her like she's dead?" I say.

Mrs. Lightly turns away and a spiteful joy rises in me, because I've shamed her.

Pat rubs his cheek, leaving a thin white scar.

"I'll find her and she'll be fine," I say.

His eyes linger on me.

"Will you?" she says, and laughs without feeling.

"Mom, please." Pat bangs his coffee cup down and some of it slops onto the white tablecloth. She darts up and begins lifting plates and dishes onto the counter. He sighs and gets up to help her. This is how they were when he was a boy and she was a widow. The two of them surviving together.

I push the undercooked eggs about my plate until she takes the fork from my hand, carefully so she won't touch me, and lifts the dish away.

I shove my chair back and it screeches against the tiles.

She turns slowly, my plate of scramble held well away from her body. "Joyce never spoke about you," she says.

"And she never spoke about you," I say. But this is also a lie.

She turns to Pat. "I've been showing Joyce all the family albums. She's very curious about us. The Lightlys."

"I never was as a boy." Pat smiles at the table. "I suppose it's because she's studying history now."

"Did she ask about my family?" I say.

"No. Joyce knows I know nothing about *you*."

"You don't seem that worried about her," I say.

"I could say the same for you."

She drags open a drawer and pulls out a new tablecloth that looks exactly the same as the last one. Why anyone would use a white tablecloth is beyond me.

"Did you find anything in her room?" I stare hard at her. She's frozen in her smoothing of the new cloth.

"That's it." Pat strides across the room and slams the door behind him. A pause of silence and then the car revs and fades.

He won't find her. She doesn't want to be found.

Now he's gone the two of us have nothing to say to each other. Just like when I first married Pat, my arguments with Mrs. Lightly are purely for his benefit. We act for him. Slowly, I leave the old woman in the kitchen. She's still staring in surprise at the door he slammed.

I climb the stairs. I need to read Felim's letter. I'm not sure how yet but it must be linked to what's happened to Joyce. After all this time, how can it not be?

The Sister

I ran from Aislinn, slipping on the road, and made it home just before morning, drenched and shivering, blood on my shins. Mam was waiting for me.

I stumbled through the door and saw her sat by the fire. I thought about running but I was so tired and already she was beside me, marching me across the room, her hand gripping my shoulder, tight. She stripped me down by the fire, even though anyone could have walked in and seen me naked. I clenched my teeth, ready for the slap, for the sharp words, for the bite of her anger, but nothing came. My fears drifted to the corners of the room, waiting, but Mam's seemed to crowd in on her. She was breathing fast, her fingers fumbling as she dropped her dry dress over my head and wrapped her shawl around me. I was drowning in waves of her clothes. Her hands were like winter. I saw then what she had seen. Me washed up on the beach dead. Me bleeding on a rock. Me a ghost following her about as she walked alone through her empty life.

She sat me on a stool and washed my face with warm water, biting her lip. Holding her hands over the flames, she told me the story of how her sister, my aunt Kate, was caught out in the snow when she went off on her own one evening. What's snow? I asked her. Cold white dust that falls from the sky, she said. I couldn't picture it. Kate was sick for weeks, Mam said. She almost died but in the end God was good. But He would not always forgive a girl for running away. It was only the once she'd make it.

She peered down at me from her tall place and said, "It's not easy. Not a bit. Don't leave me again, Oona."

She sighed, fetched herself a drink of water and went into the big room.

For days, thoughts of Aislinn took me away from the cleaning and digging and praying. Mam would cry out, "Are you away with the fairies or what?" and I would think, I am. I am. My secret of seeing the sea-fairy thrilled through me. It kept me full.

I wanted to see her again.

*

Mam was sad again. One day Bridget and Pegeen joined her spinning. Pegeen battered on about her husband, Liam, who made her knees and shoulders ache from the worry of him drowning. I dipped my hand into Mam's basket but her threads were never as smooth as Bridget's. The door opened and the wool blew like clouds across the earth-packed floor. Pegeen had left.

"She's not herself," said Bridget.

"Is it just Liam?" Mam's voice had no music.

"Aye. Liam's away longer than most and doesn't bring the fish or birds back to show for it."

Mam turned to look at Bridget. "You mean he's . . . ?"

"I wouldn't like to judge."

"Who?"

"You know what people say, but there's no knowing." Bridget squinted at the wool frothing through her fingers, impossible to draw back. "Pegeen's still going out at night to that beach to watch her."

Aislinn. The sea-fairy. I wished Pegeen would take me with her. I wanted to see the beautiful English woman again. I wanted her to love me like I loved her.

"It's only talk," Bridget said.

"It'd kill me if I was her," Mam said.

"You're not yourself as well," Bridget whispered.

After Bridget left Mam stood for a long time, staring at her hands.

*

The flames chased me across the island, burning. The yellow rye fields, the white cottages, a washing line of red skirts. The faster I ran the closer the fire got, until my feet were swarmed in flames and I was the one setting the world alight. I stopped and let the flames swallow me and I was full of joy.

"Jesus, Oona. Will you ever be quiet?" Kieran said in the darkness.

I heard the creak of the straw as he rolled over. I pushed off my blankets, my nightie clammy.

"Bad dream?" Enda whispered.

"I was on fire."

"Tell yourself a story and you'll forget it."

They were soon breathing heavy but I kept thinking how Aislinn had drowned her husband. Did he still live under the waves with the sea-fairies? Many fishermen said they had seen ghosts across the sound, between Inis and Éag, and on the still air their voices begged to be buried so they could rest.

I lay and watched the dark until a cry from the other room broke my thinking. A fear slithered into me that the fairies had finally got in. Mam never put the feet-water out like Bridget and the other island women, as she said it was superstition and unchristian. I climbed out of the warm nest of my bed and into the bitter air of Mam's kitchen. Moonlight poured through the two windows that faced the sea. I stepped towards the hearth, peering into the dark. The doors were all shut. Not a whisper of the little people. A black shape by the dead fire was shifting. A strange groaning. Sour rose into my mouth. My feet were stuck and I couldn't run away.

"Aislinn?"

It lifted a head swinging with long, dark hair and it was Mam. She held out a shaking hand. Red. All the water in me chilled.

"Oona?"

I collapsed down to her.

"Mam? I'll get Dad for you. You'll be all right."

"No." Her voice was made of flint.

A wetness pressed against my skirt. Mam quietly sobbed and I stroked her hair. She shook under my touch. I was too afraid to hold her hand.

"Mam," I whispered. "It's blood. I need to get Dad."

"No." Her breath was harsh and fishy. "If you tell a soul, I'll kill you."

Winter entered me, crawling through my door and chilling every corner of my body. I focused on stopping the tears, on wiping Mam's face with my nightdress. We sat a long while.

"Help . . . help me outside," she said.

I took a deep breath as I stood and she slowly pulled herself up, using me as a post, leaning so heavily on my shoulders my legs shook. As we walked towards the door, a small thing flopped out of her dress.

Outside, Mam turned her face to the wind. The water barrel was by the little room's window and she dipped her hand in it, lifted her skirt and began running the wet up and down her bare legs.

Shivering, I splashed my hands too and washed her feet but no matter how much water I used there was still more blood. It was pouring out of her like rain.

"I'll get a cloth."

She didn't hear me. She shook, staring into the barrel like she had dropped her wedding ring in it.

I left her balancing against the barrel and went back inside, keeping close to the wall, eyes up, away from the floor where I might see it, lying there still. I grabbed a bit of soft cloth from the rag basket and backed outside again, holding my breath.

Mam's blood had slowed so I could wash it away from her legs. When the stains were wiped, she went back into the kitchen and I watched the ground soak up the dirty water.

Close to the dead fire, she pulled off her dress and I bundled it into a knot for washing. Then she stood naked, her hand over her eyes, and her fingers had a dark crust. I walked her towards the big bedroom and put my palm against the door, ready to open it.

"Oona," her voice cracked. "You'll clean the floor. Before anyone wakes."

"I will, Mam," I whispered. There was a lump in my throat so big I couldn't say a word more.

She grasped my wrist and bent it so I had to bite my tongue to stop the yelp. "Don't leave it somewhere people would find it."

"I'll not—"

"What if they guessed I meant . . . ?" she mumbled. "I prayed and prayed. I did, and I found an answer then, a way."

The sharp taste still burned my mouth. "What are you on about?"

"Don't speak to anyone," she said with the quickness of her own voice again. "Not a word. It's our secret. Me and you. If they knew, they'd tear us apart."

"Mammy, did you kill our baby?"

"God's will." She was all calm. "His will. I'm not meant to be a mother again."

She disappeared into the bedroom and I watched moonlight swirl at my feet. I didn't want to look up. I breathed deep. I was brave. I was brave. I was—

The small white-red thing was closed like a flower bud. I stepped closer. Her arms and legs were thin and fine. I put my ear by her face but heard no breaths. She was still as if she'd never once moved. There were no rags soft enough in the basket to wrap her in so I went into the little room where the boys still snored, and fumbled around my bed until I found my skirt and shirt. In the kitchen I tore off my nightdress and pulled on my day clothes; I laid my nightdress beside her and lifted her by her finger-length arms and placed her on it. She was so small I was afraid to break her. Her face was damp so I smoothed away the wetness. Her eyelashes were as wispy as an insect's wing. She was tiny, perfect and clean.

Eyes were on me. I looked up. The Virgin watched me from above.

"Please, Mary," I whispered. "Bring her back."

I waited but the small girl curled up like a white shell inside my clothes didn't move. I left my prayer with the Virgin, but I knew she'd do nothing. She was only ever silent, judging.

Stones cut my soft shoes. I held her close. My sister. She was light as a mackerel. I stopped at our cows' field. Purple flowers burst from the walls there. I could place her beneath them so the petals would fall onto her closed eyes to kiss her awake. But no, someone would find her there. They'd hear her cry when she woke. They'd steal her.

Breathing came rough because of the tears. I couldn't wake the cottages all around. I couldn't scream.

Mam had killed her.

She had killed my sister.

I was running, along the top road to the other side of the island. I passed the beach and kept running, tripping but catching myself with speed before I could crash to the ground. I cradled her in my arms, holding her close so my warmth would pass into her.

I went through the garden, all the flowers shut, rapped on the door and opened it. The fruity air hit me. I stepped inside and the black turned greyer. Near the gaping hole of the hearth was the lumpy mound of a floor bed.

"Aislinn," I called, and my voice sounded as strangled as Mam's had been. "Aislinn."

A slippery movement. Two heads or one? And then she stood and crossed the small space.

"Child? It's the night."

"I— I heard you were a healer. Bring my sister back." I held out my nightdress parcel and for a moment I felt her search my face but there was nothing an eye could see in the dark. She took my sister.

"Be gentle."

She glanced at me and placed my nightdress on the table and unwound the cloth. She sucked in her breath.

"The baby is dead."

She rewrapped my tiny girl.

The tears stung my eyes. "But you could . . . you could bring her back. You change the sea with your wanting. You took Felim's daddy's life. You could bring her life back. You could."

My hand rested just above the little parcel.

"She was too small to live outside your mam."

The voice was distant. A small head bobbed up from the sea of blankets on the floor. Felim. A hand stroked my shoulder and I pushed it away, lifted my sister from the table and ran. The wind screamed in my ears.

I was on a long flat rock that slipped into the sea. Water sprayed us. Cold, gentle. I heard Bridget once say a baby lives like it's underwater inside a woman. She could swim, escape for ever. Go to America. I laid her on the rock and freed her from my clothes. In my open palms I cradled her and held her like a wish. I waited for my prayer, for Mary to bring her back. No one else could. I waited and waited until I was hard as a stone and couldn't move. I waited and then I cursed Mary. I cursed myself. I cursed Mam most of all and dropped my sister in the sea.

The Cave of Dead Children

Mam did not appear in the morning and I wondered if all her blood had dripped away, leaving her empty, clean, ready for a wake.

I stepped out the back to get the eggs and found the small white parcel tied with string on the ledge of the little room's window, just where the bird wing had been left before. The night's bitter taste seeped back into my mouth, but it wasn't a tiny sister hidden inside the cloth. It was a bunch of dried herbs and it could only be from Aislinn. I'd been awake all night, knowing I would never sleep again. Lying just below the window until sunrise, I heard nothing. Aislinn could have hovered there through the dregs of the dark without me knowing.

Mam appeared long after sunrise, whiter than fishbone. Nothing passed her lips. Not food or tea or words. The guilt made her mouth full. She just stared at the hearth. I had scrubbed and scrubbed and scrubbed it the night before, but I couldn't get rid of the dark stain. Dad lifted Mam's hand and covered it with his own. She never met his eye and he never once looked down at where his dead daughter had lain, so he couldn't have known. As they were all leaving, Enda whispered I was to keep a good eye on Mam and let her rest. I watched him to see if he knew but he glanced at her with only worry but not fear or anger dragging at his cheeks. The words were rubbing against my teeth to tell him she was evil but I caught sight of the shadows under his eyes from late-night Bible reading and realised it would be too tiring for him to know she was a murderer.

The day went slow. Mam didn't move from her stool. I tidied and sewed up the holes in Kieran's socks. When I came back from getting water, she'd lit the dry dung and was bent over, prodding a white bundle into the flames.

"Mam! That's my nightdress."

She poked it with a stick. "You got it all bloody."

We watched the flames devour it, then she walked into the big bedroom and bolted the door behind her. I didn't even know it had a bolt until I heard it clunk into place. I sat on the floor and let the tears come.

*

The sitting still and lying in bed went on for days. After a week, in the afternoon when no one was about, I boiled water and made the herbs into a tea in the pot the way Bridget did with Aislinn's flowers when I was small. The smell of it brought her out. She strode up to me as I poured a cup and grabbed my arm, making the water slosh across the table. Her dark eyes sparked with light again and her fingernails drove into my skin.

"You went to see that woman."

"No."

"Don't you lie to me."

"The tea was outside on the windowsill. That's where I found it."

"I won't touch another drink from that woman. It's poison. It'll kill me this time."

I knew then how it'd happened. A great darkness had come into Mam to make her walk across the island to Aislinn's and drink herbs that killed babies. I decided I would never let it into me.

I looked down into the yellow depths of the liquid. Petals floated near the rim. I took a deep breath, stared straight into her twisted white face and drank.

She snatched it from my hand, fixed her gaze on me and lifted the cup to her mouth. I looked right back at her. We said nothing. Silence was agreed between us and the dead weight of all the island women dropped on me. I gritted my teeth.

For days I waited for Mam to come to me and ask where I had laid my dead sister down to sleep. She would weep and make me pray with her by the sea, asking God to bring the baby's soul up to heaven. I waited and waited but Mam behaved as if her child, my sister, had never been.

*

My sister visited me most nights. She wafted in through the shutters and soaked into my chest. We ran the fields, her as tall as me with wispy hair like a crown and me hanging on to her hand because she was so thin that if I didn't she'd drift away. Sometimes in my dreams we were drowning and I would wake gasping.

Mam sat all day spinning or staring out at the water in summer and the shut door in winter. At first I was sure she must know where I put her baby but when I looked closer I saw that her eyes were dull. She wasn't looking at anything at all.

In the past year my limbs had grown as quick as the grass in the summer and they carried me faster than ever before. Growing meant it was easier to escape from Mam's silence, and she didn't seem to bother when I left.

I was sat on a wall, far from the village and alone. Below me was a beach I'd not been to before and at the far end, carved into the cliff, was a cave. Kieran had told me it was where women left changeling babies. He said if you walked along the road at night you could hear them crying.

"I've been looking for you."

I jumped, scratching my hands against the rough rocks of the wall, and blinked in the blinding sunlight until Felim took shape before me.

"Did you follow me?" I asked.

"No."

I waited for him to ask about my coming to his cottage in the dead of the night. Dead.

"I'm going to Éag today," he said.

He'd seen the baby. He knew Éag was where I should have taken her.

I swallowed. "Why do you want to go there?"

"My mother and me could live there just us, no one to talk about us and say bad things about her." He smiled and it was all wrong on his face, like sun shining at night. I had to look away.

"How will you get to Éag?" Fear was turning my arms and legs stiff.

"Daithi will row us," he said. Old Daithi and Bridget never had their own children so I believed that to make one child smile, even Felim, he would take his fishing boat into dangerous waters.

I peered across the water but Éag was hidden in clouds. "It's too far and I can't even be seeing Éag just now. Daithi would never find it."

"I can see her." He laughed and then stopped suddenly. "I need to go there."

"No one goes there unless someone's dead."

He shook his head. "I'm not right. I'm sick."

I looked him up and down. He seemed to shine, blinking heavily under his own brightness.

"Sick?" I said, doubtful. I slid off the wall and prodded his arm. "Does that hurt?"

He shook his head.

"You look fine to me."

His face was such a blank it made me want to take his hand and squeeze it to force him to laugh or cry, but I didn't, knowing it wasn't right to touch someone like that without them wanting it.

"Why do you think you're sick?" I asked, holding my hands behind my back.

"Father Finnegan told me I was ill. He said God will kill me soon."

"He never said that."

Felim shrugged.

"You really shouldn't listen to what the Father says."

He stared at me, his mouth slightly open, revealing his yellowed teeth. "Father Finnegan speaks the word of God."

"Well, yes, but if there's nothing wrong with you, you won't die. He's from the mainland so he has to make things up to keep himself from jumping off a cliff."

My brothers would've laughed at this but Felim just looked at me all serious, like what I said was true and the Father would kill himself out of boredom.

"You'll be punished for that kind of talk," he said.

"By who?" I laughed, and he searched my face like he was looking for the reason I'd say such wicked words, and I had to look away.

"You sound like you don't believe in God."

"Well, He's never listened to me. Has He ever done anything for you?"

"Yes." Felim smiled a small smile just for himself.

Out at sea, bruised grey clouds piled while wind blew them fast towards us, over the waves, and for a moment I felt a thrill of terror. I had made the storm clouds come after all, but then I looked at the pale boy born on the beach to a murderer mother and I knew he'd done it. All my power fell away.

"The cave'll be dry." I was more afraid of returning home to the empty kitchen with its stained patch on the floor and Mam locked in the big room than the stories about the cave, the dead children, and how if you kept walking down the passage the air would turn warm and you'd end up in hell.

Felim pressed his lips into a white line.

"You're afraid, aren't you?" I said.

"I don't like the dark." He wasn't like other children. He didn't seem to lie.

"Enda says you've to face your fears." I jumped down and marched towards the shore.

I glanced over my shoulder at him, laughing, but his face was smooth as a stone, like he had no feelings at all now.

"You're queer, Felim," I called, as I strode away from him towards the beach. "You could just talk to people. They might like you if you did."

I ran ahead, worried the fear would get me if I slowed, and

already the rain lashed my face and cut through my clothes. Just inside the cave I waited for him, squeezing out the wet ends of my hair, knowing he would follow. The air was salty and the floor grey with pebbles and shells, but no tiny bones, no skeletal white fingers grabbing from the walls, and only the dark stood ahead. Felim arrived at the lip of the blackness and hovered there, stepping a little further in when I took a step backwards. The light vanished from him and the stones clacked under his feet.

"Quiet," I hissed. "You'll wake the ghosts."

He sucked in his breath and held it in his mouth, then let the air out in one great rush. And he laughed, a short cackle, his eyes wild and wet with rain. I caught it and together we barked into the dark. But our joy echoed back from the depths and it was broken. We stopped.

We crept into the gash of the island, feeling our way along the wet walls until it became so black my eyes stung. I clung to the rough rock, afraid I'd fall through the earth and into nothing. I reached out behind me for Felim's hand but there was only empty space where the angel boy should have been. I heard the clack clack of feet stop, then start again but quieter until there was no sound at all, only my heart battering inside my ears. And then I was falling, sliding down the slippery insides. I tried to shout at him but the dark had swallowed my voice. I listened for the babies crying but all I heard was the drip drip of water. I saw the row of those mothers, a hundred empty-eyed island women with their shawls pulled over their heads, leaving those baby bundles to die in the blackness alone.

My breath came short and thin again. Step, step, step. Light.

It was so bright and in the brightness was a shadow. Felim stood with his back to me. Rain beat down and the land shook with thunder. As I got closer his voice came to me, strange and small. He was singing. He was calling to the sea-fairies to slither out of the water, grasp me in their damp fingers and drag me under the waves. Felim must know I dropped the baby in the sea and he was punishing me. A whisper from the spirit of the dead children entered me and I screamed with every last bit of air in my chest. Felim leapt to his feet and spun to face me. There was a panic in his loose limbs and it jumped into me too and sent me tumbling back. For the briefest breath his face looked torn in two by the gaping hole of his mouth. From somewhere inside me a deep laugh burbled to my lips and rolled out of me, on and on and on.

He ran up the beach, becoming another dark smudge among the rocks, and when I stopped laughing a bit of childhood, a bit of light, had torn away.

He was stood on the seaweed line, the barrier between the sea and the human world. I ran to him, the stones sliding under me, and soon I was more drenched than I'd ever been. Felim turned and his face belonged to a life-worn fisherman, not a boy.

"You left me with the ghosts," I said, panting, rain slipping into my mouth.

He stared out at the waves blossoming and scattering.

"People say your mam is a murderer," I said.

He flinched and my mouth tasted sour. I couldn't stop it.

"You were afraid," I said.

His eyes held mine. And then his arms shot out and shoved me. My cheek slammed hard into a rock. My ear rang. He stood over me, staring down, and again his face was blank. Then his hand stretched out. I touched my head, looked at what had come away and then gave him my bloody hand. He paused for a breath and hauled me up.

"Sorry," he said, and walked off up the beach. I didn't follow him. He was right. My mam was the murderer.

*

Aislinn's cottage was a good walk, but I didn't want to go home with a bleeding face and Bridget always said the English woman was good at healing.

I found her in the garden. No sign of Felim. She was bent plucking twigs and humming a sunny tune. She straightened and pushed her loose hair back from her face with a muddy hand. She smiled, glowed almost, at me but said nothing and I passed through the small gap in the tall wall and breathed in the green smell of damp soil and dripping leaves.

Her eyes were rockpool green-blue.

"I fell," I said in English.

She frowned. "Come in. I'll look after that for you."

I hadn't noticed the night I'd been there, but their cottage was smaller than any other I'd been in. Plants hung drying from the beam and filled the air with a brown, mouldy taste. It was dark, only one small window casting in one ray of light. The whole cottage was one room with one bed, but the night I had come there had been a second head, Felim. But he wasn't there.

"Where did you fall?" she asked.

"On the beach."

She tilted my chin up, drawing my face into the light falling through the door.

"How is your mam?"

"She doesn't notice when I'm gone now."

I sucked in my breath as she dabbed at my forehead with a cloth. "Did she talk to you about what happened?"

She was looking closely at the side of my head, like she cared about the hurt there, but her hand was still. She pressed harder and I felt in its force that she guessed what Mam had done and judged her.

"It was Felim," I said.

Her hand dropped from my face. "What was?"

"He pushed me over because I laughed at him."

"He hit you, Oona?" She was all still, her eyes on mine now, making me all squirmy under them, but I had to distract her from Mam. She might make the sea take Mam like she did with Colm, and I still needed Mam.

"Tell me just how it went," she said.

"We were in the dead babies' cave and he left me in the dark by myself and I heard a little girl crying. I scared him when I came out. I did want to scare him, but not like that, and then when I ran after him he pushed me."

She licked her bottom lip and drew a hand over her eyes, and I worried she'd guessed why he'd really hit me.

"He did say he was sorry," I said.

She nodded. "How have you been, Oona?"

"Why did you give my mam that poison drink?"

"Every woman deserves a choice. I think your mam will heal eventually."

"How did you get so good at healing?"

"I used to be a nurse."

She strode to the little bed on the floor and began shaking out the blankets. Mam had once told me the English live in big houses with giant comfy mattresses.

"Why did you come to Inis then?"

She dropped down onto her stool, hands limp in her lap. "It seemed like a place lost in time, you know." She lifted the rag and began dabbing my face again. "I wanted to live off the land and have a quiet life with . . . But, well, that's life, isn't it?" She stopped her dabbing. "Your face will heal just fine."

She handed me a shiny flat thing the size of her palm.

I had never seen myself before, except as a moving, rippling blob in a bucket of water and Mam's mirror in the big bedroom was still too high for me. The scratch had stopped bleeding and was now only a pale pink line but it was the rest that held me there, staring. I had Enda's pointy chin; my skin was almost as milky as his but with freckles over my nose and under my eyes, which I pressed at in a kind of wonder. My eyebrows were bushier and my hair was a dark mess of knots so I could see why Mam nearly ripped it from my head with the comb on Sunday mornings.

Aislinn laughed. "Shall we go out?"

I nodded, the reflection nodding back at me, and for a moment there was Mam's frown. My hand dropped and the mirror clattered against the table.

We went to the beach to fetch seaweed and plucked green leaves from the garden and took them back inside to make a soup. And all that time I tried not to think about my face and tried not to think how I longed to steal her mirror.

She ripped the leaves into the pot hung over the fire.

"Do you remember two summers ago when the men killed the whale?" I asked. "Why were you so angry?"

Her hands stopped their tearing. "I hated seeing them cutting up that defenceless animal."

"But we needed the meat and it kept the lamps alight all winter," I said, echoing Dad's and the other men's words.

"But they didn't wait for her to die."

"What will the whale do?" I said with a shudder.

"What whale?"

"The one that's the island." And I told her the story Bridget sang to me when I was small.

Aislinn delivered the soup to me in a small bowl.

"Do you think the island whale will punish us for eating her sister?"

"Oh, no," Aislinn said. "From what you've told me, I'd say she's forgiving."

The soup tasted sharp and bitter.

"Should we always forgive?" I asked. "If people, or one person, does a bad thing, should we forgive them?"

Aislinn was quiet, and I thought she wouldn't answer. Then she said, "You never know the reasons behind why a person behaves a certain way. Even if they hurt someone else or do something you can't understand, then they will have had a reason. You don't have to forgive them but you may feel lighter in yourself if you do. But sometimes it is too much to forgive."

No one spoke to me like this, like I was a grown-up. I tried to think of the right words to say so she'd keep thinking I was old like her.

"Do you ever miss your husband?" I asked.

"Sometimes." She laughed and it sounded like her voice was full of water.

I left soon after and again, with a sigh in her voice like she was much sadder about it than me, she said she was sorry Felim had hit me.

I ran along the road towards home, the wind nipping at my heels, waiting to walk until I was well beyond the shore, the cliffs far off with the smudge of their cottage on the tip lashed by the wind and rain.

When the daughter was almost as tall as the mother, she begged to be allowed out alone to pick flowers and collect eggshells. The woman looked out the window and saw it was a flawless, blue-sky day. The curlews were calling from the long grass and a gentle spring breeze was blowing. There was no good reason to deny her child.

"You may go," she said, and her daughter cried out with joy and kissed her on the lips.

"I will return soon," the girl called over her shoulder as she ran into the fields.

The mother sat, her fingers trailing her child's kiss across her mouth, and sewed a dress. She tried to push away the fears pressing at the corners of her mind. Their homeland was safe after all, and the woman knew every God-fearing person who walked the fields and shores. There was no threat she knew of or could name that might harm her daughter, but still the mother left the front door open, still she was afraid.

———————————

The Childhood Friend

I drag Felim's letter from my pocket.

I'm perched on Joyce's bed. Mrs. Lightly is in her room, and Pat drives the streets of Ottawa searching for our daughter. Out the window, the sun paints a glow over the white houses all along the road.

I tear the letter open. It is light, written on thin paper like a Bible page.

> To Oona,
>
> I never was good at words or writing but I could see no other way to let you know.
>
> Your daughter phoned for me at the pub on Inis. I'm on Éag now so when I was over on Inis one of the men told me. She said she is coming. You'll want to stop her.
>
> I still think on us and Enda. I miss those days when we were children and nothing mattered.
>
> God bless.
> Felim

I scrunch it up, slamming my fist into my knee.

Enda promised to never talk to Joyce about the island, and I know he was loyal. I drop to the floor and feel about under the bed, my fingertips brushing the fluff. He never betrayed me in life so it was something else: my fingers brush a box. I drag it out, dust shivering off it. Inside are letters. Bright postcards from Enda's friends: Mexico, Paris, Japan. I never saw Joyce take them when we were clearing out his apartment in New York, but that time is so blurry. His home was so beautiful, so full of things, so unlike the almost empty rooms of our childhood. Full of plants, the walls packed with shelves of books and prints from artists I'd never heard of, tasseled lampshades on at least fifteen lamps. All the figurines he collected on his trips. We kept so much but I never noticed the postcards. Did he give them to her before he died? Or did she take them without telling me? A memory thief.

I drag out a letter. It's from Aunt Kate and her handwriting is just as precious as when I was a child and we waited with longing for her words to brighten cold evenings that stretched on for ever. There is no date but it must be years old because it's yellowed. She says she is married and misses us. The address on the back of the envelope is Galway. She is where Joyce would go for answers.

I'm sure Mrs. Lightly knows. She left the box here for me to find.

The hall has the same vinegar smell it had when Pat and I were newly married and Joyce was beginning to swell my belly. I slip out the front door and head to the bottom of the street, wrapping my arms around my chest in the lukewarm air. At the payphone I call a taxi and book it to bring me to the airport.

I lean against the front door and light a cigarette. Just a few hours to wait.

There's a rap on the glass behind me. A pale face and tall hair hang just behind the door's window. I step backwards and she opens the door and looms out from the darkness.

"Give me one of those." She points at the cigarette glowing in my hand.

I pass her one, flick a match and illuminate her thin face. She breathes in deeply.

"I don't usually but I found them in the car," I say.

"Sometimes they're unavoidable," she says, almost casually, like we are two strangers who just met at a bus stop on the way to somewhere better. "Joyce wants to be alone. Leave her alone and she will come back when she's ready."

I laugh. "You don't know what people are like where I came from. You don't know what they're capable of."

"You never thought to warn your own daughter?" The bitterness is back in her voice.

I flick ash onto her roses. Small satisfactions.

"What will you tell him when I'm gone?" I ask.

"I'll think of something."

We both lie to him. I taste guilt like the cigarette flavour in my mouth, but I can't tell him. If I tell him Joyce is in Ireland, I'll have to tell him why she left.

When I was small Mam made me promise to always tell her the truth. She listed the tortures in hell, salting my dreams with huge flames and sharp-toothed monsters and endless night. I still couldn't help it. The taller I grew, the more lies raced out of me. Hell didn't frighten me. I was a child and far from death. I didn't know hell was real for the living too.

Of all the lies, I deserve my torment for the ones I told Joyce; but when a lie is repeated the liar starts to believe it. And I did. I wanted my new life to remake me. The future was light and the past would only drag it down so I pushed it away like it never happened but truths left unsaid rot like old clams.

"I love Joyce," she says.

"I know."

We breathe smoke together until the cold gets to me and I go inside.

In Joyce's room I curl up again on the patchwork, a square of my old red skirt against my cheek. There's no wedding white among the stitched-together fabrics. For my First Communion Mam argued with herself and Bridget about whether to cut up her old bride's dress to make my gown for my marriage with God. In the end she decided to keep her virgin's costume intact, carefully preserved for my own wedding day. But when it arrived I just wore my old red skirt.

I used to bring the ironing to the bedroom window and stand there in the summers to watch Pat and Joyce in the garden below. Joyce dug holes in the dirt outside his shed, cupping bugs in her hands and trotting inside to show him. I'd picture the exchange: him cooing in appreciation; her face proud, superior. I would iron everything, even knickers, just to stand there longer soaking them both in.

A car engine is silenced outside and I run to look out. I want, by some miracle, some change of fate, for him to have found her. Head down, he walks up the path alone. It's me who knows where she is and me who has to follow her there and if Pat comes with me he'll see the cracks that were always there.

My breath fast, I sit at her desk.

I miss you, he had said.

After I bring Joyce back I will return to the lake.

All I write to him is: *I'll find her and bring her back to you.*

An Aunt Blows In

"It's against God to kill, isn't it?" I said to my aunt Kate.

"Jesus, Oona." She dropped her lit pipe onto her navy trousers. She always wore what I knew to be the latest fashions. "I was just starting to relax here." She nipped the glowing tobacco between her thumb and finger and popped it back into the pipe's bowl.

It was Kate's first evening with us and the whole village had gathered at ours to welcome her. Everyone liked Kate, despite her painted fingernails, because she was Mam's sister and quick to laugh at people's jokes. I was only small the last time Kate took the ferry to see us, so when I'd heard I was cheerful for a week. Outsiders were rarer than sunny days, but already Kate was losing her shine for me. She was too bright and joyful, and soon she'd be gone back to Galway, leaving me behind to the days that were always the same, always inside with my murderer mother.

"What are you asking about murder for?" Kate said. "There's never been a theft here, never mind a murder."

"I know."

It was a year since I put my sister in the sea but I still dreamed of her.

We were sat in the hearth nook and the voices of everyone had dimmed to murmurs beyond us.

"What stories has that priest been filling your head with?" She glanced at Father Finnegan, whose greasy face was bent close to Enda's, whispering fiercely.

"Father Finnegan never told any story about a murder," I said. "I'm usually too tired to listen to his sermons anyway."

She laughed. "You sound like an old woman, Oona."

"I know." I sighed. "Please don't laugh at me, Kate. I am being serious."

"Well, if you really want to know, some men get away with murder in every way, not just killing. And women can't get away with a thing. We get blamed for men's crimes too, you know."

"And if a woman does do something bad?"

"She'll be burned at the stake."

"That's a bit much."

"A bit. More than a bit."

"Well, some punishment is needed."

"Believe me, if a woman does do something wrong, she's sure to punish herself far more than anyone else will."

"I see."

She blew smoke slowly through her lipsticked lips.

"You're ten now?"

"Eleven."

"That old. Time's flown."

That afternoon she and Mam had sat outside with tea and I crept out to look at them. Mam was collapsing. Kate's head was thrown back like she'd just been laughing and I thought how different my life would be if I were her daughter.

Kate's eyes narrowed on me. "What's going on?"

"Nothing."

"Good." She smiled and puffed her short hair from her eyes, the sign she was about to get up and leave me.

"What's your life like, Kate? Is it really different to here?"

She settled back against the wall. "Well, I suppose a lot of my life is easier," she said. "I get all my food from the shop. I only live with one woman and work inside in an office."

"Is typing hard?"

"Not a bit."

"Could I come and live with you in Galway?" I asked.

"They'd be broken-hearted without you." Her eyes danced about my face.

I looked at my dirty feet. "Do you not like me, Kate?"

"Don't be like that. I can't just steal you away. When you're grown up you can decide to leave yourself if you want. But I bet you'll marry some rosy-cheeked boy here."

"I'd jump off a cliff if I'd have to stay here for ever." I gulped.

"What's the matter? It's good to talk things out."

Words pouring, easy. I told her about waking up and finding Mam on the floor, my dead baby sister under her skirt.

"Mam killed her," I finished.

Kate rubbed her lips, smudging her lipstick. "Christ, give me your shawl." Kate wiped her face.

"I know babies don't always stay but Mam wanted her gone. She drank a poison from Aislinn."

"Listen, being a mother is not easy." She pulled on the pipe and knocked it out in the fire. "Women don't get a choice often but your mam was able to and I'm proud of her for it."

"Proud?"

I'd wanted to tell Kate how I had brought my sister to Aislinn's to heal her and how I'd had to throw her in the sea.

"God, I'm sweating. How do you all sit in these hearths so long? I need some air."

I wanted to call after her "Don't tell Mam on me," but it was too late. There was a pain in the back of my throat from speaking and Kate was gone. She didn't go to Mam and instead sat with Pegeen and a few others, chatting the evening away with them. I did catch her now and then glancing at me, and when our eyes met she'd give a forced smile that looked all wrong on her.

Kate watched Mam too. She watched us all. She was the outsider who might have seen us better than we saw ourselves.

Evening wilted into night and the villagers drifted away until it was just us family. All the lamps but one had been blown out. Dad was dozing, head propped against the wall. We were lulled by the soothing sound of Enda carding the wool for Mam. Even Kieran's chewing of his nails had slowed and he was only spitting the bits into the last glimmer of the fire, not at me where I hid in the nook, hoping Mam wouldn't send me to bed, but soon everyone went except Mam and Kate.

Long into the night the women's voices whispered. I strained to hear, but caught no meanings. It was all a tangle. Like all that lived in the adult world, I was still somehow unable to unravel it.

In the morning, while the cottage was still filled with gentle snores, I crept through the kitchen where Kate slept in the hearth bed and out into the wet behind the cottage, lifting my face up to the rain.

"You told her." Mam was stood by the barrel, her eyes red-rimmed.

"I couldn't lie, Mam."

"You're never to speak to Kate again."

"You told me God punishes liars but you lie to everyone. You never told Dad."

The slap rang in my head. Mam had never hit me before.

I turned and ran back inside.

"Oona?"

Kate was sat at the table and beckoned me over.

"Your mam's just upset. She's been through a difficult time of it over the last few years."

Tears were pressing at my eyes and I turned so she wouldn't see them fall. I wouldn't beg her to take me away with her. One day I'd find my own way out.

"Listen, Oona," Kate said. "It always gets better."

She left that afternoon on a gust of wind.

Broken Wings

It was late summer, the wind picking up its winter nip again, the soles of my feet beating the road on the way to school. Ahead of me the younger children were clustered, laughing and shoving each other as they walked to the schoolhouse. Many were missing, taken out by dads to finish up the rye harvest. None of them had tried to become my friends, having formed their groups before I came. My first day Jonjoe appeared even though he was too old and sat beside me but the boys hooted until he slunk away, lobster-coloured.

Enda had got the priest to tell Mam a girl of twelve needed to go to school; my brother had freed me, but schooling wasn't what I'd dreamed. I was years behind the other children, and Father Finnegan was as sleep-making in school as he was in church, but still, every day I focused on everything he scratched out on the board, trying to catch up. When I came home, full of new knowings, Mam still made me pray but the skin on my knees had thickened. The days sped by and before I knew it it was winter and my backside had to thaw the school bench and I learned that the good

Father Finnegan lit a small gas stove under his desk while the rest of us shivered together. The warm rains came again and I longed to be out and off, not stuck indoors listening to his droning.

I scuffed my cowhide shoes on the grass as the children vanished around the church. I didn't want to go. My cheeks burned just thinking about how yesterday I jammed against the words of Acts, how slow they came to me, how Father Finnegan and all the children laughed. The days after Jesus's death aren't meant to be funny.

Enda had sat up with me, to help me make the floating words stick to the page. We only had the Bible at home, but I stole a few books from the schoolhouse. The best had pictures. One was about America, with illustrations of birds in rainbow colours.

The wind was high and squealing but curled rising over it was a twittering. I followed it, climbing over a wall, and found the nest perched in plain sight in the short grass. Inside one wet baby bird opened her beak up to me, crying out her hunger. The shell was cracked and scattered around her. The other eggs were still full. I found a worm under a rock and she slurped it up and opened her beak again, tweeping. Her eyes were black and shiny like Mam's, like mine.

I touched the damp feathers. She was so ugly.

"Oona."

Above me, Felim blocked out the rain. His brown clothes were darkened with the weight of water and he didn't have a coat or waistcoat, just a jumper that was too small, with the sleeves halfway up his forearms. He knelt beside me, his elbow brushing my arm, sending a cold shiver up into my shoulders.

"You've killed it," he said.

My hand flew to the nest, but she twittered, beak wide again.

"She's fine."

"Its mam and dad won't feed it now you have," he said. "It'll die."

"No. She'll be grand. I only gave her a worm."

"Do you never get out? Do you never see how the island is? How birds and animals and fish and men live?"

"You don't know everything, Felim," I snapped.

"The bird will die."

I lifted her out and held her close, gentle in the cup of my hands. I'd show him.

"I've to go to school," I said. "You take her. I'll get her off you later."

I passed the little bird to him.

"Will Enda be at school?" he asked.

"He always is. Why do you care?"

"I'll come with you."

"You've never been to school."

"I have. Father knows me, but last time the other children chased me off."

The bird chirped in his hands and I knew it was wrong, the priest would be angry and Felim should stay away, but I said, "Come on."

Rain pressed against the high schoolroom windows and damp hair and damp clothes got damper in the unheated room. I twisted to look over my shoulder at Felim, who was hunched at the back, watching us like a tourist off the steamer. We all held our breaths, waiting for the priest to see the outsider in our midst.

Enda stood at the front, reading the Psalms, the priest hovering behind him. Enda was fourteen and the oldest in the class. Kieran, like most boys, had left at twelve to work the land and sea; but over the last few winters Father Finnegan had taken to Enda, teaching him in the evenings at his cottage beside the church.

Enda finished his reading and the lilting tweets of a bird flowed up; giggles rippled from the back row while Father Finnegan recited the lesson, English, a poem about a mountain. Every now and then the priest stopped midway through a sentence and fixed his yellow eyes on someone, but the chirping went on and on. I glanced back at Felim, a wickedness in me, a longing for him to be caught because he was always running, always free, and I needed him to know the other side of childhood. I wanted him to suffer like me.

Before I could pull it back and tell Jesus I didn't mean it, my prayer was answered. The priest strode across the room, a blackthorn stick clutched at his side, and yanked Felim up by the neck of his jumper and shook him. Felim opened his hands and cupped inside them was the baby bird.

"The mother pushed it out of the nest," he said.

A boy bubbled with laughter, setting everyone off again.

"Get out," Father Finnegan said, his voice thin, controlled.

"No," Felim said.

"Right." The priest nodded, thoughtful almost, and stepped away from Felim before lunging back and dragging him down the room and out the door. There were clatters and bangs as everyone jumped up from benches and pushed against each other in their rush to follow. They scattered in front of me across the grass, the rain pelting down, the rush of it the only sound as the children formed a circle around the two figures. No one spoke, not a single voice rose up, just bright eyes staring, unable to look away from Felim curled on the ground, shrinking, his knees pulled up to his forehead. The priest licked his flaking lips and with the blackthorn stick hit every part of the thin body again, again and again.

"Filthy. Filthy. Filthy," the priest said over and over, only he wasn't the priest any more but some man with all his certainty turned upside down in him.

Enda was beside me, his chest rising and falling with each jerk of Felim's body. He made no sound. This was what my wishing had done.

I reached for Enda's hand, to feel skin, the realness of a touch, but Enda wasn't beside me. He stood, arms outstretched, over Felim. The blackthorn whistled down, slashing my brother's wrists. Father Finnegan dropped the stick like it had burned him and staggered away, a hand clamped to his mouth, but he smoothed his fingers through his hair and strode, head held high, back into the school.

We stared down at Felim curled up and inside the boat of his hands the baby bird was dead. I took it from Felim and it was so light the wind could have carried it off on a breath.

"Felim, stand up." My voice was a shout. "Stand up."

I was a giant above him.

The children had all drifted back to the schoolroom and now it was just Enda and me.

Enda knelt and bent his head down to Felim's, whispering words I couldn't hear. Felim rolled over and was sick on the grass.

"I'll bring you home?" Enda said.

"No." Felim spat the word. "She's not there. She's with him."

Enda gripped his shoulder and helped Felim sit up. He was struggling to breathe, great pants coming out of him, and his hair was dark and flattened to his head.

"Can you walk?" Enda asked. "Oona, come here, we'll bring him to ours." He pulled Felim up and draped a limp arm over his shoulder. "Take the other side."

"Felim, I'm sorry," I said. "I shouldn't have given you the bird."

Felim sucked his breath through his teeth, staring between his feet, and a little bit of anger at him lodged in me because he hated me more than ever now.

I tucked the bird into my skirt pocket and we walked home slowly, Enda and me balancing Felim between us.

I didn't know what capsized inside Father Finnegan to make him attack Felim. It must have been a fear at the fairy-boy's far-off beauty, the way he seemed to live in another world where God was forgotten, powerless. I wanted to go there too.

"Why does Father Finnegan hate you?" I said as gently as I could.

He said nothing.

*

Mam was sat in the middle of the kitchen peeling potatoes into a tin bucket, dirt smeared on one cheek. Guilt tricked at my insides. If I were home with her, I would make sure she was always looking right for visitors. Her eyes caught on us and the potato clanged against the bucket. Her mouth opened and I saw the bitter words hanging like spit from her tongue, ready. I pushed my softness for her down somewhere deep.

"Mam," Enda said. "He's been hurt. Will you help?"

"Help?" she whispered.

Enda peeled Felim's shirt up. Red stripes stood out across Felim's back and chest. Mam stepped forward, one hand outstretched to him, one fluttering at her ear. A smile. A frown. Her hands dropped.

"Father Finnegan did it," I said.

She'd not moved towards us. "This boy must've done evil." She stared at me. "Father was called on by God to punish him."

"No," Enda whispered.

Mam flinched.

"It wasn't God's work," I said. "The Father went mad."

"Shut your mouth. I told yous to stay away from those people."

"Why?" Enda said.

"There's nothing wrong with them," I said.

"Is there not? What about his mother and all she gets up to? She leaves this boy wild and dirty to watch us at every turn." She rounded on him. "Oh, I've seen you. I know you're after my daughter."

Enda let go of Felim's shirt and the boy flinched and mumbled to my brother, making him shake his head.

"The Kilbrides are not right, Enda," Mam said. "You know this boy's not right."

Felim stepped slowly out the back door, his fingers flickering at his sides.

"You judge them, but you won't be judged," Enda whispered. "You let us all think you're so holy but you're a liar."

Something in Enda was unrolling out of him and across the floor to her feet.

"Did you know they were close to starving last winter? She has no man to get food. What would you do if you were her? Felim tries to take care of her but he's never had a dad to show him how. I bring them food because God would want us to help them."

"You're too young to know what God wants."

"I know enough." Enda glanced around. Felim was gone. My brother sprinted out into the rain without looking back.

All these years, when I had thought Felim and Aislinn were mine, my secrets, and Enda had known them better than me. A precious part of me had been stolen, but I couldn't blame Enda. I could only blame Mam.

She went at the potatoes, slicing most of the white meat away with the peel.

Behind the cottage I dug a small hole and buried the baby bird. I placed a purple stone on the mound so I could find it again. This tiny body I could visit.

I searched the fields that rose towards the castle ruin at the top of the hill but the island had swallowed Enda and Felim.

Far off, the woman heard her daughter's scream. It echoed off the rocks and gurgled as if drowned in sea water. Birds shot screeching into the clear sky. There was a pain in the mother's throat and she couldn't find her voice to shout for her daughter.

She ran to the meadow, and it felt like she was in a dream. All that was left of her child were blood-soaked petals and broken blue eggshells.

———————————

Motherland

As the plane screeches and bounces down into the mist and rain of Ireland, I picture Joyce flying this route, peering out the window, alone.

The bruises are healing on my arms but I've not slept much on the flight. I don't dream about my sister much, there are other ghosts now, but recently while I was at the lake she visited me— her and Joyce—but I always turned and ran away each time I saw them walking hand in hand towards me.

My hands shake as I step down the rickety ladder. My feet in their canvas sneakers are unstable on the tarmac. It's the first time in twenty years I've touched Ireland, touched the solidness of her, but this is not the land I knew.

Before me is a squat grey building and a wire fence all around. This concrete place is a foreign country.

When the taxi pulled away from Mrs. Lightly's house, I didn't look back. I forced my mind ahead. I couldn't let my thoughts take me back to Pat's collapsed body, asleep on the sofa. He will never forgive me for not telling him I knew where Joyce had gone.

I can't see beyond finding her.

I exit from Departures and go in search of a car rental. I changed all my money before I got on the plane. Every last dollar I saved from sewing dresses, kept in a tin under the bed, is now just punts that will trickle away every day I'm here. I don't know what I saved it all for except some half-formed thought that if I ever needed to run, I'd be able to.

I find a crooked booth manned by a spotty teen and he gives me the keys to a Ford Escort and directions to the city, but his accent is near incomprehensible.

I'm twenty minutes down the road when the exhaustion hits and my vision blurs. I wind down the window to breathe fresh air and roll it up again as the rain slices through. Cold settles into me. The sky has lowered; needles of rain prick the windshield; the odd tree and white-licked house blaze by and vanish in the wall of water. I'm driving fast. I catch a flash of sea—grey, dark, surging—and I lean towards it but it's already vanished behind a rise of green.

The car shudders to a stop beside a farm gate. My foot is on the brake. On the steering wheel my knuckles pop white.

Once Joyce was just a weight against my chest, a warmth. My life was just me and Pat and a baby on my hip, but then suddenly she was upright, jabbering with thoughts and opinions of her own, and I was afraid for her.

A flock of seagulls in the grass are indifferent to the rain-hammering they're taking. Water jumps along the glistening red car bonnet. It's the only bright thing in this muddy green and grey.

Felim's letter burns in my pocket.

The car roars back to life and I continue speeding towards Galway.

Sitting on the dashboard is a piece of paper with Kate's

address. I still don't know what I will say to Joyce when I get there but I hope she's gone no further.

*

The city is a rainbow of umbrellas. I park outside a tall house on Sea Road. On weighted feet I climb the steps and tap twice with the golden mermaid knocker. I wait but no one answers. The net curtains move like someone's breathing on them; a shadow retreats. It's been over twenty years. Surely she couldn't recognise me, and there is no need to hide. Last time I saw her I danced inside a long-haired, windswept girl. Now I'm greying, tied back and wearing jeans.

I knock once more.

The Big Room

I bounded, slowed by skirts trapping between my legs but still there was a release in me. I was out, away from the stench of peat smoke and frying fish and Mam's soap. I grabbed a hank of my hem, tucked it into my belt and sped on with the sweet cool slap of wind against my skin.

The pier was already heaving, piled high with crates of tea, bricks of turf, pouches of tobacco. The damp smell of food from the mainland. I stretched into my arms and breathed it all in.

Liam, now greying, and Old Daithi paused in their lifting to wave to me, both grinning, Daithi gap-toothed and Liam still with all of them.

"Oona!" It was Pegeen, who, because she was so short, had a way of appearing without me ever seeing her approach. "Did you ever see the Virgin Mary with her dress up to her oxters?"

"No."

She yanked down my skirt. "Is right you didn't. She wouldn't be caught dead in your state."

"I was only running."

"Aye, for now. But you'd all the men half-distracted. Get on with you and then get home."

I laughed as she marched off towards the village. Chuckling at his wife, Liam gave me his twinkly smile; we were in on it together, but it'd be all over the island by teatime and Mam was sure to get me on my knees for it. Bare legs hadn't mattered the summer before, when I was still thirteen, but being fourteen and no longer at school meant wearing clothes with shame to hide my body like all women must.

Since Enda and I had brought Felim into our kitchen, Mam's sacred space, she had realised the threat was closer than she had thought. It had woken her up and she kept me at home with her more often. Sometimes I managed to get away, like I had in the years after my sister, and I would meet Felim at his cottage to show him his letters. Once, while we sat on his beach, while I went over the English spellings on my slate, he said, "Did you ever think of marrying?"

"Mam wants me to marry Jonjoe." I laughed, shaking my head.

"You could marry me," he said.

"Felim, we're too young."

He darted up and strode down towards the water.

"But I will," I shouted. "If we can leave Inis together one day."

He clambered slowly back, frowning, a worried look on him, and I held out my hand to him and he took it in his cold one and I squeezed.

After a morning with Felim I would stop with his mam to drink her teas and talk about the villagers, making her laugh at my descriptions of Pegeen's eyes popping at the least whiff of gossip. I stored up this latest encounter to share with her, although I didn't know when I'd manage it. Mam noticed when I tried to leave, finding new tasks for me she'd never even thought of before. We knitted and sewed by the basket-load, and the pot of coins on the dresser was getting heavier as she sold almost everything we made.

Enda kept teaching me and reading with me but two short years of learning was all I had to know my English, writing and numbers. That small bit of freedom was gone and this small slice of day I'd snatched while Mam's back was turned to search for a piece of the outside, the world beyond our shores.

I dodged heaps of turf and baskets.

"Anything?" I yelled to Old Daithi, who was bent over a box.

"And what will you give me for it?"

I laughed. "Nothing. Give me the post, Daithi."

He handed me a clean white letter, which I hid under my shawl to keep dry and told him I'd to get home. He gave me his sad smile and I ran. Mam lived for letters. Whenever one arrived from Aunt Kate or her mother a watery joy would come into her eyes and she would hold it to her chest as if the people who'd written the words were right there with her.

I was drenched with sweat when I got back and the letter had a small patch of damp on it. As I went through the door into the kitchen I whispered a quick "Please" to the fairies that Mam wouldn't notice. Her back was to me, digging in the wool basket like there was a bag of money at the bottom. Her bun was unraveling like the slimy coils on the pier but I knew I could light her up, make her smile.

"Mam, we got a letter," I said.

The rustling stopped and she turned, her lips tight as she crossed the room to me. I held the envelope out and she snatched it.

"Where did you go?" She was too close to me.

"I went to see if we'd a letter. I wanted to cheer you up."

She searched my face looking for hidden sins and I knew Pegeen had already been up, and Mam was ringing with the story of my bare legs. She smiled despite herself as she ripped the letter open but as she read her smile fell away like a feather dropping from a wing. She scrunched up Kate's letter and threw it on the fire where it uncurled, as if trying to escape, before turning black and fraying to pieces.

"Mam? What did Kate say?"

She sank onto the stool with a look of a lonely child. My anger faded. I stepped towards her, ready to put my arms around her neck and kiss her cheek, but she stood up.

"Kate's met a man. He has a grocer's in Galway and she's going to work there."

Before I could say anything she was striding past me, out the back door without even picking up her shawl to protect her from the rain. I stared after her, sure I'd seen a tear on her cheek, but already her bent figure was halfway up the road. She had abandoned me for the priest.

*

It was later than usual when Dad and the boys came home all salty and sunburnt from a day on the water and with two large baskets of glittering fish ready for scaling. They were full of the wind of excitement for the trip to bring the cows to Connemara, but I couldn't catch their joy. Women and girls almost never went to the mainland.

I lay awake and waited for life to still, Kieran's ragged snores and the woolly silence that meant Mam and Dad were gone to bed.

I climbed out of bed and opened the door into the kitchen.

Enda was sat near the hearth peering into the Bible, chewing at the corner of his mouth.

"Where are you at?" I whispered.

"I'm just revisiting the flood," he said, without looking up. "Father Finnegan is all about the New Testament, but I still love the Old."

"Aye, the stories are wilder, aren't they?"

I knelt beside him and warmed my hands over the humming turf.

"What's got you up, littlie?" he asked.

I was too old for him to call me that name but I didn't care. He softly shut the Bible, smoothed the cover and looked up, giving me his full attention.

"I'm coming on the boat with you all tomorrow. I'm going to see Kate."

Enda pulled a hand down his face like he was trying to wake himself up. "Mam won't let you go."

"I know, but I've a plan."

"Tell me why you want to come."

"I need to see Kate." I'd already told him about Mam burning our aunt's letter. "I've never left the island. I've never even been to Éag. I don't go to school now and I need to get away for a bit, Enda."

The red glow of the fire played all down one side of his face. "All right."

*

The morning opened bright and new with freshly carded clouds and thrills in all of us. I woke before the boys to brew a big pot of tea and fetch bread and milk and butter, but when I crept into the kitchen, mind awhirl going over my plan, the table was set. Mam was already up. She was plucking a chicken, its head lolling against her leg, its feathers scattered at her feet.

"God bless," she said. It was her usual morning greeting but this time she looked up and gave me a smile. I almost let it all gush out, all my hopes of getting away to Kate, almost regretting wanting to leave Mam alone.

"Mam, I—"

"What's cooking?" Kieran called from the little room.

"A fish each to keep you strong for your long journey away." Mam dropped the chicken, strode by me without a glance and began spearing the mackerels with a fork.

There was no fish for me.

I chewed slowly on my black bread, letting the sharp taste roll all around my mouth because soon I'd be eating biscuits and apples with Kate.

Dad and Kieran grunted over their food, piling it into their open mouths.

"That reminds me, Mam," Enda said. "Father Finnegan was asking me if you'd go up to the fields with him to bless the cows for the journey."

She gave him a startled look, and said, "I'll go up to him soon."

I didn't dare look at Enda, afraid we'd give it away, but still my heart soared. She'd bitten. She would leave the cottage and I'd be free to race to the shore, get in Old Daithi's currach and be rowed out to the ferry. My sack was packed with spare clothes (a dress far too tight on my newly bulging chest and a woollen shawl), my sewing needle and an old loaf.

"Right, that's us," Dad said. He wiped his chin and pecked me on the cheek. "See you in a few days, girleen."

I smiled my sweetest smile.

He went to kiss Mam too but she flinched away, nodded them all out and shut the door on Dad's worried face, plunging us into the dark.

"Well," Mam said and beamed. "I'd better be getting up to the priest."

"Aye. I can clean up here and start gutting the catch."

"Good girl. Will you just get me my prayer book from the bedroom? There's a verse in it I want to ask Father Finnegan about the meaning of. Most prayers are clear as glass to me, but this one is difficult."

"Sure," I said. I was curious, as I'd not been in the big room since I was small and crept in to look at the place forbidden, my blood beating against my skin with excitement and terror. She'd dragged me out and told me not to be prying in the adults' place.

"I'm bringing Father Finnegan a bit of sugar," she said. Her back was bent over a basket, next to the hearth. "The poor man loves it and he's never enough."

I passed her, opened the thick door made of a proper wood, not like the flimsy one that shut me and my brothers off from the kitchen while we slept, and stepped into the big room. It was just like before, the bed's cover smooth as a church window, as if it'd never been slept in. From above the headboard Jesus stared down from his cross. There was a faint smell of piss and turning fish that pressed damp against the back of my mouth, the result of the door never being opened, never airing the room out. The prayer book was on the stool under the window. I grabbed it, eager to escape from the stale air and away from Christ's knowing stare.

Three things happened: I turned away from him, the door slammed and I dropped the prayer book on the floor.

"Mam?"

Nothing.

I ran to the door and tugged but it was stuck.

"Mam?"

I hammered on the wood.

"Mam, please. Let me out. I have to get out."

I ran to the window, but even before I reached it I knew I was too big to fit. I'd grown too much in the last year, my shoulders were too broad to make it through the opening. I could shout but no one would hear me; they were all down on the shore cheering on the cows, and even if they did what would they do? Nothing. No one would help me.

I pounded my fists on the door. "Mam! Let me out of here."

From the other side there was only silence but I knew she was there. She'd put something in front of the door and it was herself.

I beat three times and sank to the floor, my back against the door while Jesus stared down at me. I swore I saw him smile. He was just like His mother, watching and judging but doing nothing.

"I wish Aislinn was my mam," I yelled.

There was no answer.

"You are not my mother."

*

I lay on the floor while the ferry left with all the men and cows, but not me. When I opened my eyes the room was darker and there was a breeze against my cheek. She had finally opened the door.

"I heard you." She was stood above me, chicken feathers stuck to the bottom of her dark skirt. "Talking last night. Thought you could trick me?" She laughed. "I know just how you think, I know the evil that plagues you, and Galway is full of them that'd lead you into sin."

"I only wanted to see Kate."

"You're not leaving. The world is a danger to you. I heard it when you were born."

I pulled my knees to my chest and curled up around them.

"It doesn't matter now," I said.

"That woman will not save you. She is wicked."

"You're not my mother. You are not my mother," I whispered over and over like a prayer.

The Island's Ghosts

"I will leave the island one day," I said to Mam's back. "You can't make me stay."

The men had been gone a week and I had barely opened my mouth to say two words to Mam. She was knelt in front of the dresser, mumbling her complaints, but at my words she crossed herself and, still on her knees, turned to face me.

"Don't fool yourself," she said. "There's two ways it'll go. You'll marry Jack O'Flaherty's boy."

"Jonjoe. I will not." It was the old discussion, repeated constantly.

"Or you'll stay and look after myself and your dad, if he's still with us. There's no leaving the island. Not for a woman."

I was out the back door before she could drag me in again. The grey sky peeled open, spilling light onto the waves. I leant against the wall, the rain cutting into my cheeks, weighing down my dress. There was nowhere to go. The sea cut off every escape.

There was no way I'd let Jonjoe tie me here; his constant grinning and chasing after Kieran like a calf after its mother would drive me mad. And not all boys were the same. Felim was different. The storm had bound us on the night of our birth; the ocean chose us to be together but it never told us it had to be here.

I whispered a prayer to my dead sister to show me the path that'd lead me away from the island and waited for an answer.

Liam passed on the road, head down, hands deep in pockets, and I called after him, "Is the ferry back from the mainland?" The wind must've stolen my voice away because he kept striding up to the top of the hill and turned away from the villages onto the thin track above. There was only one place he could be going, only one cottage at the end of that path.

I didn't need to ask because already more men were trudging up the road, tired-looking in their heavy shoulders but also with small smiles they gave to me, which I struggled to return. They'd enjoyed their trip to Galway.

I followed Liam's footsteps through the rain towards Aislinn's. As I passed in front of the cottage I heard her voice, joyful and full of laughter, but I didn't stop, knowing I would disturb whatever warmth she had found. I walked down to the little beach, where Felim was sat close to the waves.

I settled next to him and he beamed at me. He'd never beamed before.

"You've not been home yet then?" I asked.

"No. Should I?"

"No. What happened in Galway then?" I yelled in the pause between the smacking sound of the water.

"Everything." He was staring at the sky.

"I'll leave Inis one day."

"I need to stay."

"Why?"

"There are people I can't leave behind."

"Aislinn does need you. Without you she'd have no one. I'll only really miss Enda."

We watched the sea, deafened, each of us in our separate imaginings, until I went home. When I reached the cottage evening had sunk into the hill and behind the castle.

"Get out of them wet clothes," Mam said when I came in. "You'll catch your death."

"I don't care if I do. What's the point in living if I'll always be here?"

"You've an awful lip on you these days," she yelled as I slammed the door of the little room.

I sank onto my mattress and looked up at the window above. The room was dark apart from that small slice of light.

Dad and the boys clomped into the kitchen with all the news of the cows freed for their summer feeding on the thick grasses of Connemara; our island meadows were too thin and bare to keep them alive for winter.

I dragged myself into the kitchen and Enda gave me a kiss. His cheeks were warm and wet with rain. "Sorry you didn't make it," he whispered. "We missed you."

"You've grown into a woman since we've been gone," Dad said to me.

"What makes you say that?" Mam snapped.

"Look at her, she's almost as tall as you, Mary. What age are you again, love?"

"She's fourteen," Enda said. "A year younger than me."

Kieran didn't give me his usual grunt. He pushed past me into the little room, his shoulders hunched by his ears, and shut the door behind him.

"What's the matter with him?" I asked Enda.

He shook his head. "He's just being . . . himself."

Mam was unwinding a ball of wool, a small puddle of red string pooling between her feet. The wool spread out.

I sat, quiet in the nook. Mam was as forcibly chirpy as a wren on a winter night pretending the sun has risen. Enda laughed with Dad, said a few kind words to Mam and winked and beamed at me. He was glowing, loud, and Mam was thrilled with him and asked question after question. He told us about the ferry ride and then how good Felim was with the cows; he had a hidden gift for animals. Felim's name was the only thing that made Mam's sewn-on smile fray at the edges.

*

I listened to the dark for what had woken me. At first there was nothing but prickling silence, then a ruffling of feathers, a spatter of wet and tap-tap-tapping on the shutter, followed by stillness again. Someone was trying to wake me.

Cold shivered over me, but still I got up and pulled on my dress and left the room. The kitchen was crowded with shadows and out the window they stood long in the moonlight. I pushed the door open and stepped into the stillest night. The stars were breathless, black clouds raced away from the bright and my heart beat rapid as a bodhrán.

A figure stood behind our wall and as I approached he peered at me, turned and began walking along the field. I rounded the wall, following, afraid if I called out I'd wake the sleeping cottage. I gained on him, and as I sped up he grew and became solid and the moon sheened off the shadow's white hair.

"What're you doing out here?" I yelled at Felim. We were now far enough away from the cottage.

I reached him and his eyes, unblinking, fixed on my lips. "You're different," he said.

He stepped close. It wasn't me who'd changed. It was him. His hand raised as if to hit me.

I stumbled back. "Don't."

His breath was hot on my skin. It smelled of day-old fish.

"What are you doing?" I whispered.

"I'm just seeing."

He trailed a fingernail down my cheek. I shuddered but I wanted to kiss him. I stepped closer and shut my eyes, but his touch fell away and when I looked up again he'd widened the gap between us.

"Don't touch me like that again," I whispered.

"Don't women like it?"

The skin still tingled but I felt wrong inside. I shook my head, thinking of the sounds of Dad grunting at night and Mam's red eyes in the morning. Whatever made Mam sad, it was like what Felim had just done to me, unnameable, and somehow shameful and sickening.

"No, Felim. Women don't like it."

"I don't believe you. I've seen it." He turned and began walking down the road.

"Seen it?" I rushed after him. "What did you see?"

But he was far ahead, striding into the dark at the turn of the road and close to vanishing behind Jonjoe's house, which bulged from the hillside, more permanent than the island herself.

"Where are you going?" I hissed after him, my belly swooping like I'd lost something important. "Wait!"

He waited for me and I ran to catch up. Somehow I wasn't cold in my dress; it was like Inis had warmed herself for me and whispered to the wind to soften and sung to make the stars shine brighter. The road bent close to the sea and curved back in again where the walls were just below our shoulders on either side.

We crossed a field and he stopped at a wall and peered over it at the tiny beach below.

As if from a tear in the thick air, a woman appeared on the shore and walked towards the water. Slowly, she pulled off each layer of her clothes until she shone white and her hair fell wild across her breasts. Her belly was as round as the moon above us, full with a child. I clung to the wall and leant out, a familiar hum gathering in my own stomach, and my chest tingled with exquisite pain until Felim pulled me back.

"She's pregnant," I said.

"I see it." Neck stretched, he stared at her.

The moon slid behind a black pile of clouds and she ducked under the swell. Felim's eyes were fixed on the spot where she disappeared. Time stretched, and in it I saw Aislinn drown in the watery underworld of the sea, but she broke the surface, spurting water.

"Felim," I whispered. "Let's go down and swim with your mam."

"I'm waiting to see if he comes."

"Who?"

"I don't know who he is yet."

My eyes stung with watching Aislinn gliding through the dark water but no one joined her, although I knew who it was.

Felim sank down the wall, his head between his knees, breathing heavily.

"Are you all right?" I said.

He said nothing. I watched him crawl away across the grass, straighten when he was down the slope and start for the road.

I turned back, just once, and over the wall Aislinn broke the stars apart as she floated across her sky-sea and a man swam towards her.

*

I ran to catch up with Felim and I said nothing to him. I didn't say the man's name. There was a reason Aislinn hadn't shared this with him. It wasn't Colm raised from the dead I'd seen when I was ten; it was Liam.

Felim stopped, and I bumped into his shoulder. The castle was just ahead and below my feet the road home dove down the hill, away from the ruin and into the dark.

"Aislinn just likes swimming," I said. "No one knows. About any of it."

"They'll know soon." His jaw was working, his teeth grinding, his face half-hidden by night, half-lit by moon.

"Are you angry with her for meeting with a man?"

"Don't talk about her." His face jammed close to mine, his breath was cool now.

"Why were you tapping on my window, Felim?"

He stepped away from me, chin dropping. "Go home, Oona," he said, voice tired.

A slippery fish flipped inside me as I headed off down the road but halfway down, the cottage in sight tucked below me in the hollow, I glanced back to wave and saw Felim duck into the ruins of the castle. Too much had happened in this night, and I was ready for sleep, but I climbed the hill again, reached the top and went through the castle's gaping doorway. The stench of moulding wet stones filled my mouth. Stars for a roof, tall shadows standing all about watching.

And there was Enda leaning against an empty window. The wind rushed through behind him. Felim stepped towards him, their heads gently tilting, hands reaching out. Felim's fingers were white, weaving through my brother's dark hair.

I ran away from them because I shouldn't have been there. I should never have seen that moment that was meant to be just theirs.

But we lived on an island, and in the end nothing can be kept hidden long.

The woman searched for her stolen daughter, and as she searched she wept, and as she wept the rye withered to dry husks, the poppies, dandelions and grass wilted, and unhatched babies shrivelled in their mothers' wombs and fell away.

She asked everyone she met if they had seen her child but no one told her what they all whispered about behind the woman's back, that the girl was no longer a girl and she had chosen to leave her mother. Years passed and the woman did try to forget her child. She filled her life with the sights of the world, the stories of the people she met, the meals cooked on open fires under the stars. For whole days, she told herself she was busy, she was happy, she was fulfilled, but a dream would land in her with visions of the child she lost and the pain cut deeper, the loss felt emptier. Her life was hollow, its circle broken.

And the earth was dying, all because a faithless daughter was tempted away from home. All because a mother wept and couldn't live without the fruit of her own womb.

————————

The Aunt

Ivy and sodden roses brush my soaked feet as I descend the steps, back onto the rain-licked Galway street. Kate must be out or she doesn't want to see me.

In the middle of the road there's a broken umbrella flapping like a dead crow's wing.

"Oona?" a voice says.

I spin, but slowly, my rain-clogged clothes dragging me down. The front door is open. I climb the steps again. All I can make out in the hallway is a shrunken woman.

"You'd better come in." She is wearing fuzzy slippers and has a hasty smear of pink lipstick across her mouth. She's softer, rounder, shorter than I remember. Not the Aunt Kate I knew, always talking, feet up, sparking life, but I don't know why I thought she'd be the same when I'm so different too.

I want to reach out and hold her, feel her warmth against me, but I can't move.

"Hello, Kate," I say.

The stairs scoop up to the next floor behind her. My heart

beats faster. Is Joyce up there? Was I right to think she'd come here first? Or, like all mothers, do I not know my daughter at all?

"Get into the other room," this new Kate says.

We perch at opposite ends of a long green sofa. The house is so enormous I half expect a large family to burst in, all with the glossy curls and laughing eyes Kate once had. But we're alone. The place is asleep, waiting for life to return.

She stares at me and I try to smile but whatever my mouth produces only encourages a grimace from her.

"I'm glad to see you, Oona," she says. "You're very different. Not the girl I remember."

Her hands clench the thighs of her grey slacks. Her wedding band gleams.

"Is your husband at work?"

She smiles, her eyes sparkling in the old way. "His shop's down the road."

"Do you have children?"

"No, but you missed a lot," she says, and I feel it. "You wanted to forget us."

"I did." I do.

There are no photographs in the room, nothing but chairs and coffee tables to fill the cavernous space. No shadow left by Joyce, and I don't know if she's been here, but I can see her with that look on her face I've only ever seen on her father: worried, very intense and eager.

"I'll make us a tea." Kate stands, smoothing her top.

"My daughter, Joyce, she's missing. She had your address and I thought she'd come here first. She mightn't have said her name. She looks nothing like me. Fair hair and young and fierce. Always asking questions."

The room is slippery like a reflection on water, never quite still. Kate is kneeling in front of me and I'm looking at her through my fingers. There's a map of tiny lines on her face. Under her eyes are the heavy places. One is Inis. One is Éag.

"You'll be all right." Her wet words almost persuade me. "Breathe with me now."

And I do. One, out. Two, out. Three.

"Sorry," I say.

"It's all right. I got a fright when I saw you there on my doorstep, looking . . . looking just like your mam. I was in shock. I didn't know what to say to you. You're like a ghost come back to life." She takes my hands and stares at them, stroking, stroking. "How're you feeling now?"

"What is it?"

"Mary's got cancer."

"Mam?"

A white light falls through the long window and onto the tangled design of the brown carpet.

"I tried to get her to move here," Kate's saying. "But she's more stubborn than ever. Won't budge from the cottage. Got some notion of dying on the island."

"But she always hated the island." I'm standing. The light blinds me.

"Don't I know. But whatever I say, she won't leave." Her arms circle me. Mam never once held me. "Will you go to see your mother? She won't be with us long."

I pull away. "You've seen Joyce."

Kate sinks back onto the sofa. "She left yesterday morning on the ferry."

"What did she say?"

"Not much. I did ask her, but she's as good as you at dodging a question. Better. She asked me a load about you and Enda, what your lives were as children. She hasn't a clue who she is."

"I told her other stories. Better ones. Stories I read in books."

"So, were you ashamed of us? Because what you told her was all lies, wasn't it?"

"I wasn't ashamed of you." I feel grey, like I could shut my eyes and sleep for years. "When's the next ferry? I need to find her."

"In the morning. Stay here tonight. I've a single bed made up already."

"Thank you, Kate."

"But where's her dad? Will he need a bed?" She says it casual, like she expects me to tell her Pat just dropped down to the shop to pick up a packet of cigarettes.

"He doesn't know I'm here."

The clock in the hallway dongs.

"Will you tell me what's going on?" she says.

I can't look at her. I don't know how to answer.

"I need some air," I say.

I walk down the road towards the river. The rain enfolds me and I can breathe a little easier.

The Whispering

Enda had kissed Felim.

I hadn't noticed, in all the years, it wasn't me who was bound to the fairy-boy, but Enda.

I flew down the hill without looking back, fumbled through the back door and sat by the empty hearth. I couldn't speak of it to anyone. If Mam knew she would be heartbroken because what Enda had done was against God. This was another secret I would have to hold deep inside me. I would have to try to forget.

Kieran shook me awake when light was trickling into the kitchen. He stood over me where I sat in Dad's chair, a look on his face like he wanted to tell me something, and I'd never known him not to speak when there was a thought in him.

"Kieran?"

"That boy of yours. The Kilbride. Does he fancy you?"

"What do you mean? No. No, he doesn't."

"Right. I thought so." He grabbed a rod. "I've to be out, Oona."

"Kieran," I yelled after him, but he didn't come back.

My limbs ached and I crawled into bed. I woke with pains like the whispers of cruel gossip digging into my stomach. Mam was banging about in the kitchen with the kettle and broom. The breath-filled air of the little room was dank with the smell of metal and fish. I leant over the side of the mattress and tried to throw up whatever had gone wrong inside me. Nothing came up. Both the boys' beds were empty. I squeezed my eyes shut.

Someone dragged the door open and light slashed in.

I looked down and my sheets and dress were stained red. I sat shaking on the bed. A cold shock hit me like a wave. I was dying. This was blood. I looked about for a small dead baby, but there was only blood.

"You're not dying." Mam stood above me with her arms crossed.

"Mam." My voice broke and I swallowed a sob. A deep sadness spread from my stabbing stomach. She didn't care.

"Arms up," she said. "Oona, stop crying."

"I'm not."

"Well, don't start."

I watched a blue string under the skin of her neck bounce.

"Is this what happened to you? Is my baby going to die?"

"What are you on about?"

"Like your baby that died?"

Her slap landed hard on my cheek, stinging worse than my stomach.

"I told you never to mention that."

She yanked off my dress and pulled me up, tearing the sheet from my bed.

"Here." She handed me a piece of cloth. "Put it in your knickers to catch the blood. There's more. You'll wash them at the end of the day."

She stopped in the doorway, her back to me. "It's the curse

on all women. We all bear the shame. You'll suffer it now like the rest of us."

Being a woman meant I was red. Shame buried deep in me. I pulled the blanket over my head and curled in a ball.

*

The truth about Aislinn's pregnancy spread fast, as all whispers did.

One evening, when the grey of day was being stolen by heather-coloured mist, she was gathering seaweed on the main shore. A few women were filling their baskets but not a one of them would look at Aislinn. I ignored Pegeen calling after me when I started down the beach towards her. Aislinn was changed from the free woman I'd seen swimming. Her dirty yellow hair was scooped up on her head, her upper body was wrapped in a brown shawl and she didn't look at me, but kept bending for the red strands of kelp.

"Oona," she said, without looking up. "You should go back to them."

She lifted another long lock of weed from the shallows, her bare feet submerged.

Up the beach, the women had stopped their work and were huddled together, watching us.

"People are talking about you," I said.

She darted a glance at me and I thought I saw a flicker of worry there.

"They're always talking but now there's something to it."

She picked up her basket, ready to go. It was my last chance to ask her.

"Aislinn, can two women . . . kiss?"

A small flicker on her lips. "Yes, Oona. They can do what they like in private."

"No, it's not me."

She stared and it felt like she saw deep into me, to the dark place I was afraid to see in myself.

"Follow your heart, Oona," she said.

I nodded.

She walked away, up the shore and past the women, and they stumbled back and leered at her new shape.

"Colm would turn in his grave," Pegeen said when I reached them again.

"He's not got a grave," I said. "It was a sea death."

"Aye, he'll haunt her for ever now."

An Immaculate Child

At church the silence of unspoken suspicion crackled through every Mass. Everyone thought it was Dad or some other man young enough who got the baby in Aislinn. Dad was known to speak kindly to Aislinn if he ever met her, but I never heard Mam accuse him, although she prayed more and went every day to clean the priest's cottage.

Every Sunday Father Finnegan reminded us that all men are sinners but women are worse. He knew the rumours as well as anyone. Women are the root of all evil, he said. People sat up straight and swallowed his words like they were delivered from the mouth of God Himself. Everyone wanted these words. They wanted God's blessing for their hatred of Aislinn and in the long winter nights, with time to think and never a sight of her, their fear festered.

Throughout the rains and heavy skies my family kept by the fire as much as we could, eating dried fish and thin soup and stacking the embers with cow dung, saving the turf for the evenings when it was even colder. And through all those long days I watched Enda for some sign of what had passed between him and

Felim, for what it meant. I searched for the courage to ask him but it always fled me. I would tell myself a man kissing a man was nothing. But the weight in my chest told me it was more real than anything that passed between myself and Felim.

On a fading afternoon Enda was reading aloud to us from Genesis. Dad snored softly in the nook. Kieran was mending a fish basket, although he wouldn't need it till spring. Mam and I sewed by the light of the lamps. I'd not been out to see Aislinn and Felim for months, so I didn't know if Aislinn's baby had arrived. Since the neighbours were all shut indoors like us, I'd heard no news, only the odd muttering about the scandal of it.

"Why don't you read from Genesis 19?" Kieran said to Enda. His words had a slipperiness. I couldn't remember Kieran ever asking to hear the Bible, and never a particular text. Enda's neck was pink in the firelight.

"Kieran," coughed Dad, awake and glaring. "Don't you be turning into a religious one too."

"Read it out to us, Enda," Mam said, yanking the thread in the skirt she was mending.

Enda scratched the back of his neck. "'And there came two angels to Sodom at even.'"

Kieran laughed, threw the basket aside and pulled off his boots, his feet close to the fire. Enda kept reading, his face unchanged as if Kieran was just a whirring bluebottle, and when he dropped the Bible into his lap, to escape the warm mould smell Kieran had released, I got up and went to sit next to Enda. He shut the Bible with a snap.

"Do you ever wish we'd been let to be friends with Felim?" I whispered, glancing at Mam to be sure she couldn't hear.

Enda's hands tightened around the Bible. "I don't want to talk about him."

"But everyone's angry at Aislinn. I'm worried about them."

"She chose to leave God behind and let herself be open to everyone's judgement. What could I do to help them now?"

He stood, the Bible thudded against the floor and I bent to pick it up while Enda vanished into the little room. Kieran spat in the hearth and it hissed. Mam sighed and got up and disappeared into the big room. Dad was whistling softly as he slept. I flipped to the passage Kieran had asked Enda to read. If the priest had given a Mass with this story at its centre, I wouldn't have understood, but in one night my understanding had grown and I knew Kieran, like me, had stumbled on a secret moment between our brother and Felim, and he saw it as wrong.

When I glanced up from the page Kieran was watching me, a frown between his eyebrows that said to me we were not to speak about our brother.

*

Aislinn's child was born and no one realised until Pegeen heard the baby's cry when she passed the cottage in the spring. We'd not seen Aislinn for months and Felim only the odd time when he walked through the village on his way to somewhere else, somewhere hidden, where I was sure he would meet Enda.

Inside her cottage the fire was blazing and Aislinn sat close, singing to a bundle in her arms. Her chest was bare, showing the smooth half-moon of her white breasts. Her nipples were flushed and puckered like lips and I stared, fascinated, as she lifted the baby to one and it began to suck.

I squatted next to them. The baby was too beautiful, even more angelic than Felim, its eyes cornflower-blue, and a soft white down clinging to its head.

"What's its name?" I asked.

"Etain."

The baby smiled up at Aislinn, all trusting.

"I've not heard that one."

"It means passion. Names can guide our future. I changed my own name when I came here. I used to be Norma."

I laughed. "Aislinn suits you better."

"Choose your own children's names well."

"I don't really want children," I said. "How's Felim? I've not spoken to him all winter."

She stroked the baby's head, her lips drawn into a tight line. "I've not seen him much myself."

"He asked me if I'd marry him."

I meant it to be funny, to make her laugh, but her face was ridged with horror.

"Do you love Felim?" she asked.

"In a way, I always have."

"Don't marry him, Oona. He's not the one for you."

"I know that," I said.

She nodded, and I thought she might tell me she knew he loved my brother but she only began to hum a tune to the baby.

"What're you doing here?" Felim was stood in the doorway. We hadn't heard him come through the garden.

"Oona's come to see me," Aislinn said. "Does that bother you?"

He grabbed a piece of bread from the table and turned and strode out the door.

She raked her fingers across her face.

"I'll go after him," I said.

"Don't. He's in a mood. Better leave him to it."

"I'll be fine." I ran out the door before she could call me back.

I found him on the beach. The sea was wild, as if it was angry with us. The shells were bluer than rockpools. The sky was somehow quieter; the short cliffs all around softened the wind and hushed the gulls.

He kicked a stone and it went skidding off into the little waves.

"You love me, don't you?" he said.

"Why would you ask me that?"

He dragged a limpet off a rock and poked at the yellow flesh.

"Is Enda with the Father?" he asked.

"I don't know. You're the one who goes with him."

"The priest won't have me in his house now. Enda won't talk to me now either."

"Because of your mam?"

His blue eyes shimmered. "I know who he is."

"Who?"

"Its father."

"Etain's?"

"Et-tain."

"What's wrong with you? She's just a baby. It's not her fault."

"It's Aislinn's fault. And it's *his*. He ruined us. He ruined it all."

"Felim, do you mean Liam?"

His eyes startled like I'd shone a light into them.

"I saw him swimming with your mam. He's Etain's dad, isn't he?"

"So it's him."

"Will I get Enda for you? He's your friend, I know," I said. "I know."

"He hates me now."

"Why?"

"Why do you think? Why do any of you hate me?"

"I don't hate you."

Felim brushed my arm, a touch so gentle like the stroke of a wing overhead, and leant in. He pressed his lips hard to mine. My eyes were wide open and so were his. I pulled away.

"No. You don't like me like that. I know you don't."

"But you love me."

"No."

He strode towards the waves and walked into them up to his knees. I watched as the rain hammered down on him.

Some loving part of me was falling away. I felt a cold hatred of him, that he could think he was allowed to kiss me.

The wind cut cold over me, rushing off to somewhere far away. I wished I could go with it.

In the meadow, the girl's voice was made of clear joy, rising up with the songs of a family of housemartins and a single cuckoo. She was alone for once and could listen to the thoughts in her own mind. She could finally follow her own yearnings.

When the earth split open and he crawled up from below, she was only a little surprised. His breath was fire and his eyes black as coffee.

The girl had never seen a man like him. She didn't run, even though her mother had told her to fear the unknown.

And so he took her away.

———————————

The Old Man

I leave Kate's road of tall houses, breathing hard still, heading for the river.

Mam is sick and wants to die on the island. I will see her when I go. I never thought I would. I counted on her being dead years ago. A mother should always die before her children. When Enda died, Pat asked me if he should phone Ireland to tell my parents. I said no one had a phone on the island when I left, but he said he'd figure it out and I didn't have the strength to tell him not to. I don't know if he reached them, but no one sent word. Enda and I were the outcasts after all.

When I was still a child Enda told me a story. I can still hear his voice, as nervous as scrunching paper.

"Once," he said, "there was a village where all the people looked alike. I don't mean they all had black hair and big feet. No, what I mean is they all looked normal. All the women tied their hair up tight and all the men shaved their cheeks. The villagers did this because if they did not they knew the sea would take them. To them, difference meant death. So when a little boy began to grow wings he told no one. He hid them under his shirt and he was always in pain because his feathers bent and the sharp ends stabbed his back. He had to wash in his room at night so no one would see him. He would unwrap his wings, spread them out and let them breathe. Even though he hid his difference, one woman felt it about him. For a long time she couldn't figure out what was wrong about him, but was determined to find out. One night she hid by his open window and watched. When she saw his wings unfold, her whole body was soaked in fear and horror and also passion, and it was this, her desire, that sickened her. She ran home and the next day she told everyone the boy's secret and the villagers built a huge stack of turf high enough to reach the sky. When they were finished some of the men fetched the boy and told him to climb to the top of the pile to see if there were any ships at sea, but he refused. Hearing this, the woman who had spread the whispers about his wings begged him to rescue her baby who she'd forgotten up there. He agreed."

"What happened to the boy then?"

"They burned him alive."

"Why wouldn't he just fly away?"

"His wings weren't strong enough."

I don't remember the day Enda told me that story, if we were in the kitchen or the little room at night, if he was sad or thoughtful. I didn't realise it had meaning, that he was telling me about himself. I'm not sure if the woman was Mam or just an example of what could have happened to him if they found out. Mam never showed any sign to me that she knew what Enda was, but then again, I didn't pay enough attention. I was too absorbed in myself.

Now Enda is gone, and she will be gone soon too. I wish it had been the other way around, but my prayers never were answered.

There's a payphone perching on the bridge. I could call, just to hear Pat's voice, the regular, smooth sound of his vowels, but he'd only ask questions, ask if I'd found our daughter, and there's nothing to tell him.

I walk on, my canvas shoes soaked by the streams rushing across the pavements. These streets are almost unchanged. Grey, grey Connemara stone, blackened with rain. It's not my Ireland. Mine is battered cliffs, empty fields, songs of curlews in the sky and old men telling stories by the fire.

I never painted Galway for Joyce in stories, preferring tales of places I'd never been, like the rainforest or desert, but if I had perhaps my memories of home would have lodged deeper in her because tales grounded in truth are always more meaningful.

I press a hand to the damp brick of a building. This passageway is just off the main street; a shop selling antiques with a peeling front is pushed in on either side by a cobbler's and a butcher's.

Inside, the floor and walls are cluttered with dusty grandfather clocks and oil paintings of cows in fields. A chipped rocking horse watches me from one corner. The ceiling snatches at my chin and tips it up, saying look, look. Model ships float as if on an ocean. Beneath the hulls, deep in the air-water, I am drowning.

A man dressed like a respectable scarecrow plods in from the back, licks his hand and begins to flatten his already wet hair with a damp palm. He looks more ancient than half the objects in here.

"Do you have any notebooks?" I say.

His bushy eyebrows bounce up. "You a foreigner?"

"Yes. No."

"Well, you are or you aren't. You can't be both."

"I've not been back in twenty years but I was born on Inis. Do you know it?"

"Course, never been myself. I hear there's nothing to do but pony rides. I'd rather the Canaries for a holiday. Sure I get enough rain here as it is. Would you like a towel for your hair there?"

"Oh." He's right, I'm drenched. "You're all right, but thanks."

"If you're sure. I've not got any notebooks but I've a few of my grandson's Aislings. Those are the copies the children use in school here." He's rustling under the desk. "I always leave a few in case he comes here and wants to fit in a bit of homework. Aisling means dream or vision in Irish, did you know that?"

"I did know."

"You do?"

"I used to know a woman with that name."

"And what happened to her?"

"She died."

"Death comes for us all. Ah, I've got them." He holds up some yellow notebooks. "I've got a typewriter, although I couldn't tell you it works."

"That's all right. I'll just take those. How much?"

He grins chocolate-coloured teeth. "What do you want them for?" he says.

"Sorry?"

"What do you want it for?"

"To write," I say.

"Yes, but what'll you write?"

"An apology."

He nods. "How many do you need?"

"One should be enough. How much?"

"Ah, it's yours."

"You sure?"

He smiles. "I wouldn't say so if I wasn't."

"Thank you."

I reach the door and one of the grandfather clocks begins to chime.

I stop in the cemetery wrapped around the prod church and

sit on a tumbled grave. The rain drips from the leaves of the branches above and onto my head. When I passed here all those years ago I heard Christopher Columbus stopped in Galway on his way to America. He came into the church to pray for a safe passage to India. He got his safe passage but he never made it to India. I didn't pray here before I left. I was over praying.

The Lost Boy

Rockpools shimmered with light. Hair stuck out like sunshine.

"Oona, wake up."

Aislinn hovered above me, the girl balanced on her hip. My head and belly still ached with my monthly bleeding. After the midday meal, when Mam went to the priest's, I had lain down.

"What're you doing in my room?" I said, sitting up and struggling to rip off the blankets. Since Etain's birth over a year ago Mam had hardly let me out of her sight, afraid I would learn some evil ways from the woman I was always running off to. Pegeen had told Mam she saw me talking to Aislinn on the beach. Every day, new whispers mushroomed at firesides. I couldn't get away from it.

"I need your help," Aislinn said. One cheek was streaked with mud and her red skirt was dark with water. "I can't find Felim."

The baby cooed and reached out a chubby hand.

I climbed out of bed.

"He'll be back," I whispered. "He'll be out fishing with Enda."

"No. He's never with Enda now."

Since he kissed me on the shore, I had avoided Felim. I

stopped visiting Aislinn and glimpsed Felim only at a distance trudging alone along the top road. I never saw him with anyone.

Her eyes flicked to the window, one hand pressed to her cheek. "He's not right any more." Her lip was bleeding. She wiped it quickly.

"He hit you," I said.

She shook her head, and then nodded. "I've walked the whole island looking."

"Why did he hit you?"

She paced up and down. The child nestled her head against Aislinn's shoulder and sucked her fingers.

"I don't know what to do," Aislinn said. "I don't know. I'm afraid for him."

There were few places to disappear for long on the island. The only way to really vanish was into the sea.

"Go home," I said. "I'll find him for you."

She breathed out, lifting the hair from my face. "He talks about you and Enda every day." She wiped a tear from her eye with the heel of her hand like it was a bit of dirt caught there. "I think he's lonely. I'm afraid he'll . . ."

A crash behind us.

"What is she doing here?" Mam stood in the doorway, a broken bowl at her feet. "You. How dare you bring that through my door?" Mam pointed with a shaking finger at Etain.

Aislinn held Etain out to Mam, who flinched and stepped away.

"You will not speak with my children," Mam said. "You'll not lead them astray."

"Mary, have you seen Felim?"

Mam laughed. "God is punishing you. I knew He would."

"I never meant any harm to you and your children, Mary. I only wanted to help you."

"Get out," Mam cried, great tears plopping from her chin and on to the floor.

Aislinn reached for my hand. "Help me find him, Oona."

I grasped her cold fingers. "I will."

"I'm sorry," she said to Mam and left.

Mam collapsed onto my bed, dragging her shawl across her face. I lowered myself beside her and took her hand. For a moment it lay limp against mine but then gripped me tight as she pulled in long, harsh breaths. Her tears stopped and she yanked her hand from my hold and wiped it on her skirts. It was worse than a slap. I darted up and was at the door, grabbing my shawl from the floor.

"How did you dare bring her here?" Mam said behind me.

"She came in while I slept."

There was a red spot on each of her cheeks. "Oona, get the supper going. The men will be hungry when they come home."

"I'm going to help Aislinn."

She followed me across the kitchen. "You'll stay here. That boy is bad."

I didn't turn to her but said, "You always say God protects us."

"I never said He would protect you."

I knew she had killed the fear that had lived in her since my birth, of death taking me from her. She had realised she would still be living, breathing, praying, if God took me. She no longer needed me.

I walked away from her. I walked the island. The usual boats hung below the horizon. Enda would want to know Felim was lost but there was no way to tell him.

The only way to escape here was death but Éag was too far

for me to reach and hidden behind rain clouds. No, there was no way Felim could be there. No one would agree to row him in this weather. The only other way to death on the island was down a dark passage with slimy walls where the souls of babies cried at night. I found him, a shadow of Felim in the opening of the cave, halfway into the belly of the island. There was no fear in me, but when he looked up it crashed over my body like waves onto a sinking ship. Felim's face was dripping but his eyes were clear white and blue. When he looked at me his gaze flicked away, as if I were just another shadow of a dead child, not breathing, not a friend.

"Are you all right, Felim?"

I knelt beside him, thought of taking his hands and blowing on them to warm him, bring him back.

"Felim?"

He was staring over my head; a brief flash of life, of hope, darted over him. Behind me stones crunched and scattered. Enda was stood above us. His face was red from running.

Felim staggered up and fell against Enda, who put his arm around the boy's shaking shoulders. Felim leant his head against Enda's cheek.

The tide was rushing in.

"I thought I'd never see you again," Felim said.

"You're a fool," my brother said. He was stroking Felim's back, like he was soothing a skittish horse. His movements small and careful.

"Go home," Enda said to me and walked Felim around me, out of the cave.

The sky drained of red and washed with purple but the thought of returning to Mam made me feel lonely. I took the road that wound outside the village and disappeared. The walk woke me. Who would care for me like Aislinn did for Felim? No one.

Not Mam or even Kate. Dad cared for me without knowing what really was in me. Enda loved me but he loved Felim more. I was alone.

I passed the lighthouse close to Aislinn's, but walked inland again so I wouldn't meet Enda or Felim. I watched my feet and leapt from stone to stone, missing the cracks that cut deep between them. The tourist traps. I stopped. A red coin shone ahead of me. Beyond there was another and another. A trail in the twilight. Blood.

I followed it across the stone landscape, losing it in the dark when I was close to Pegeen and Liam's cottage. A deep moaning sound leaked from the open door.

The Dead Don't Talk

Pegeen was sat on the floor by the unlit fire. Her dress was pulled over her head and she was shaking, moans and sudden gasps shuddering from her. Kieran leant against the wall, his face as white as salt, staring at the table where Liam lay with his green woollen hat still on. One red droplet on the floor by the table leg. I stepped closer. His eyes were open like the windows of a house, but no one was at home. I swallowed.

"He's dead," my brother said.

He looked up at me and tears were chasing down his cheeks.

"I was only over to see if he'd come out in our boat tomorrow," he said. "His was leaking. I told him I'd help him tar it again soon."

"Kieran," I said. Nothing else would come out.

"He came in," Pegeen whispered. "Said he was feeling light in the head. Said he'd just lie down on the table and sleep it off but he's not got up since."

"Will I get Mam?" Kieran said. "You'll have to get Liam ready for the wake."

A wail rose up out of Pegeen and curled into me with a wet weight that hung in my chest.

"Mam won't come," I said.

Kieran, deaf to me, left. I lit Pegeen's lamps but they fluttered in a draught I couldn't find. Pegeen groaned on and on to lift the roof, to lift the horror. I knelt beside her on the floor, held her hand and she didn't push me away. I moaned with her and it was like releasing all the anger I'd tied up. All the tears I'd not spilled for my sister or for Mam's coldness or for Enda moving away from me rolled out. I was on the edge of some kind of peace when Pegeen stopped, her eyes wide and fierce.

"You," she hissed.

Aislinn balanced at the head of the table, at Liam's head. Her fingers were tangled into her wet hair. "No . . . no. Felim, no."

"It's not Felim," I whispered, but she didn't mean the body.

Behind her stood Enda, his back pressed against the wall and head dropped into his hands. Aislinn clutched at her throat, gasping like she was drowning. My mind was in flight. I had told Felim Liam was Etain's dad.

Mam strode in with Kieran. She would know what to do. She would know how to care for Pegeen and Liam. She looked at me without surprise, as if she expected to see me in this place of death. She went straight to Pegeen and took the woman's hand, wrapping a dry shawl around the shaking shoulders.

Kieran went close to Enda. "Tell me," he whispered.

Enda shook his head violently, as if to get rid of the thoughts, the knowing that was racing into him. Kieran went quietly out the door again.

Aislinn began to keen and her voice was one of such beauty, such sadness, that it ripped through all of us. She didn't know you're not meant to keen until the body is being taken out of the house and you're sending them on.

"Get out of my house," Pegeen shouted. "Get out, you devil, you. You whore."

Silent now, Aislinn stared down at Liam.

I took Aislinn's hand, led her to the door and watched her weave, unstable, on the rocks off towards the cliffs instead of the way home.

I stared at the dead man. Already the handsome face was drooping, waxy. He wasn't Liam any more.

Mam crossed herself.

Pegeen slowly walked out the back and returned with a bucket of water. She poured it over Liam's head.

"Will you help me wash him?" she asked Mam.

Liam was the first man I saw without clothes on.

*

Everyone came for the wake, passing around Liam's pipe for a puff and whispering kindnesses to Pegeen. Outside the cottage I heard the other whispers. People were saying Aislinn's bastard belonged to Liam. This caught like fire in the dry tobacco. Their eyes were sharp as flint.

They whispered Liam was too stable on his feet to trip and fall like the tourists, even if he'd taken the drink he'd never slip. They whispered Felim must have knocked Liam down.

Enda stood by the wall and watched the road but Aislinn and Felim didn't come.

*

That night, I was shaken awake by Enda.

"Get a bucket," he hissed.

"What?" I rubbed my eyes, sat up. "What's going on?"

"Felim's house is on fire."

I stumbled into the kitchen but no one was there. I yanked on my shoes, ran outside, grabbed the bucket under the window and raced up the hill and along the top road. The closer I got, the stronger the smell of burning. When I reached the cottage all was dark but smoke billowed towards me on the wind. I tumbled over the wall and through the garden, my free hand covering my mouth.

From the blackness, a hand reached out and grabbed me.

"Fill your bucket on the beach," Enda shouted in my ear as he raced past.

When I got back I was half-drenched with the water I carried. Enda snatched the bucket and threw it on the smoking thatch.

"Are they still inside?" I shouted.

He shook his head, panting, hands on his knees watching the smoke shoot into the sky and the sparks finally hiss against the roof. We were just two small people and we couldn't stop the fire.

I walked back to the beach and sat there waiting. As the light turned grey in the distance, Enda came to sit with me.

"Why was no one else helping? Where were they, Enda?" I knew, though. No one wanted to help the boy murderer or the mother of a bastard. "How did you know their place was on fire?"

"I tried to stop them, but they'd been drinking."

"Someone lit it? They could have killed them."

"Yes."

"Who did it? Etain's just a baby."

"Jonjoe and some other lads."

We watched the water creep up to our feet and suck away again.

We returned to Aislinn's cottage. The thatch was singed and blackened and broken by holes wide open to the sky.

I knocked and Felim pulled the door open. There wasn't a candle lit in the place. It was black and stank of wet, burned straw.

Felim said nothing, just stood in the middle of their wrecked home.

Enda hung back at the door.

"Felim," I said. "Where's your mam? And Etain?"

"Get out," he whispered.

"What?"

"Get out. Get. Out."

He came towards me and stopped when he was close enough to touch me.

"They wanted to burn us alive, Oona." He said my name and looked at me but it was Enda he was speaking to. "They thought we were inside. You told that mam of yours about us. You told the priest." He meant about him and Enda, and I realised the priest had had words with them, had pulled Enda away from Felim with God.

I turned to see my brother and the sadness under the streaks of black on his face told me I was right.

Felim's breath moved a strand of hair across my face. Tears cut white lines through the soot on his cheeks. "Leave," he shouted, his pooling eyes fixing on me in hatred.

Enda took my hand and pulled me away.

*

I found Aislinn later in the orange evening light, staring out to sea. She was alone, without Etain. She came up to me and grasped my wrist.

"Come with me now," she said. "If we go home, we'll be happier."

"I'm Oona," I said. "Not Felim."

"I know who you are. You want to leave the island. Now's your chance."

"I'm sorry for all that's happened to you, Aislinn."

"You don't know my son," she said fiercely.

"No. I'm sorry."

She blinked at me and peered at my face as if it were for the first time.

"These are not my people," she said.

"So why did you stay?"

"For him."

"For Liam?"

She smiled and turned back to the water.

I left her, and the memory of the cold grasp of her fingers on my wrist clung to me until I fell asleep that night.

*

Two mornings later Aislinn returned to the sea. Old Daithi found her washed up on the shells.

I wept bitterly when her boat was rowed over to Éag. Felim's glass eyes were dry. He never came back that winter. The little girl, Etain, was left with Bridget. I never asked Daithi which shore Aislinn had come to rest on. I was sure it was the little one below her cottage, where she swam with Liam, and where she had pushed out her son.

Sometimes, when the nightmares woke her, the woman sat up alone by the fire wondering whether her daughter was afraid, alone as she was in the underworld.

She regretted the words she didn't tell her girl, the stories she didn't whisper over the crib. She sometimes wished she could see her child again, make a bargain to have her back, even just for a day so they could sit in the meadow and sing and weave their separate tales together until the sun set.

Family

In the little room at the top of her house Kate has left me a cup of tea, now stone cold, and there's a lump under the covers of the bed that, when I investigate, I discover is a hot water bottle. I wandered Galway for hours, walked along the pier and then out to Salthill where I stopped in a pub and took out the Aisling notebook the old man gave me, but I couldn't think of how to tell Joyce I was sorry. Aislinn would have told her daughter the truth about everything if she'd had the chance. I finished my pint and left. When I got back it was late evening and the windows were dark, but Kate had left the door open.

The chilly edge is kept at a distance by the gas stove in the corner. The room is small, made for a child, and the bedding smells of lavender and mould. At the end of the bed is a blanket made of wool spun by Mam. I'd know her uneven yarn anywhere. I sit and look at it, without touching, but then I can't resist and lift it into my lap. I run a finger along the ribbing. It was knitted for us by Bridget, who was always the best with the needles. She would make patterns as delicate and complex as the plants that weave over each other in a meadow. When I was small Mam and I had walked up to her little house to ask her to make it for Kate's birthday. We'd brought the cream to give her as payment, but Bridget wouldn't hear of it, batting her hand at us and laughing. When we were halfway down the road home Mam had sent me running back, the dish balanced in my hands, to leave it by the door for her. I had forgotten Mam took me out that day. I have forgotten many of the good times.

My face pressed against the cold window, I search for the stars but find none. When Joyce was about twelve she'd roll out a rug in the back garden with her dad and crane her neck to the heavens while I watched from the kitchen. Sometimes she'd kick her legs in the air and laugh, and I knew he'd told a joke. Out there, together, they were in another world and I could see it as if through a film of water, but I never could break through and enter.

Once she splashed through, banged open the back door and called out to me. I was lying under the table, tracing the grains of wood. Her earth-smudged shoes appeared and I did see her, I did hear her say my name. But just like she and Pat had a world of laughter, I had my own silent one and I never invited her in. I didn't want her to suffer the loneliness there. She waited. It must've been for a long time but eventually she went back outside. I think about that every day now.

If she's at my mam's, the old woman will be whispering lies and truths into my child's ear while she sleeps, like she did to me.

I pull on my shoes and go downstairs. The hall is draughty, the air pinching my bare arms.

"Leaving already?" Kate's voice echoes along the hall.

She's sat on the bottom step of the stairs, her hair a sleepy fuzz. "Come into the kitchen with me."

I follow her down a tiny wooden staircase and have to duck to avoid hitting my head on the beams above. The kitchen is small with a squashy sofa in one corner, an unlit stove and a green glass bottle on the windowsill.

"Tea or a whiskey?" Kate asks.

"Whiskey."

She lifts two tumblers from an oak press and rinses them in the sink.

"How long have you lived here?" I ask.

"An age. Almost as long as you've been gone."

"Right."

She pours two generous glasses.

There's a rapping above. Someone's knocking at the door. We wait for them to give up but the knocking continues and Kate gives me an anxious smile.

"I'll tell whoever it is I'll ring the Guards if they don't go," she says and leaves.

I pick up my whiskey and swallow. I strain to hear Kate but the walls and floors are too thick in this old place and silence rings around me. There's an ache in my belly and I remember I've not eaten much, not since Mrs. Lightly's overcooked dinner. I open cupboards in search of biscuits, stumble only on cream crackers and inhale a few.

Behind me, the sound of someone clearing their throat. I turn slowly, a cracker suspended in front of my mouth, and there in the doorway is a grey-grizzled Kieran.

"Well," Kate says from behind him. "A family reunion. I'll make us a pot of tea."

She widens her eyes at me, some secret message, but I can't take it in and she glides towards the sink.

I should embrace him, but I can't move.

He is frozen too. His skin is a cobweb of red veins and his bristly horse-hair has thinned like Dad's did.

"You're back then," he says.

"I am." I let out a breath, glad we're saying something.

"You came over from America."

"Canada."

His eyes dart about the room, never resting on me.

"I heard Mam is sick." I step towards him but stop just short.

"She'll not see you." He shoves his hands in his pockets.

"It's been twenty years."

"Did ye really think Mam would change her mind about you?" Anger flicks at the corner of his mouth. "You'll always be a traitor and a whore to her."

The words cut me because I know he believes them too.

"How is Mam?" I say.

"Holding on. Holding on. I'll not stay long."

"You will stay for a sup of tea at least." Kate puts a teapot on the counter.

"I'd rather a drop of something stronger." He perches his large frame on the sofa. For such a large man, he's almost dainty.

"How did you know I was here?" I ask.

"Kate," he says.

"I knew you'd not get in touch with him," she says to the tin of tea leaves. "So I went down to the pub this evening while you were still out and found him. He's your brother. He deserves to see you."

"Sláinte." Kieran holds up his glass.

I answer with mine.

"It's a miracle to have the pair of you here," Kate says. She walks to Kieran and holds out her hand and he shyly gives her his. "I've missed this."

Kieran empties his glass.

I knock mine back too and it stings my throat on the way down.

"Tell us about yourself," Kate says.

"There's nothing to tell you."

"It's been twenty years. Something's happened."

I try to say, I've abandoned and betrayed my husband and he'll never forgive me. My child is missing. But the words are too heavy.

"When did Inis get a phone?" I ask.

"A few years back," Kieran says.

"I can't picture technology there at all."

"But don't you remember we had the radio?"

"Who had it?" I have remade my childhood the way I want to, cutting out what doesn't fit.

"The O'Flahertys."

"Jonjoe's family?"

"Aye."

I never went to their home but still, people must have talked about it. I must have just tuned out what didn't seem important for me.

"What are you doing in Galway, Kieran?" I say instead. "I never thought you'd leave the island."

"I come for the summer work," he says. "Farm labouring, and then I go back to them in the winter. Life isn't what it was on Inis. It's all just about the tourists now. I like to get away when they flood in."

"How's Dad?"

He shrugs. "His sight isn't what it was."

"Can he still work?"

"Not much. That's a bit of why I come here. The money helps them."

"That's kind of you, Kieran."

"I never thought about it, did I? It's just what you do."

Kate leaps up and goes to the sink again. Kieran pours another glass for himself, not meeting my eye.

"I was sorry to hear about Enda," he says, and I can't look at him, can't bear to see his pain.

"Did you see much of him?" Kate asks. "I know you lived far away, but it was nice to think of the two of you over there together."

"I haven't really spoken about him. Not since it happened."

Kate squeezes my shoulder and it gives me the strength to smile at her.

"He was happy, I think. We saw a good bit of him. He loved my daughter. Joyce. They had all these private jokes together."

"I was always jealous of the pair of you," Kieran says to his glass. "I was never brave like yous."

"Of course you were, Kieran."

"No."

"The things you did to keep us fed when we were young."

"I was a coward. I was the one who riled the lads up to set the Kilbrides' cottage on fire."

You could snap the air like a sheet of ice.

"They all could've been in there," I say. "Etain was just a baby."

"They were in there. I don't know what got into us. I'd never want to hurt any of them now."

Kate smiles. "He'd like to marry Etain but she won't have him."

Kieran's ears are flushed and he rubs at his neck. "Oona, do you think Aislinn did herself in because of us?"

"She felt alone. A nothingness in her, everywhere, and she couldn't get away from it."

They are quiet, not looking at me.

"Aislinn thought," I say, "like the rest of us, that Felim killed Liam."

"Do you think he did?"

"Yes."

"Jesus." Kate knocks back her drink. "Can the two of you not be a bit lighter? Talk about the good things that happened since you last saw each other. You're making us all depressed with these memories."

Kieran laughs, gently, and shakes his head.

"I saw your Joyce the other morning."

I turn to Kate.

"He was dropping off the bike he borrowed from Jack," she says.

"She looks just like her dad, what I remember of him anyway," he says. "But prettier, of course."

Kate laughs with him.

"I'm sorry," I say to their beaming faces. "I'm so glad to see you both, but I need to sleep. I'm wrecked."

I leave them, cross the hall and go out the door. Night folds around me. Galway is punctured with lights, some blinking through the thickening dark.

It feels like a shadow is clinging to my footsteps, echoing them along the narrow streets, but when I look over my shoulder no one is there. Joyce is not there.

He Came from the Sea

Everyone thought the death of Aislinn was the end of our troubles and life would be uninterrupted again, the tide rushing in and out, the bright half of the year giving way to the dark.

No one let the sea-fairy's name pass their lips, afraid it would invite her ghost to melt through their bolted doors and press her wet lips to their ears, whispering curses. I could have told them it was dreams she entered. Most nights she came to me, joyful, laughing silently.

The priest had words after she washed up, said there was no need to get the Guards over, poor Liam had tripped on a rock, poor Mrs. Kilbride tripped into the sea. Perhaps he didn't want anyone to know his parish was thick with murderers and suicides. God knows what he wrote to the officials on the mainland, but no one came to check. Everyone always trusts a man of the cloth.

Every day Mam and I stopped in on Pegeen to cook and clean. She wandered around dropping plates and smiling sweetly at me, mumbling about "that woman." Pegeen was gone.

Felim hid on Éag all winter. The priest could say what he liked; people still had their own notions and he still lived at the heart of them. I was glad not to look at him. Sometimes I even forgot what he had done to Liam. But most days I couldn't.

One night, in the early summer, more than a year since Felim had been living on Éag, I could hear from his smooth breaths that Enda was awake too.

"He said Liam just fell, like a tourist," Enda whispered.

"Do you believe him?"

"Liam was sure on his feet. Surer than anyone."

We'd both felt Felim's anger, and he'd been controlling it, but he was always on the edge of falling into rage.

*

Summer wind whipped salt in off the sea, cooling me from the rare warmth of the sun. I was up digging the thin earth of our field with my brothers. It was only a few days until I'd be sixteen and then I would be closer to leaving, to getting the ferry and arriving at Kate's, and she would help me find a job with her or in a shop. This thought had got me through the winter while I was at my sewing. I'd make money for myself and not see all my hard work go into Mam's stack of coins.

These days Enda was always off with the priest, so the three of us being together was as rare as the sun. The holy disappearances were what me and Kieran called Enda's time with Father Finnegan. Dad had the fear that his second son was wanting to become a priest. Mam feared he wouldn't, and Enda was too distracted to notice their tense glances.

When Kieran wasn't fishing or hunting, he and some other lads went about following the girls and running races to ready themselves for the Saint John's Eve games.

The smack, smack, smack of metal rang around us. Limp

potato leaves crushed by my spade lifted a smell of rotting soil. Enda and Kieran's arms glistened with dirt and sweat. My skirts scratched my prickly, hot legs and I longed to rip off my shirt like them.

My back strained pleasantly with each slice of the spade and I wished the day could stretch on for ever. I lifted my head and there was Felim walking along the road with a loaded sack over his shoulder. He must have come to labour, but who'd take him on and risk the judgement of everyone? The only person I could think who enjoyed the presence of a sinner was the priest. I wondered what Felim had told the Father, if he confessed at all.

He'd grown taller and even thinner than when I last saw him, and there was a growth of straggly hair on his chin. Felim's shadow stretched across the field. Kieran hadn't noticed and Enda continued pounding the earth. Felim disappeared around the turn in the road.

In the neighbouring field rye wafted its moist, green smell. Far off, above the water, clouds stacked quickly with a wind I couldn't feel.

I went to the wall and watched the sky and sea blur together.

Something hard smacked my thigh.

"Wake up, you clod." Kieran laughed. "You're away with the fairies."

I threw a sod back at him, but it fell wide. My mind was all a-wander, unfixed, unfixing. The sky and sea were boiling. The wind picked up, clouds rolled in to eat the blue behind us and fat drops tapped my face, splattered the turned soil and darkened the pile of potatoes at my feet. The sky spun, darker and darker.

Far too close to the shore, I saw the ferry; it was late and no large boats ever came to this part of the coast. My gaze fastened to it. Everyone knew the shallows rose almost out of nowhere, sharp-toothed and starving. I tried to shout but my voice was gone. Moments dragged like a nail on flesh. Lightning scarred the sky and thunder rolled along the waves, up the beach, across the broken walls and through me.

"Enda! Kieran!" I roared.

Over the howling of the wind their voices yelled and their bodies ran towards the beach. My feet chased after them. The air was thick with water. From where I stood at the top of the shore, I could make out that the ferry was already swarmed by waves.

Kieran wrenched open the door of the hut where we kept the breeches buoy. We'd never used the life-saver before. No islander in the past had reached the wrecks in time.

Enda hooked the coil of rope over his shoulder and grabbed the swing. He darted past me and Kieran snatched the rocket and launcher, his eyes alight with something like excitement, and I would've hit him, only I felt it too. Nothing like this had happened before.

I tasted salt in my mouth. On the ashy sea the ferry appeared and disappeared behind black waves. I stood still, searching for what to do, who to run for, but there was nobody about except Felim in the shallows.

No one could risk taking a boat out to rescue them. The only chance was the breeches buoy. Shapes of men slipped over the rocks. If they called out, I couldn't hear. Rain battered me and my dress sucked to my skin. Women joined me on the seaweed line.

At the edge of the waves two men in oilskins planted the rocket for launching the rope. They aimed it at the ferry, marked by flitting bird-like lanterns.

A bright flash, a brilliant whooshing noise.

The ferry was all lit up. It tipped and waves swamped it. The flare went out. We'd missed. There were only two rockets left. I ran closer to the water, to the breeches buoy. It was Enda and Felim holding the flare between them, clinging to one lifeline. They pointed it, fired, and the flare lit the tar-coloured sky. The rope had missed.

They aimed the last rocket. We watched its course across the sea. A heartbeat. It took hours. I knew somehow it would bring my future to me. The light died. A hand grabbed my wrist, squeezed all the blood out. Shouts cut through the wind. Everyone shouting. They'd done it. The voices faded. The hand released my wrist. It was Mam.

I saw the words on her lips. Come home, Oona. Come home.

No. There was beg and sharpness in her eyes but nothing could make me miss this day. People would tell stories about it in the years to come. There were raindrops or tears on Mam's cheeks. I turned to the sea. She walked away.

The rope wavered between the shore and the boat. Enda and Felim and the other men slowly winched out the sling. Fear sliced the air.

The waves crashed up to my knees with brittle coldness. The women scattered. Enda stood in the shallows, steadying the rope. Felim's hair blazed when the lightning flashed. My eyes stung with the black and salt and cold. I dragged myself out of the sea. The men waited, but I didn't know what for. It grew darker. The cold began to bite at me. I watched and waited. All around was black and rain and sea lashed from above and below. How many people were on board? Just the ferryman and his lad, or more? Tourists, or what if Kate had come to visit us?

A whooshing filled my ears and out of the dark flew a body that crashed onto the stones, the waves lashing in behind it. The men ran to him—it was a him—and I was close behind. He leant against Enda.

Someone yanked on the rope and the sling whipped away again. Enda beckoned me over and shrugged the arm of the man onto my shoulders. His limbs were so long and he was floppy, as if half-asleep. My legs wanted to buckle under the weight of him. It lessened a little and I looked and Felim had taken the other side.

"Take him home," Enda yelled, and already he was running back to the sea, away from Felim and me.

Salt water was pouring off the man. He shook head to toe. He stumbled, dragging Felim and me with him, but we steadied. I felt all the weight of him in my chest. My breath came in quick bursts.

When we got to the cottage, I kicked the door open. Mam was bent over the fire. I roared over the shriek of the storm and almost in the same instant she spun, crossed herself and frowned at Felim.

"Bring him to the fire, Oona."

We placed the stranger in Dad's seat. His long body made it seem like a child's chair.

"Get out of my home," Mam said, but Felim had already left.

One hand hovering at her chest, she glanced at me, then at the man I'd brought in, and peeled off his coat. He didn't move to stop her, just allowed her to take away his layers until he was in only damp shirt and trousers. I was the one who'd carried him back. I should have been helping him.

Mam went outside to fetch water from the barrel.

The man was lifeless, empty as a shell, as if the sea had somehow taken his mind, his soul.

I stood above him. He had hair across his jaw like Jesus. I reached out and brushed it with my fingertip. His eyes fluttered open; blue. He took my hand. His skin was clean like a rainwashed sky.

The door crashed open and Mam was back in the room, her face tight and her hard black pebble eyes stuck to me. She smacked the bucket down. The man let go of my hand.

Mam led him into the small room, my room. She was gone a long while, long enough for me to boil a kettle on the fire.

Mam and I sat in silence, cups of tea growing cold in our hands while we waited for news. Not a word passed between us, because those words would have been about death.

When the sky had whitened, Dad came back alone. He said the few men on board had been spread among the villagers.

"Get the man awake, Oona," Mam said. "And bring him in. He'll have to sleep out the rest of the night in the nook."

I opened the door to the little room. The smell of sweat and sea touched my nose and lips.

I sensed him stand up.

"I'm Oona," I said in English.

"Glad to meet you." He fell against me. My arms flicked out and grasped him. As I lowered him back onto Enda's bed, I wondered if he was dead, but his hand gripped mine. He mumbled and fell silent.

A Song for a Man

In one night the island was changed. The air was warm, full of moisture and heavy with the smell of flowers. I reached the highest point of the land, near the castle, and looked out at the wreck far below. Men were on the water, rowing towards it still stranded sideways, pinned to the dead place between land and sea. Watching them under the gaze of the castle, I felt oddly lonely.

The night before Dad had helped the stranger out of Enda's bed and into the nook. Still shivering and wet, I collapsed onto my mattress but I lay awake until I heard Kieran and Enda talking and the stranger's low voice answering them. They fell quiet and I shut my eyes, waking to silence.

When I came through to the kitchen the sun was well up and no one was about, not even Mam.

I ran outside and stopped Jonjoe on the way down the hill, ignoring his blushes, and asked what the news was. He said tomorrow the four men from the boat would be rowed over to the big island beyond Éag to catch the ferry back to the mainland.

I rushed up the road, yelling my thanks over my shoulder. There was still time to see the stranger again.

I climbed down the cliff, hung with ferns and ivy, lay flat on my belly and thought of the stranger. Purple sea stock, sage and yellow samphire kissed my cheeks and forehead. The wind picked up their soft scents and made its music. There was a pooling in my navel that spread out and I rolled onto my back. The sky bent and starlings darted in and out of my sight. For once, I felt all was right.

My fingers climbed under the band of my skirt. A strange purpose came into my hand, an unknown need in my thighs and upwards to my groin. I was blank, except for need. My hand moved, urgent, fast. Then slow. I smoothed. I stopped, and my breath was a panting, shuddering. I flung out my arms, released, and breathed in the sky.

*

Mam was kneading the bread, white for special occasions, but the stranger wasn't there. The door to the little room was wide open. The beds empty. The warmth, the thrill I had made inside me, dropped away. He was gone back to the mainland. I was too late.

"He's not here," she said. "Did you see him?" She was in her church clothes, her blue dress, and it wasn't a Sunday.

I picked up the basket of washing and went down the road to the shore.

*

The sea was bitter cold, the air soft with rain. I stuck out my tongue to catch the moistness. At the other end of the beach the men were black smudges against the stones. A few currachs were out. Someone flicked the fishing line, an arc of beautiful, ordinary entrapment. I plunged the stiff laundry into the water, beginning with the men's clothes, then changed my mind, my new dress in my hands. I'd saved the money all winter, sneaking pennies from Mam's coin pot, and bought the material from a tinker. When Mam was out at the priest's I sewed it, pricking my fingers in my haste, but when it was done it fit like skin, sky-coloured and pierced with red flowers. It was the dress I'd wear to leave the island.

A man broke away from the group by the pier and walked towards me. Slowly, he grew into the tall body of the stranger. My breath came fast. He stopped above me on the stones, the water licking his boots. I looked away. His gaze, long and blue.

"Thank you," he said.

"What?" I kept my fist under the water, not wanting him to see the dress.

"The men told me you're the girl who carried me back."

"I was. You seemed to fly out of nowhere. Were you afraid to be the first to try our sling? Why were you the first one to come?"

"I volunteered to test it."

"Lucky for you it held."

He laughed. "My name is Michael. You're Oona?"

I scrubbed the sleeves of the dress against each other.

"You'll have to thank your friend too," he said. "He helped carry me back as well, didn't he?"

"He's not my friend."

Michael smiled and I bent down, stretching my arms deeper into the water.

"I went out early to explore." His hair was light now it was dry. "It's a pretty spot."

"I've not been anywhere so I couldn't tell you if it's *prettier* than anywhere else."

He didn't say anything for a moment and I watched my dress drift to the surface.

"Where I'm from it's all forests and snow and lakes." He grinned, thinking thoughts I'd never know because I'd never see the places he spoke about. I wanted to reach into him and grab them for myself. "Here life is on the edge somehow. The sea is your master."

"I'd say it was more yours after last night. I think the sea got the better of you."

He laughed again. "I guess you're right."

"I'd hate for you to get notions about us."

"I wouldn't dare."

"Are you leaving with the other men from the boat?"

"I was told there's a festival that can't be missed."

"Saint John's Eve," I said. "Yes. It's on the other island, Éag."

"Will you be going?"

"I've never gone before."

"But it sounds like it's the biggest event of the year."

"It is, but my mam never liked me to go when I was growing up."

"Well, it can be our first time together."

"I'd like that."

He was a giant, the wind catching at his leather coat. It had dried since I'd carried him back.

"Aren't you getting cold in the sea there?" he asked.

"We always do the washing this way." The sea was well up to my knees, the tide coming in. I pulled the dress out, squeezed it and walked through the shallows towards him.

"Are you a yank?" I asked.

"Something like that."

"I never spoke to one before. You're free in yourself. Not like us at all."

"You are the freest people I ever met."

"You don't know us well."

"But you don't know *yanks* well either."

"No." My neck was warm. "But I will. As soon as I can, I'm going to America."

"Why?" His eyes were sad but his lips smiling. "It's a long way. So far, you'd probably never see your family again."

"No. I never would."

A group of men passed and called him over. He was gone with a smile and a wave but he was staying on the island longer and he would come to Éag.

*

When I saw Michael again it was evening and the sky had turned the colour of heather. Our cottage was bursting with people. All the children were there, collected in their various heights. The oldest villagers were perched on stools carried from hearthsides by their daughters. The men had brought bottles of new-made potato poitín and whiskey. The doors were thrown open to leak out the heat and clatter of voices.

I felt the hum of excitement as I wove through them, trying not to watch him where he stood at the centre, willing him to glance at me with all the force of my eyes looking anywhere but at him. Instead I drank in the room the way he might, seeing the lit turf and pipes coughing blue smoke, hearing the drone of conversation in Irish, smelling the burn of cow dung and scrubbed flesh and tobacco.

While I stumbled around in my dirty red, Mam floated about in her blue dress, a sparkle to her, as if it was a wash day, as if it'd been her who'd carried him home instead of me.

"He's in your dad's chair now," Bridget said to me. "Not moved yet."

I allowed myself to peek up from her sun-creased face. His butter hair stood out among the tartan hats and white heads. Above his rough beard his cheeks were warmed by the heat of the fire and his eyes took in everything about us.

I hopped over sprawling legs, away from Bridget, and hovered by the table to listen to Old Daithi speaking to Michael.

"Where are you from?" Daithi asked.

A real quiet had fallen, as if the wind had dropped, and Michael seemed to sense it too because he blushed a little.

"My mother's family were from Ireland," he said.

Daithi nodded. "There are a lot of us over there. Is that why you came? To see where you're from?"

"I guess it was. I needed time to myself and I wanted to get away for a while. See new faces, you know?"

"Oh, I can understand that feeling," Daithi said.

People laughed and Michael grinned.

"Tell us in your own words what happened on the boat. That's what we're all dying to hear."

As he described his journey over the ocean he moved his hands like the waves and cupped them into the ferry. Somehow, I was so close to him but he didn't turn his head to see me.

"When the storm lit on yous," Daithi said, "were you not afraid you'd drown?"

"My father threw me in a lake when I was five years old, so

I learned to swim just after I hit the water. That's how we do it where I'm from. Do you throw your kids in the sea?"

The room was wintry.

"We don't learn to swim here." Dad's voice cut cold across the kitchen.

"Aye," Daithi said, breaking in before Dad could go on. "It'd be tempting fate to learn swimming. Sure I never learned and look at me. Still alive."

"That makes sense," Michael said. "But I suppose I prefer to tempt fate. I'd like to trick death, if I can."

There was a light in Michael and I wanted it.

"Why don't you sing us a tune, girleen?" Daithi said.

Everyone was staring at me.

"It's time we had a bit of music," Daithi said.

A few lamps had been lit, filling the room with the smell of burning oil.

"What'll it be?" I asked Daithi.

"A ballad or a love tune," the old man said. "I've a wish to cry."

Mam stepped in front of me, leant down and poured Michael a drink. Her dress brushed his knees and he glanced up, smiled and thanked her. Anger gritted my mouth. She was claiming him as hers.

I made the room vanish, as if it were only Michael's eyes on me.

> A hundred farewells to last night,
> and my sorrows begin anew
> With this handsome young fellow
> who beguiles me awhile on his knee
> You placed your claim on me,

O my fair love, but I'm not meant for you
For, a hundred sharp sorrows,
the ocean lies between you and me.

As the last note rang out, the room held quiet until Daithi banged his fist on his leg and wiped a bit of water from his eye and everyone broke out with murmurs and smiles.

Someone gave me a whiskey and water. It was rare for me to get a drink so I swallowed it quick. Tight-jawed, Mam beckoned for me to help her hand out biscuits Kate had sent over the week before. I retreated with the warmth of Michael's eyes on me.

Maebh, near a hundred years old, or so she said, grabbed my skirt and yanked me down so I could hear her. "It's a joy to be seeing something so fine as that new man. God did himself proud." She laughed, shaking her entire wispy frame. "Ah, sure look at you, girl. You're smitten. Keep your skirts on and don't be getting ahead of yourself. Sure he could have a wife at home."

I walked away with my head high and stumbled over someone's foot.

"We like a nickname here," Dad said, his words thickened by poitín. "I'm Ardàn, meaning tall man in English." Swaying, he motioned for Michael to stand and when he did he towered over Dad, who threw up his arms in defeat and laughed.

Mam delivered Michael a bowl of stew, bending close to his body again. I licked my salty lips and watched him eat. His hands moved slow and careful, wiping his beard and the small crease at his eyelid and along his bottom lip. Those hands were the only scarred thing about him. The cuts lit up, white, but his face was unmarked. No man could live without ageing. Even beautiful Enda had furrows in his seventeen-year-old brow, and Michael had to have seen at least twenty summers.

I looked about, wanting to share this thought with Enda, but I couldn't find him. The priest hadn't appeared either, although he would never have approved of the drink being passed about so freely, especially among the women.

I stepped outside and the cuckoo, traitor in the nest, called out a lonely cry.

The stars and endless black blinded me.

"You're sick," Felim's voice said.

He was just a solid shadow pressed against the cottage. How long had he been there, watching and listening to us? His lips were bleeding and his cheek was purple.

"Who hit you?"

"Enda."

"He wouldn't."

"I saw you," he said. "In the field, touching yourself, and I know you were thinking about him, that yank."

"You watched me." The skin on my neck felt like it was tightening, choking me, but I stepped towards him. "You're sick, watching me like that."

He moaned. "God will punish you, Oona."

"God has never punished me for a thing," I said. "And He never will. I am happy with myself." I knew the words were true. I was grown and soon I could leave and none of them, especially not him, would matter.

"You know, Felim," I said, "I pitied you when your mam died. I felt bad for the way everyone was treating you, but your mam killed herself because of what you did to Liam. I spoke to her before she went and, whatever it is you think about her, she loved Liam and she tried her hardest to love you. I don't want to be anywhere near you now. And Enda doesn't either. No one wants you. Why don't you just go back to Éag?"

He pushed himself away from the wall and I saw tears on his bruised cheek before he disappeared into the dark.

The smoky warmth and dim light inside was a relief. I slept deep that night with the memory of Michael's eyes dancing on me, in me.

I forgot Felim.

The Fires

My body woke early, traced with dreams of the stranger's imagined touch as gentle as grass against my leg. A lightness, a floatiness, lurked in me for this day. Every June I ached to go to Éag but this time the ache was sorer. Soon Michael would leave us. Every day would be the same women's work with Mam, every night empty. I begged Mam for my brief freedom and she nodded. Yes, yes, she was saying. You can leave. And I wanted to weep with joy, but I held it in.

I was light.

Not a cloud dirtied the sky and gannets rode up gusts from the water. All the currachs were loaded with turf. Everyone, big or small, had to bring a lump for burning on the great fire.

Each time I breathed in, a sense of possibility filled me. There Michael was, on the road just ahead. I ran towards him, just a few more steps.

"Oona!" Mam yelled. "Come here to me."

I dragged my feet back to her. She pressed a hand to a pink cheek. In the sun she was older. Flints of grey in her hair and under her eyes, which were on me but I looked out to sea and thought of America.

"Where'd you get that dress?" she asked.

It was my escape dress.

"Kate gave it to me," I lied.

"You'll catch your death in it." She handed me her woollen jacket.

As I got into the currach, she called after me, "Be a good girl."

I was sixteen, no longer a girl, but no one had remembered it was my birthday or perhaps just Mam, who'd let me go as a gift.

Michael was sat at the top of the currach with Enda. Neither of them looked back.

"How're you, Oona?" Jonjoe was perched opposite me, oars in hand. "You look . . . nice."

I didn't answer but looked away at the sky and towards Éag.

Excitement rippled from boat to boat. There would be races through the day and evening would have tales of the dead and ever-young, and the fire.

They rowed far out in an arc to avoid the sound between the islands, where most men were taken. As we got closer the dark stack of Éag sprang out of the green water. Waves danced through the stone arch where, Bridget had told me, once early islanders left coffins to be taken back by the sea.

We landed on the only beach, a narrow grey stretch of stones, and from there the island climbed up towards the cliffs on the other side. Everyone rushed off the boats like calves hurtling towards a fresh meadow. I jumped into the shallows and the bitter water tongued up to my knees. This was the dead land. This was where we left the drowned who washed up, the people who fell, those lucky enough to reach old age.

Everyone was crowded together, moving as one along a steep

little road that cut up the fields and past roofless empty cottages long abandoned. Enda's voice floated down to me. His head was bent close to the priest's. I searched the back of the group for the head above the rest and found Michael. As if sensing my stare he turned, and I waved. He nodded and bent his head to talk to Dad. My hand dropped and my fist clenched open and shut but he looked at me again and he was grinning under his beard.

"We'll be stopping halfway," Daithi said, making me jump. "It's flat and right for racing."

"Who is it you think will win the race?" Jonjoe asked me.

"Enda."

Jonjoe laughed. "You're very confident in your brother but he's not as strong as many of us."

"What? You think you will win?" I asked.

"You see up the top?" Daithi said, pointing towards the lip of the island, high above us. "That's where Éag falls away into the sea. There's the fairy houses up there."

Small round stone structures protruded into the sky. Michael looked up at them too and smiled back at me.

*

The day stretched and I ran and sang and danced with the rest of them, free to be wild for once. My legs won the girls' race because I tucked my skirts up and the fresh damp air bit at my skin. Most were younger than me, at fourteen or twelve even, but one or two were older so I whooped.

I left the small crowd with a thought that he'd follow and took a narrow path through taller walls where the branches of brambles bent down to scrape the earth and cut my legs before giving way again to a field of long grass with a small cottage crumbling against a wall and Enda stood in its doorway. I was about to shout to him but stopped myself. He was talking to someone inside. His voice rose high with anger and sadness. I couldn't hear what he said but it was clear he was falling apart. I turned and fought my way back through the thorns. Michael hadn't followed me and I was sure it was Felim who'd made my brother angry. Later I saw Enda out on the water, rowing like mad, face gleaming with sweat. His boat won the race and the men ran into the water to carry him and the other winners away for celebrations. Felim wasn't among them.

After the races we all walked to a ruined church, where we prayed to the dead. I thought of my sister, of Liam, but mostly of Aislinn. Death was always so close. Life should be lived. My eyes played on Michael where he was propped in the doorway, watching all of us like he'd never seen people praying before. He was smiling and it came to me he didn't understand why we were in the church. The women began sean-nós, and the lilting sad songs entered all of us, and only then did I see him catch the meaning of it. He straightened; his eyes roved the faces but his body was still, listening. I rose my voice up too. It was the only way to stop from weeping.

When it was over he sucked on an old man's pipe and told stories with the best of them, as if the music had released him like it had the rest of us. I was given a long drag of whiskey by Jonjoe. A few groups away, Michael laughed. Our eyes met and he didn't look away.

The evening closed in and the great fire was lit and the men started drinking. The children had been put to sleep in the old church, and Dad was already singing, arm around Daithi, laughing between each song. I tossed turf sods into the flames, even though girls weren't meant to tend the fire. Jonjoe gave me his poitín bottle. It burned my mouth on the way down. The hot eyes of men were on me, and the whisper tongues a-gagging. The wet of wind rode up my skirts and made the whispers all the louder. Whiskey hissed in my ears and I spun and spun and spun away with giggles and sure hands on my waist, leading me out of the crowds and away to the woven dark and the moaning sky.

I let the night carry me on and on, up the hill, and when I tripped hands I knew caught me.

It was him. I knew his smile was murmur-smooth across his lips. He was too tall for me to reach his mouth but my body tugged me upwards anyway.

"Oona?"

The moon revealed herself from behind a cloud and brushed white across the bulging backs of the stone fairy huts.

"That boy was making you drink too much. Thought you could do with a walk."

His face was turned away. My mind begged for what he was thinking, so I asked him.

"I'm too old for all this," he said.

"How old are you?"

"I'm twenty-seven."

"That is old."

He laughed. "You should go back to your family now."

"No. I'll stay with you." Keep him talking. Keep him here.

"I'm not staying on the island and I can't stay with you now. God, I wish I could. You're . . . you are *you* and . . . you need someone like you."

"I hate them all. I hate it here."

"That can't be true."

"You don't understand us."

"No."

White light danced on him. My mouth hummed with the taste of whiskey and longing.

"You took me out here," I told him.

"I know, but I wasn't thinking. You're just a child, aren't you? This place is so strange."

"I'm not a child." Not any more. "Can I come to America with you? I wouldn't be a bother."

"No. No, you wouldn't." His voice had softened and he was closer to me.

"I love you," I said.

He was quiet and behind him the sky was all big and black.

"You don't," he said at last. "You've just had . . . too much to drink. You don't know enough men; if you did you'd never choose me. Tomorrow you will say somethin' different. If you're lucky, tomorrow you won't remember anything."

I wrapped my arms around his waist, and his body was hard and cool and perfect. I felt his head dip to the crown of mine, his beard tickled my forehead, and I moved my face upwards but he pulled away.

"Sorry," he said.

He walked away from me, a tall man with hunched shoulders who only looked back once.

I sat on the rocky ground and wept in anger and frustration. I pulled out a small bottle of whiskey I'd lifted from Kieran's sack and drank.

As I wandered, the sea loudly shushed. I crawled into the open mouth of a fairy hut and lay down in the quiet.

*

In the dark someone was calling.

My head rang. Arms stiff, cold. Little bells jingling close by, the sweet voice of my sister calling me away.

A scuffling. Someone coming in. Michael had come back. My heart lifted and I tried to sit up. A word whispered. A cheek against mine. None of the prickle of Michael's beard but the smooth skin of all island men.

Leave me, I said. No.

I lunged up, but the ground smashed into my head and sparks stung my eyes. A heavy weight on my chest. Tears or rain on my neck. Above me, someone with no face.

I pushed up, but my arms were pinned to my chest. Fingers tugged at my skirts.

A fish smell in my nose.

Teeth nibbled my mouth like a child testing, playing. Kind and soft and I laughed at the tickle of it. A hardness struck my cheek and I was seeing lights again.

I pushed, somehow I pushed.

Sour mouth. A strange laughter in my voice, but not my voice.

I would crawl. That's what I'd do, but the weight was so heavy. I shoved, but only at air. Heat and weight pressed on my legs. A ripping sound. My beautiful new blue skirts. I was so angry. I yelled, but it turned into a scream.

Fire tore up from the gap in my legs and burst into my spine, my skull. I kicked and twisted and bit, and tasted blood in my mouth. My skin scorched. I needed out of it, out of this place, this body.

I swallowed sour, but it kept coming up. I spat and it dribbled down my neck. I watched for fairy lights. I saw none. I listened for the bells but none came.

I heard sobbing and I was sure I was dead. Someone had

stolen me and dragged me down to the underworld, to the dark of pain and nothing.

The weight on my chest lifted. My mouth was thick, bruised. I snapped my neck to one side and spat an evil taste from my mouth. My legs didn't work.

Hush, hush, hush, said the sea, but I was screaming.

Sobbing. I touched my cheeks but they were dry. I think the shadow touched me. I think he pulled my skirt back down. But it didn't matter. I was gone.

He must have left my body too.

*

I stood on a cliff. Far away, a flicker. Mam would be boiling water on the hearth and humming some tune her mam taught her. The doors would be shut against the dark and she safe in the bright of the lamps. I wanted to hurl this body into the sea like a stone. I crumpled to the ground, rocks slicing my arms and chest, and the flicker of Mam's light across the water went out. I was alone in my body.

The wet sucked my skirts to my legs and belly. Day came clear, as if night had held nothing, as if it was nothing but the passing breath of darkness. Only it stayed in my body. It clung moist in my clothes, my skin. I needed off with them all. I peeled my nails back—tearing. I could toss away my skin and let it float on the water.

A river lay between the green world of her mother and the grey of her husband. No living person could cross it. The waters, deep with the memories of all the dead, were poison. The girl could only cross with a guide, so her husband lifted her into the belly of the boat. She knew it was too late to change her mind and return home and still she looked over her shoulder to see if her mother was chasing after her. But when she looked her home was gone like a candle blown out.

On the journey across the river she went hungry but forced herself to keep her eyes ahead and not look down at the swirling mist, the nothing of the dead waters. The acid in the air burned her nose. She blocked her ears to the shrieks that ripped up from under the hull. In the end, she squeezed her eyes shut and waited for it to be over.

———————

No-Body

Galway is silent at night. A fine mist of rain shrouds me. As I walk beside the canal, the street lamps drip pools of light. I stop and stand outside them to think in the dark.

A swan is sleeping on her nest, sheltered by a tree, her head scooped beneath a wing.

I need to sleep too, to have strength for my return to the island, and to Éag.

I can't stop remembering Joyce, but I always drift back to the early times, when she was too little for me to lie to, before she could really hate me. These are the memories that keep me going, keep me here.

I walk the streets of Galway all night, heading out to Salthill along the water and then back to Kate's, but I don't go inside to get my bag. I just start the rental car and drive out to the pier.

As the ferry bumps away from the mainland the waves swell and beat and burble, flipping my insides round and round. It will arrive too quick; already the hills of Clare are shrinking.

When I left Inis with Michael, Mam stood on the beach and watched me disappear. Michael said later she didn't move from the spot. I didn't cry for her. When you are broken with pain, when the loss makes you want to walk into the dark and silence of the lake, sometimes you still can't cry.

I look now at the mainland, the sea, the sky, anything but the island, which I sense is growing behind me.

There are specks of blue in the sky. I cling to them even as they slide away.

Joyce used to sing when I put her down to sleep. She'd nuzzle her head against the baby pillow, shut her bright, lively eyes and pretend she was dreaming but as soon as I left the room I would hear her voice. She couldn't talk yet, she was only just two, but I would stand outside her door to listen to the squeaky la la la of her songs, and when Pat passed we'd laugh. She brought us together. But then he would open the door and go to her, and I would walk back down the hall and lie alone on my bed.

Seaweed

Dad took my hand in his, led me along the cliff and down a crooked path to the beach of broken shells. Tears ran down his rough, grey cheeks. It was Kieran who lifted me into the boat. The men kept their heads down. I lay in the bow, pulling in all my edges.

Hands held me up on the road from the pier to home. Clean washing flapped on the line. Inside, Mam was bent over the fire, stirring the flames with the poker.

"So the lot of you are back."

She turned, her hand flapping to her throat. Her knuckles were red and the skin was cracked and wrinkled.

"Ardàn," she said. "Kieran, get out of here."

They let go of me and I was clutching at nothing.

She banged about the kitchen, setting water to boil on the fire. I stood by the door, scraping at my skin with sharp fingernails, and watched the floor, the table legs. She dragged me to the tub. It wasn't set up in the bedroom like usual but in the middle of the kitchen. She pulled my dress over my head and tossed it on the fire. The red flames licked up the sea-blue fabric.

She pushed me into the scalding water, forcing the breath out of me. She tore my skin with a rough brush. The tears began to fall.

"Stop that."

"Mam?"

The scrubbing got fiercer but I couldn't stop the tears. The slaps were no surprise. My head bounced off the back of the tub.

"You let him. You filthy whore."

Nails scraped me. The tears kept coming. It was Dad who had to pull my mam off me.

*

Sleep didn't come.

I stayed in the little room, afraid of Mam in the kitchen, more afraid of who was outside the cottage, what faceless man passed on the road. Any one of them could've been him.

Days ground by. Enda sat with me on the bed and chatted, telling me little things. He was going to be a priest. He asked me to pray with him, but prayer turned my mouth to dust.

"Oona?" Enda whispered. "Will you talk to me?"

I shook my head.

"Michael was with us most of the night on Éag."

I stuffed my fingers in my ears. I didn't want to hear.

The little room became my cell. I sometimes slept but in my dreams I was on fire. I woke screaming.

I woke and ran.

*

The water bit my legs. My skirt sucked and sloshed, pulling me further out. I watched the horizon and pictured myself in a new country, a new life, a new Oona. The answer was so simple. I would leave.

"Oona." The sea was calling me.

I took one last gulp of air and slipped under. The cold, the dark, wrapped around me. I was with her, my sister. I reached out to her, to comfort her, and felt her arms wrap around me. She whispered my name.

I pushed at the weight on top of me, struggling, and light and air burst through the dark. I was coughing and a stone weight pressed on my chest and I shoved at it and crawled across the sharp rocks. My eyes stung and there he was, beard dripping onto me.

"Oona?"

It was him. Michael. His fingertips were fumbling about my chest.

"Get off me," I cried, and slapped his hands away.

"Keep breathing."

The rocks were slippery but I hauled myself up.

"Here." He offered me a hand.

"No."

I stood to face him on my own. He was drenched and trembling. It began to rain and he lifted the camera hanging on a leather strap around his neck.

"I think I might've lost all my photos," he said. "You can't get a camera wet."

"Why did you jump in the sea then?"

"You were—" He pointed at the waves.

"You don't know me," I said.

"Will I take you home to dry?"

"No." My teeth chattered.

"I'm leaving tomorrow on the ferry," he said.

"So am I." It was sudden but it was true. The sea had thrown me out; my sister hadn't wanted me. I would travel away from them both. I would be that other Oona.

He nodded. "Where are you going?"

"Anywhere else."

"You could come with me."

*

Sleep never came. I left the cottage before sunrise. My brothers were still sleeping, and I didn't wake Enda; if I did, if I told him I was leaving, I knew I wouldn't go. I met Michael on the pier and almost felt glad to see him. He'd spent the night at Bridget and Daithi's and was fresh and rested and smiling. It was a lovely smile and it made me sad. He was with two men I didn't really know, who were there to row us out to the ferry. I felt them watching me, but it didn't matter: I would be gone soon, for ever.

"I didn't know if you'd come," Michael said.

"Let's go."

One of the men pointed out that the ferry wouldn't be in the bay for a while yet. We sat in silence, waiting. A few more people gathered on the pier and I tried not to look at them. Eventually we were rowed out.

From the back of the currach I looked out at the grey-green back of the island, the old whale, for the last time. Along the thin stretch of yellow beach Mam was running towards the pier. Her red skirt slowing her. The small smudge of her blank white face was the last piece of the island I saw before I turned away.

"So," said Michael. "How far would you like to come? To Dublin?"

"I want to come all the way to where you're from."

"There's not much there and we don't know each other."

"Please, you could marry me. I wouldn't be a stranger then."

He coughed. "You want to be married?"

"Please, Michael. I need to leave."

He looked me in the eye and I didn't look away. There was nothing left in me to see.

"Okay, I'll marry you."

*

We landed in Galway and stopped in the church where Christopher Columbus prayed before he journeyed to America. The priest was in a panic with us. He'd never had such little notice for a wedding. For a start, he said, the banns hadn't been read and what about my parents' permission? Michael said words to him quietly but the Father shook his head. It would be done on the boat to America instead, Michael told me, and asked me again if I was sure and I said I was.

The city was full of noise and heaved with more people than I'd ever seen. My breath came in raggedy gasps. I wondered if I should stop at Kate's work, to be warmed by her familiar face, but I stopped that notion. She'd ask me questions, and when I answered she'd make me return to the island, to Mam.

I could tell Michael was getting unsure when he started pacing up and down on the steps of a bank where we were waiting for the bus.

"How old are you?" he asked.

"Nineteen." I didn't even blush at my lie.

On the bus to Dublin I pictured lots of things: what food we'd have at the hotel, what a hotel looked like, whether there would be buildings as tall as the ones in Galway; but beyond Dublin my mind couldn't stretch. He tried to describe it to me. How big the "ship" would be at Holyhead. How long the "crossing" was. I know boats, I told him. But, he said, you don't know any like this.

*

We stopped in at a hotel with red carpets and gold doorknobs. There were long mirrors just inside the door. Reflected back at me was a short girl with wild hair and a blackbird's eyes.

The man at the desk asked twice if we were married, and Michael got annoyed. It was the first time I saw his stillness ruffled. I climbed the stairs slowly. You could fit a cottage in the bedroom. The bed was big and white and looked soft like a cloud. I didn't go near it. My eyes were heavy and I stood blinking and bleary in the bright light hanging on a string from the ceiling.

"I'm sorry I can't really afford two rooms," Michael said. "I'll sleep on the floor. Are you all right?"

I nodded and he went into a small room and shut the door. I dragged off my dress and put on my nightie, but even though it was warm in the room I shivered. I stared down at the street where cars shone their bright lights and flocks of people hurried by. The door of the little room opened and he stood there in the blinding light. He treaded towards me.

I stood still.

He stepped closer. He was smiling. I looked away.

"Don't get any closer," I said.

He halted. "I just wanted to look out the window."

"I need to go." I rushed past him into the small room.

It was strange and white and shiny. I ran my fingers along

everything and tried to figure out where I could piss, and where I'd get some water. I fiddled with things. He'd want to touch me. I let the cold run and scrubbed my body until it hurt and shone pink.

He'd taken up my position on the windowsill.

"Do you believe in fairies?" I asked.

He laughed, but his face was serious. "I don't."

"Do you believe in God?"

"No."

"I've not met many people who are brave enough to believe in nothing. Do you not find it scares you? What if you're wrong?"

"You mean am I afraid of hell? No. Things in this world scare me more."

"I know what you mean."

"Do you believe in hell?"

"I do. Sometimes."

"I wouldn't have . . . you know, touched you."

"I know."

I walked slowly to the window and sat, leaving a good gap between us. We were quiet for a while. He gazed through the glass, at the building opposite. A little smile crept up his lips and he began slowly to shake his head and chuckle.

"This is the weirdest thing I ever did," he said.

"Me too."

"Why did you come with me?"

"I always wanted to go to America and I liked you and your beard."

He stroked it. "Glad you noticed. I've worked hard on it."

He lay down on the floor, yawning. I lowered myself onto the bed.

"I was afraid to go on my own," I said.

"It scares me too."

"You can come up."

"No. I'm all right."

"You won't be in the morning. You're a tourist, you're used to sleeping on a bed."

He lowered himself down beside me and rested rigid as a plank. In the yellow light his chest rose and fell gently, and I wondered what it would've been like to lie in this bed with him as the old me.

The morning after, we bought new clothes: a blue suit and a straw hat. He laughed at my choices but said they were "just great." Next, my photograph was taken in a studio off Grafton Street and brought with my documents I'd taken from the dresser in the kitchen before I left to make me a passport. We got the night-mail boat, *Princess Maud,* to Holyhead. There were some folk from the West onboard and I was able to speak Irish with them. It was only then I thought of my brothers fighting over dinner for the last lobster, the clock ticking above the fireplace and the smell of Dad's pipe smoke. My eyes stung in the wind on the deck.

I never even left Enda a note.

The first day on the big boat to America, Michael got the captain to marry us. That night we went up on the deck and looked at the stars, the same as the stars I used to see on the island.

In a cabin with bunks I threw up in the bucket on the floor. I wiped my mouth and took the drink of water he offered me and went to sleep in the bottom bunk.

The next day, when the boat was in the Atlantic, I threw up anything I ate and lay in bed shaking. He came to tell me what had happened, what he'd seen, and I listened. It was all so new. He told me about Saint Patrick and I couldn't stop laughing that he, a Canadian, was telling me about my country's saint. My dad loved him, he said more enthusiastically than he'd said anything before. Soon I named him Pat when I was teasing him. Soon it had stuck.

I decided to get well. I decided to forget.

Cold Wings

I was a bird dropped out of her nest, tumbling on a sharp wind. I didn't weep much in the New World. I held the shock of it inside.

We were released from the boat into the sticky air of New York. Red-yellow-white cars flashed past, screeching and honking when I stumbled off the sidewalk. Sidewalk. There were new words Pat reeled off as if I knew them. Train, trash, chaps, attorney, diner. I got tired of the sound of myself asking him what he meant. I just nodded and soaked it all in. I had finally arrived in America. I was free and I searched in myself to find a sense of soaring, but instead I was falling. It wasn't the beautiful country of many trees I had pictured; it was full of people in bright clothes and strange hats and dark glasses. There were neck-creaking skyscrapers that shot up like giant pins to pierce the sky. I longed to stand on top and see out across the whole world. But we never went up. We never saw the sea again either, even though we stayed for two days.

He bought a new camera and took pictures, and when he got them developed we laughed at the ferocious black-haired creature he'd frozen in them. I didn't know you were meant to smile in photos.

In one of his diners we ate frozen cream and I'd never tasted anything so delicious in all my life. It sent shivers all through me. Pat laughed at how I vanished it and ordered us two more in different flavours. I told him I would be happy to eat ice cream for every meal.

We took a bus north and I threw up again and again, and had to get out at every stop to breathe. Each town was the same, sun-drenched with square buildings all together in neat lines. They didn't seem natural. I slept too and woke surprised to find my head on his shoulder.

We stopped in Montreal and Pat got us a room in a motel with pink flowers printed on the curtains. I'd slept so long on the bus, I sat awake by the window with nothing outside to look at.

I could leave but I didn't know where to go or how to live alone. I was in the place I'd always hoped to reach, America, or what he kept telling me was now Canada, but this country was so much larger than I'd ever imagined. I didn't fit here and I didn't know how to survive on my own. I was a wife now.

I sat beside him and quickly, without thinking, I pressed my mouth to his. We were married and I wanted to wipe out the past. Are you sure? he whispered, but his voice was already muffled in my hair. I could say no, I could, but I nodded. I was a wife. I remembered Mam sobbing and I didn't want to be like her. I wanted to be like Aislinn. I gritted my teeth. We undressed before I could think, and he gently kissed my face. He kissed me down my body and I couldn't move, and then he kissed me down there, making shocks of fear and pleasure, making me want to cry, and he stopped and it was worse. While he was in me, I felt like I would throw up, but I swallowed it down. After, he wrapped his arm around me and told me we should've waited and I felt my anger at him down low, in my belly. I wouldn't do it again.

In the morning we went early to catch another bus but he stopped first at a shop and picked us up two sugary buns with holes in the middle. While we ate them at the stop, I asked him, "Why was it you married me?"

He coughed and his Adam's apple bounced as he swallowed his mouthful.

"I liked you and everyone knew it," I said. "But you didn't like me."

"I did like you," he said. "But I always think every little thing through, sometimes so much that I end up never acting at all. The first impulsive thing I ever did was buy my ticket to Ireland. I used most of the money my dad left me, which most people would say was a bad decision. But with you, I can't explain. It wasn't an impulse but more like a need."

The bus pulled up in front of us. He didn't move to get our bags so I reached out for them.

"Wait," he said. "I want to explain it right to you. I felt like I needed to take you away from there."

I looked down at him on the bench and felt oddly tall for once, but he didn't glance up.

"I'm sorry about last night," he said.

I picked up my bag and went to stand behind the other people getting on. He stood behind me.

"And you're also pretty," he said, "and funny, and I knew my mother would never like you."

We arrived in his city, Ottawa, and she was waiting for us on the porch of a big white house with windows all along the bottom and the top. She looked like a doll. Not one of those cheap plastic ones but a tiny one made for a tiny house with a tag around the neck that said "housekeeper." She wore a stiff grey suit-dress and a face to match.

"Michael," she said. "I didn't know you were coming today."

He laughed. "You knew." He was carrying his bags and I stood beside him with my little sack slung over my shoulder.

He kissed her on the cheek and she beamed but her smile fell away when she looked down at me.

"And you are the new wife," she said. "Well, she's very young and short, Michael."

"This is Oona. Oona, my mother, Joyce."

"Mrs. Lightly," she corrected.

"Good to be meeting you," I said.

She sighed. I followed her into the giant hallway.

"Is it just you who lives here?" I asked.

"Yes. Michael's father died twelve years ago."

"Sorry."

"You'll be staying upstairs. Are you hungry? I'll get you something. Blueberry pie? Coffee?"

"I've never had blueberry pie. We had coffee in the city. It was awful. Do you have tea?"

"No."

She gave Pat a look of disbelief. They towered above me but I could still see their faces. He was grinning like a fool, without a notion of what she was thinking, all her judgement. I wanted to hit the pair of them.

"I'll drop the bags upstairs," Pat said, and left the old woman and me alone. She coughed. She had to be at least fifty but she was as straight as a stalk of rye and her face as smooth as Mam's. No. I'd told myself not to think of her, not to think of the past. I'd have to teach myself better.

Mrs. Lightly shuffled past so as to avoid touching me and

strode away down the hall. I sniffed my armpit; a little overripe but not that bad. I wasn't catching. I stomped into the big room and found it stuffed with dark, sharp-edged, shiny furniture. Above the fireplace there were photos in cold silver frames. Most were of a light-haired, smiling boy. In the best one the boy looked about ten and was sat on a shore by water, laughing up at the photographer. I stroked his little face.

Behind it was another picture of a grown woman. She was half-turned away and had round glasses pushed into her short yellow hair. She was beautiful, laughing too.

Mrs. Lightly marched in with a tray stacked with cups and slices of what I guessed was pie.

"Is she Michael's sister?" I asked, pointing at the woman with the glasses.

"No. I only had one child," she said. "Michael," she added, as if I had no sense at all.

"Who's this then?"

"Sally was Michael's fiancée three years ago." Mrs. Lightly's grey-green eyes were pinned to me.

"What happened to her?"

"It was a car accident. Terrible."

My feet itched to run but I had nowhere to run to.

*

Pat's room was too hot. I sat on the bed and waited for him. It was still early but I had complained of illness so I could get away from Mrs. Lightly.

Unlike the other rooms, Pat's was almost bare of furniture. Just a bed, a press, a shelf full of books, and a honey-coloured rocking chair in one corner. I pulled the chair into the middle of the room and sat on it. It shaped against my body to hold me, smooth as a pebble.

There was a knock.

"Are you sick again?" he asked.

"I don't know what's the matter with me." I gently rocked.

"It's all new to you." He lingered at the open door.

"Come in," I said. "It's your room."

"It's yours now too." He walked to the dresser and lifted a brush. "We won't be here long. I'll get us our own home."

"That'll be grand. This is such a big house, but it's not a home."

"I guess not."

"I'm going to read those books." I pointed at his shelf. "I'll finally be able to put Enda's teaching to use. We only had the Bible at home, and a few others I stole from school."

"Tell my mother that. About the Bible, not the stealing. She loves that book." He pulled a thick one off the shelf. "Herman Melville. My favourite when I was a boy."

"What's it about?"

"A whale."

I sank onto the bed beside him. "I know a story about a whale."

"I bet it's a good one."

"It is."

"Michael!" Mrs. Lightly's voice cut between us.

"I'll go down," he said.

*

Three weeks of almost nothing whipped away from me. I found some books on Mrs. Lightly's shelves that told me about the country, its cities and people. All the words I didn't know I skipped, but I soaked in enough to make me thrill at the thought of living somewhere so vast and unexplored. One book said you could walk for days among trees and never see another person. One day soon I would leave and breathe in the forest air.

Pat went back to his job running the family furniture factory. He was saving money so we could buy our own house. I said I'd go out to find a job myself but Mrs. Lightly sighed. "You can't work. What would people think?"

Sometimes she reminded me a lot of Mam.

When I told Pat I wanted to work, he scratched his head. "I know it's boring for you . . . but I don't know what you could do here."

"What about a shop? Or I can always dig. I'm good at farming."

He laughed.

"I'm used to always doing, Pat."

"Why don't you help my mother?"

"She doesn't want my help. You don't cook like I do. Everything I know doesn't make sense here."

"I'm sorry." He did look sorry, but he never found me a job.

Some days I enjoyed the ease of doing nothing, but my legs began to ache with the lack of moving. I went walking one day, past many, many houses, and found the city. It was smaller than New York, and much less exciting. I went into a huge shop with clothes hung everywhere. I flicked through them, overwhelmed. I found a short yellow dress that would swing just above the knees. It was the kind of outfit I'd always imagined I would wear when I worked as a secretary with Kate. I walked up to a woman with her hair fluffed up on top of her head and asked her to hold it for me while I went home to get money. She sniffed and said, "We don't *hold on to* our stock. If it's still here when you come back, you can buy it." She gave me a look like she didn't expect I would be able to afford it. I had been planning to ask her if they had any jobs going, but swallowed my question. I never went back there and stayed inside Mrs. Lightly's more and more.

Pat's book made me ill. It was impossible to make the words stay still. When I could focus, I found Ahab's whale was nothing like the island whale, or the mother who washed up on our shores; but the men were like the ones I knew, ready to slice a creature apart.

*

I was sick when I woke up.

Breakfast was tasteless white bread and pink jam, or jelly, as Mrs. Lightly said.

She took me to her doctor, who poked inside me with cold fingers and asked me about my last bleeding. I told him it was about seven weeks ago.

"I thought so. I'm happy to tell you you're pregnant," he said.

"But how?"

He blushed, and explained quickly to me what he meant.

I counted in my head from when Pat and I were at the motel, and it was all wrong.

I thought back further, but my mind blocked me.

When I came out of the doctor's room I couldn't stop the shakes and Mrs. Lightly rubbed my back.

"Silly child," she said. "I wondered why he married you. I should have known."

"If I'm pregnant," I said, "I can't leave here."

"And where would you have gone? Come on."

She held my hand as we walked out into the street, where cars screamed past and children shouted, and somewhere far away a baby was crying.

*

Mam told me island women sometimes died giving birth, usually as a punishment for some sin, but even when I told Pat this the notion of becoming a father burst new life into him. He bought diapers and bibs and a big dress for me. I didn't wear it until my Dublin clothes wouldn't fit me.

Birth was as unknown and terrifying to me as Éag when I was small. All I had was my tiny sister falling out of Mam's dress and the stories of my birth and Aislinn pushing out Felim on the beach.

"How was it when Michael came out of you?" I asked Mrs. Lightly one morning.

"I don't want to remember it." She didn't meet my eyes. "After Michael, I decided no more children."

"You can stop it?" I said. "But how?"

She walked out of the room. She was the worst person I ever knew for holding a conversation. And there was no Aislinn here to ask these kinds of questions, or even Enda. It was just me, and I didn't know anything about this kind of life. I wanted to cry but when I tried nothing came out.

*

I was stretching, lengthening, pulling. My body was no longer mine. It was a boat carrying a child to shore.

Mrs. Lightly told me a woman with a child in her belly cannot work. Pat grimaced at me but nodded. I told them where I came from women worked until the day the baby came out. She gave him her look above my head.

I woke with the sun every day and while they were still asleep I left the house and walked to the edge of the town and into the woods. They were my first trees and they sang to me. Branches creaked in strong winds. Leaves kissed noisily. The sounds reminded me of the sea.

This was what I had dreamed America would be. I walked through the trees, going deeper and deeper each morning, saw leaves catch fire as the weather turned cold and the flames fall to the ground and die. I woke one day to find the ground solid, pressed my fingers to it and the bitterness shot through me and snapped under my feet. It was hard to walk but moving absorbed my concentration. Next came the ice-rain that needled my face and hands, and after was the snow that made the trees shiver and drop white dust on my head.

With white roofs outside we ate Mrs. Lightly's meals of chewy meat, sliced bread, mushy carrots. I offered to help, told her I was good at making a tasty fish supper, but she said it was hard to get fish this far inland. How far am I from the sea? I said to her. Her answers changed every time I asked and I realised she'd never seen the sea.

Pat came home one day with a pomegranate. At the door he knocked the snow off his boots and approached me where I was sat on the lowest step of the stairs, stroking a swollen belly. Instead of taking off his icicled coat, he pulled the blushing fruit out of his pocket, brandishing it like a prize, like it was the medicine that would cure his sick wife. The shine and hope of his eyes, the pure faith he held in the fruit, in its miraculousness, made me smile at him and eat it when he sliced it open.

It tasted like the sweetest, most holy food, and while the juice was still on my tongue he kissed me tenderly. That night, I let go and I was no longer thought but feeling. I curled against him like a seed and fell deep asleep, waking late in an empty bed, just me, and the baby, leaping about inside me.

When the girl was a small child, her mother whispered stories about the underworld, telling her it was a land of golden fields and magical orchards.

As the girl stepped off the boat she was shocked to find it barren, bare rocks mantled by an inky sky. The flowers piercing the broken soil were red and when she plucked them they wilted in her hand. In her new house that she was meant to call home, it was always night and there was no moon to light her kitchen. She could not sleep and sometimes on the knife-sharp wind she heard the screams of tortured souls. Her mother's lullabies were gone and she had never felt so alone.

———————————

The Island

My shoes are thick against the rough island road and I can't feel the stones beneath. The rain comes down so heavily it's hard to see beyond the low wall in front of me. The ferry is lashed to a new quay, all bulky concrete.

It's twenty years since I've been here but the island is the same. There are no trees, not one. Just low rolling green slashed by the knitwork of stone walls. I keep walking, leaving a fork in the road behind, but I know this is not the way home. The land should be rising and instead it's falling again.

The waves splash in a haze of quickening darkness and the rocky land slips down to the sea. I had forgotten how the sky stretches here, rippling with clouds that race towards the Clare mountains, north to Connemara and beyond, to the ice and winter of my New World.

I find the back roads and keep my head down every time I pass a cottage. The windows reflect black like empty caves. I can't see in but they can see out. I want to stop the stories from being spun but I can't. They'll be on the lookout for me because Joyce, with her bright young face and questions, will have started the whispering already. I can't help glancing up at them, wondering if Joyce is inside.

I walk along the coast road and ahead a boy of about twelve is splayed on the back of a tractor with a collie on his lap. His blue eyes rove over me, but in a lazy way like he's only mildly curious to see yet another tourist. The driver in a hat, who has to be his dad, slows the tractor as they come to a gate. The boy jumps down, dog bounding at his heels. He grins at me and there is something of Enda's spark at the curl of his mouth. My fist rises to my chest.

"Are you looking for the wreck?" he calls to me in English.

"I am," I say as I gain on them.

The man barely glances at me and I don't recognise him. I pass them, smile and glance at the boy again. He's opening the gate and the man drives the tractor through.

"You'll find her just over the rise," he calls. "Can't miss it."

"Thanks," I shout back.

I didn't need anyone to tell me where the boat wrecked and Pat shot through the night to be delivered to me like a damp present. Would he have changed his mind, not married me if he knew everything that would come later? All the trouble I'd bring?

The wreck is huge. A rusted orange metal carcass, hollow and gigantic. It reminds me of the whale, but every part of her was used. She lit our lamps with her oil. Filled bellies for weeks with meat. Her bones fashioned needles so we could clothe ourselves. She nourished us like a mother until the harvest came and she was no longer needed. But the metal of a ship could never be sawn away with the tools the men had, and what would they have used it for anyway?

I sit for a long time with the wind biting my ears and stare at the wreck. The cold is deep in me when I stand and shake myself off. I shouldn't have stayed so long but I am afraid of finding Joyce. I'm afraid of what I have to do and say.

*

I stop outside our old home. Grey and red washing flaps on the line. The wooden door flakes with salt as I push it open. Inside, the air is stale, floor swept and table scrubbed. On it rests a brown loaf, a pat of butter and a steaming pot of tea. The dresser still has the blue china on display, Mary stood proudly in its midst, and by the hearth in his old chair is Dad. His skin is more weathered, lined like a map of his life. He can only be in his sixties, but the island has drained his life away.

I run to him and he looks up, but his eyes are milky.

"Dad," I whisper. "It's me, Oona. I'm come home."

I kneel by him and a faltering hand closes over my head. He strokes the short strands of my hair, leans down and kisses me.

"I knew you'd come back," he says.

He smooths his rough hand over my cheek and my tears slip over his fingers.

"Your girl is just like you, love," he says. "Just like you."

Red Milk

Pains tore across my lower back.

"Ssssh," Pat whispered, stroking my shoulders ineffectively. Mrs. Lightly was asleep so I bellowed louder, curses rolling out of me as easy and loud as waves crashing against a cliff. There was a massive rock stuck inside me, pulling me down, and it had been getting heavier all night. The bed was wet. He bundled me out of the house, guiding me over the spring ice and into the cold car. His braces were loose around his legs and he had no coat.

Street lights flicked by and became a blur. It hurt my head. Mam's pale face pressed close to me. I didn't know what would happen. She never told me anything. She never told me what to do.

In a room, in a bed, they looked inside me. I roared at them and Pat squeezed my hand but they whispered to him and I yelled at him to tell me the truth.

"The baby's the wrong way around and you're not breathing right."

He said more, but I stopped hearing him.

They took me away from Pat, placed a mask on my face and

while I slept they cut me open. The smell of sweat and bleach woke me.

I saw the baby first through a fuzz of medicine. My beginning was magic, delivered to Mam by the Virgin Mary. My new baby was sliced out by people in rubber gloves. An ugly story. I sniffed her and she smelled of nothing, just skin. Clean. That was when I decided I would never tell her the story of her beginning. I'd tell her nothing.

*

I sat in the front room with the six-week-old baby on my lap. Out the window rose bushes weren't yet blooming, a boy streaked by on a blue bike. A cat shrieked.

Mrs. Lightly watched me like she was sure I'd drop the baby or forget to feed her. But this morning she was at one of her church meetings.

Pat rocked the chair with his foot to lull me because, he said, since the baby's birth I was jumpy.

"Quiet, isn't she?" He went to the door and perched himself there, wearing a relaxed smile and his ironed work shirt. Somehow he slept through her midnight cries, waking content and rested in the mornings. The baby screamed and screamed and I would sit in the cold moonlight downstairs.

The chair's rockers squeaked against the floor. Pat reached down and stroked the baby's head, his mouth creased with love.

"Any ideas for a name yet?" His daily question.

"No. I can't think, Pat. Leave us be."

I was afraid to name the baby. Names have meaning. In Irish, Oona is a lamb, a sacrifice. In the story Bridget told me when I was a girl playing by the fireside, Una was queen of the fairies, a cursed mortal woman forced to live in Tír na nÓg, a frozen life, a marriage to an immortal fairy king. But that Una could return home every summer. I could not.

If I gave the baby a name, I would curse her with all the weight of one.

Another car passed. The baby mewled. I put my nose against her soft forehead and hummed a song from childhood. For a moment she quietened, her blue eyes full of knowing.

She was heavy against my breast. Limp strands of black hair had fallen into my eyes but I couldn't move to wipe them away. I couldn't disturb her. It was days since I'd washed. I was moored in my seat, tied to the harbour of mothering.

As if she were listening to my thoughts, the baby began to cry, her flushed face scrunched with effort.

"What about Joyce?" Pat said.

"What?" I asked. She was roaring.

He leant on the doorframe, peaceful, somehow deaf to the monstrous screams.

"The name. Joyce," he said. "For the baby?"

"Isn't it your mother's name?" I asked, bouncing the baby, trying to dampen the sound.

"Yes. You don't like it?" He frowned. "We could call her after your mother. Mary? It could be a nice reminder of her and the island."

"No. Joyce is grand. I don't care. You choose, but not Mary."

"Joyce then." He smiled.

The name Joyce means cheerful. Joyce shrieked in defiance at this daft new christening.

"Do you think she doesn't like it?" he asked.

"Babies don't have a choice about anything," I replied.

Joyce's howling filled me up and I couldn't hear anything else.

Pat stood staring. I unbuttoned my dress and placed her to my breast. Her rubber mouth was strong, her cheek already smeared with blood. My hand clenched the wooden arm of the chair, to focus the pain and stop me from squeezing the life out of her. Deep breaths. She needs it. I have to. This is what mothers do. I longed to unclamp her, even brushed my fingers close to her mouth to test, but Pat was smiling at us because I'd drowned her screams in a river of motherhood. It was the first time she and I played our game of lies for Pat's sake. In some way we both must have wanted to protect him. So many lies are built out of a wish to shield the ones we love from the horror of the truth.

The next day when Pat returned from work, grey under the eyes but beaming, he presented us with a piece of paper.

I squinted at it. "Nice bit of writing there."

"It's got her name on it. It's official," he said. "We'll have to christen her later, of course."

There was no escape. She was bound for ever by words to the name Joyce.

Running

One morning, deep in the bitterness of winter, I returned from one of my walks and pushed the back door open to find Mrs. Lightly stood in the kitchen. She was shoving bread into the toaster.

She turned. "What are you doing?" Her eyes were sharp as metal.

"I was out walking," I said, sidling around the table towards the hall door.

"It's freezing out there." That's all she said, but I heard the rest. She never needed to say more than a passing phrase to be understood. I knew she was saying, *You're mad, you left your daughter alone, you're a terrible mother.*

"I'm fine," I said, as if I'd not heard the rest at all.

She drew her lips into a tight line, dipped her chin a little and left the room before me. I watched the red glow of the toaster. A stinging, burning smell hit my nose. The white bread slowly transformed to black. I put my finger out to touch the glow, the black.

"Oona!" Pat grabbed my hands. "What's wrong with you?"

"Wrong? Nothing."

"You were touching the fire."

"I know."

His hands floated into his hair. "You can't go out in the cold like this. It's dangerous for you. Okay?" His eyes were too close together.

"I need it," I said. "I need the air and to hear the trees. They sound like the sea."

He examined my tingling fingers. "You scared me. What if Joyce woke up and you weren't there?"

"Our daughter sleeps in the morning, Pat."

"I know, I know, but—"

His mother was stood behind him. A shrill sound rang in my head. I told them I was going to bed.

*

" 'Can a woman forget her sucking child,' " Mrs. Lightly was reading the Bible to me. " 'That she should not have compassion on the son of her womb? yea, they may forget, yet I will not forget thee.' "

It was autumn. We had been in this high-ceilinged house for more than two years. The baby was just over a year and I was eighteen and my days were dull and empty. I couldn't escape to the forest any more, as Mrs. Lightly was always watching me.

She sat solid as a cow on the dull striped sofa, the style the women at her church approved of. The Lord's book was held in front of her face and I was perched on a hard chair, tangling my fingers. Together, apart, together.

Dust spun in a rod of sunlight. A car horn blared down the street and it seemed like the first real sound I'd heard all day. The house was dead.

I strained to listen for the baby's cry. Mrs. Lightly was always there to take Joyce from my arms as soon as she was finished feeding, to "put her down to nap" or "give her a bath" or "take her for a walk." She pretended to clean or cook, but she always made excuses to watch me, to check. I always had to be two steps ahead of her with my "But I washed her this morning" and "It's fine. I'm not tired. I'll walk her now."

"'Even so every good tree bringeth forth good fruit,'" Mrs. Lightly said. "'But a corrupt tree bringeth forth evil fruit.'"

I often got the feeling her Bible reading was just for me.

"Did you hear what I just said?" It was Pat.

"I did," I lied.

He and Mrs. Lightly gave each other the look. He knelt beside me, nibbling his lip. Through the window, the wind was blowing leaves yellow, brown and red.

"Oona?"

"Mmmm? Where's Joyce? I need to be feeding her."

"Mom's giving her a bottle."

I looked up but Mrs. Lightly wasn't there. When had she left?

"No. I have milk. The baby needs my milk. Where's she taken Joyce?"

I headed down the hall and into the kitchen. Mrs. Lightly was stood by the sink, holding the baby against her hip. Joyce's short legs kicked as the teat of a bottle was forced into her little mouth.

"I can feed the baby," I said. "Give her to me."

Mrs. Lightly stared at me with her wide, clean face like I was the madwoman. I held out my hands. Joyce looked down at me from Mrs. Lightly's hip, afraid, her hair all tangled in a nest of straw. It's all right, I tried to say, but Mrs. Lightly held her tighter, making her cry.

"Give. Her," I cried.

Mrs. Lightly was gazing over my shoulder and I wanted to slap her.

"She's my daughter, not yours."

Pat talked, Mrs. Lightly talked more, and the baby wailed. I grabbed her and rushed down the hall and into the street, but the noise chased me. I ran into the next street and the next, on and on, and she kept crying and crying and crying.

I didn't cry but I was lost. I looked and looked but couldn't find myself and a man grabbed my arm but I slithered away.

"Where are you running to?" he shouted.

The water, I'm heading for the water, but there was none in this city, only the rain and puddles in the street and it hadn't rained in days.

We were on a long straight road, the houses all painted white with a car out front. This world was measured, everything the same, the nature here so controlled. I ran, but I was slow and heavy, and my breath rasped inside me, trapped against my ribs. My eyes hurt from the cold and dust, and I blinked and blinked and hot tears seared down. There, just ahead, was a tree. It stood in a garden at the end of the road and was so tall it reached up and over the house. At its roots it had scattered hundreds of red and gold leaves. I stepped over a low fence that only came up to my knees and the grass was damp on my feet and the leaves crunched and I walked across more just to hear the sound. At the base of the tree, I lowered myself to the ground and leant my head back against the trunk like it was the hearthstone in the cottage. Above, the leaves brushed against each other in the wind like flames, rustling their dancing reds and oranges that blurred as my eyes filled up.

It was gone dark when a car with a flashing red light pulled up by the little fence and two men got out. The one with grey hair walked slowly towards me.

"Are you all right, miss?" he said. He was crouched down like I was a wild horse that might buck or bolt at any moment.

I only realised then how much my body was shaking.

"What's your name?" the man said.

"I'm Oona."

My voice was so small I could hardly hear it myself, but he said, "Oona Lightly?"

I nodded to him, trying to make my lips smile at his kind face. He was wearing big leather gloves with tufts of fur coming out at the wrist. I could see this well because someone in the house beside the tree had turned on a downstairs light.

The other man, whose hair was so brightly lit I couldn't look at him straight, stepped over the fence too and went up to the porch.

"We can take you home, if you'd like," the man said.

"I'm grand here, thank you." I whispered the words as it hurt my throat less.

He knelt in front of me, one hand raised to me like he was waving. I wanted to laugh but knew this was the wrong reaction.

"Mrs. Lightly, your husband—"

"Oona," I cried so loud I made myself jump.

A high-pitched cry shattered all other sounds.

"Would you like me to take your baby?" he asked.

I looked down and Joyce's tiny face was scrunched up and red. She was all wrapped up in my jumper and very unhappy about it.

"Thank you," I said, and handed the baby to the grey-haired man. He bounced her in his arms, and I knew he'd done it before because soon she started to quiet again and I felt sure she'd be all right.

*

Pat was stood on the porch, his hands jammed into his pockets, but he dragged them out and, as if finding them empty was unbearable to him, shoved them back in again. His silky hair was chaotic and his face, it looked scared. I had done this to him, to the unshakeable man, and I couldn't breathe. The ringing inside me got louder and I wanted to scream again and again.

Joyce was handed to me. Her head rested against my shoulder, a warmth and weight that somehow anchored me to this road and this place. Pat looked as if he was about to speak or reach out and embrace us. I waited for him to hold us, to hold the baby and me together in the circle of his warm arms, safe, but he walked past me and spoke to my grey-haired man, who put his arm around Pat's shoulders and whispered to him while I stood shivering on the path.

I turned away and searched above for pictures in the stars, but the street lights with their sickly glow blotted out the sky. I started when a hand, Pat's, touched my shoulder and Joyce woke and wailed.

"Don't touch me." The words came out before I could stop them and I saw how much they cut through him.

He opened the front door and I stepped in with Joyce screaming in my arms. Mrs. Lightly stood right in the entrance, a solid barrier, and dragged my baby from my arms.

"No—"

Without her warmth, her weight, I felt unstable, so I rested my head against the wall.

"Joyce needs to sleep," Mrs. Lightly's voice said somewhere far off.

I pulled myself up the stairs, a soft hand on my back, guiding me, stopping me from falling.

The Winter

I was sick for days after I ran away, my throat burning, my feet colder than the ice on the ground, and my dreams were of drowning and night. In these dreams I remembered what I had managed to push away while awake and I clawed at them, trying to break through their walls, but the blackness was thicker and harder than stone. Voices sometimes broke through, Pat's, and sometimes Mrs. Lightly called me, but when I woke they were gone and I was alone.

Sometimes I opened my eyes to the dark, shaking, my forehead burning and a smooth hand on my cheek, my shoulder. And then I slept, but far off a baby was crying.

*

The next time I heard the bleats, they were gentler, weaker.

She's sick, I thought.

I pulled back the heavy drifts of blankets, dragging each leg out, listening out for my baby's cries, but there was only sickening silence. The floorboards were an ocean to cross but I hauled myself, holding my body up with the wall, and reached the door. The stairs were slow but her crying had started up again and I'd never heard anything so terrible and wonderful. She was alive and she was deafening me.

The sitting room door was ajar. My breathing was quick. The stairs had taken all my strength away from me but I put my hand on the door and it fell open wide.

The light was blinding. At first I could see nothing, only stabbing pain in my head. Through the enormous window everything outside was white, the world covered and life hidden.

Mrs. Lightly was sat there, in the snow light, her head bent, her hair loose. She was the Virgin and in her arms the baby. I only noticed then the room was silent, the crying had stopped and everything was brilliant white and clean. I was what didn't fit in the picture. I was dirty.

The old woman gasped, words pouring from her mouth, shattering the silence. Ghost, I heard. Ghost, and Joyce heard it too, and she began to scream.

I looked down and there was the rug against my cheek, so I shut my eyes.

*

I woke on the soft mattress and in the corner of the room was Pat's carved wooden chair. He or his mother had pulled back the curtains and outside the air was chalk. There was a thirst in my throat, but the pain in my head had eased.

I remembered he had brought hot water bottles to thaw me, but nothing helped.

"The winters are tough here," he'd said once. "You got a really bad flu, almost pneumonia, but the doctor said we warmed you up in time."

"And I thought island life was hard."

He was good enough to laugh and wiped my forehead with a cold cloth and waffled on about his work and how his mother was taking good care of me. He said I would be fine.

I stepped out of the bed and saw myself in the dressing-table mirror. My face was skeletal, like a starving gypsy horse. For months I'd forgotten to eat, putting Mrs. Lightly's dinners in the bin. I had no hunger in me. No hunger for anything.

I was frozen and nothing sparked me alive. I couldn't hold my baby or even look at her. I had nearly killed Joyce, taking her out into the winter with only her tiny romper, not even a pair of booties on her feet. That is not what mothers do. Even my mam knew that.

I couldn't bear to be near my child. To be reminded. I let Mrs. Lightly do her work. She kept us apart. She knew.

Pat knew too, but he would bring Joyce to me, prop her in my arms and, limp, she'd fall against me and my chest would hurt but no tears would come. I saw her face, already confused. Sometimes she'd wail. As the months passed she'd hold out her arms to him. And he would talk to her like she was grown, saying, "This is your mommy," and she would blink at him like she knew he didn't understand what he was talking about but she was humouring him, to keep him happy. I did the same. I held her. And I couldn't help but notice how warm she was in my cold arms. More months passed and she wriggled more, wriggled to get out of my cold grasp.

I couldn't look at him and he couldn't look at me.

*

"Are you going to speak today?" he'd ask me.

I kept my mouth buttoned shut. It was the game he and I played. Me: the silent madwoman. Him: the questioner.

At night I sometimes tried to cry, but there was no water in me to weep with.

I was not stony-hearted, as Mrs. Lightly thought, but I was afraid to open my mouth, afraid what might come roaring out, and once all that had been kept inside me was released, well, then I was afraid I would never see my child again. I couldn't put words to the waves that drowned my mind. Not in English or Irish. Pat wanted me to speak so I'd be cured. He wanted me to be happy so I'd be a good mother. He wanted the wild island girl he first met. But she was long gone, if she was ever even real.

"I feel nothing," I said. And he looked so sad.

*

Late at night I would lean over Joyce's cot and watch her dreaming.

I always kept the curtains ajar and the yellow glow from the street lamps would filter shadows across the little mound of her. In this shifting light I couldn't see her nose, her mouth, and I could imagine she was Pat's.

In daylight, Joyce perched on Mrs. Lightly's lap, I saw all their faces, all the island men, and I had to look away. I'm sure Mrs. Lightly saw the sickness on my lips. How the sight of my child turned my stomach. I know she judged me. I judged me too. I wished I could forget.

I would dart up and take Joyce from her arms and she'd

wail and reach out to the old woman and I would sit on the stairs in the hall, Joyce weeping in my arms, and press my face into her feathered hair and squeeze my eyes shut so I couldn't see her.

*

Pat and I spent so little time alone together we forgot how to talk. One day in summer, he was driving me. I watched out the window as the grey-black of the road skimmed by. I didn't care where we were going.

He stopped the car on the edge of tall trees.

"Look, do you see it?" he said. Glinting between the branches was water, silver and black water. Ever since I came to this new place the closest thing I saw to the sea was a thin river.

I opened the door and jumped out.

"Oona," he called.

"Yes." I turned back to him.

He came to stand next to me, lifting a hand like he'd touch my face but dropped it again.

"It's a lake," he said.

I didn't look up at him but walked along the path towards the water. Rain softened my dress. He squelched through the mud behind me.

The lake moved with falling drops. My heart pitched away from me. It was nothing like the sea that joined the sky at the horizon and whipped up into the air as if struggling to reach it. The ocean would never sit still and silent. Dead.

I sank to my knees under a tree. Like my shadow, he was soft beside me, sinking down to the earth too. Take him away. I sent up a prayer like a wish to the sky, but he stayed, breathing behind me.

"Do you miss your island?" he said.

"No." I stood up, pulled off my shoes, strode into the shallows and waited for the water to still.

"You don't miss your mom, your family?"

"No." I turned to him to see if he knew what I meant, but he looked upset, confused. He didn't understand.

The rain moved too fast.

*

When we got back to his mother's, Pat said I should write.

"What?" I asked.

"Anything you like. Why don't you write about the island?"

At first I ignored him. I cleaned the house with Mrs. Lightly, but even though it was much bigger than the cottage it took little time to wash and dust. I would watch Joyce playing on the floor with her wooden bricks. Then one afternoon, while she was sleeping, I took out a piece of paper and wrote a letter to Enda, telling him I had come to Canada and about the snow and tasteless food. I didn't post it, because I was sure he had left the island and I didn't want Mam reading it. I tried to think who would know where he was, though, and put Felim's name on the envelope and a small scrap of paper with my address on it and slid it in the post-box at the end of the street.

*

I read the books on Pat's shelf, as often I slept better when I did. Joyce was sleeping better too. She cried less. Mrs. Lightly kept Joyce in her room and it was far from the one I shared with Pat.

I was just settling myself down on the bed with a book when there was a knock at the door.

"Will you come for a walk?" he said.

Pat and I walked down the road, away from the houses to where it was thick with leafy shrubs and the shade of adult trees. The wind was nippy and I wore only slacks and a blouse.

"God," said Pat. "You're so thin."

I held up my hands. They were long and white, but hadn't they always been?

"And you're cold." He threw his coat around my shoulders, the light breath of his warmth still clinging to it.

"I don't know why women never wear a good thick jumper here," I said.

He smiled. "They do. In winter."

"I didn't notice." I looked at my stiff leather shoes. I missed soft shoes.

His fingers pressed into my shoulders and I was forced to look up and see him. His face was different, somehow caving into itself with blue shadows and lines in the wrong places.

He stepped away and continued walking; light fell across his back. Soft rain dripped and then fell heavily.

We ran to the shelter of a tree and craned our necks towards the thrum of water on leaves. He looked at me and his face grew tight with feeling, as if a little part of him had broken off and fallen away. The rain fell through the branches.

"I failed you, Oona," he said. "I thought bringing you here would be a good thing."

"It's not your fault. I couldn't have gone on with my life on Inis. I am here now but I wish I saw more of you."

"What else do you wish?"

"I want to see the forests that grow in Canada."

"Let's start again," he said. He chewed the nail of his thumb, let his hand drop and fixed me with the long, blue gaze of his that had hit me when I was washing the clothes in the sea on Inis. "Oona," he said. "Will you be my wife?"

"Yes," I said. "Yes, I will."

On the horizon of the underworld, the girl began to see glimmers of light.

"Is it morning?" she asked her silver-bearded husband, and he said, "Not yet, my sweet young wife, but soon, I hope. We will go to my orchard and you can eat as much of my fruit as you like."

"Oh, I am glad. I am so very hungry."

*

Far away from her sleepless daughter, the mother in her withered land committed the greatest sin. She stole a baby from his mother and dipped him in flames to make sure he was strong enough to resist the growth and questioning she now knew moved each new life beyond her earth. And for a while, the mother told herself she was happy with this stolen child.

Mam and Dad

"You're back," says a voice.

I lift my head from where it rests against Dad's warm leg. The room is dark, lit only by the sparking fire and the thin light from the tiny boxed windows, but I can still make out the girl in the doorway of the little room. She is familiar, only a few years older than Joyce.

"You look just like Aislinn," I whisper.

She frowns but says nothing.

"Etain," Dad says. "This is my daughter. She's come home."

Etain lifts a stool and sits beside us.

"How does she look?" Dad asks.

"Like her mam," Etain says.

"She's waiting for you." Etain takes Dad's other hand.

Dad clutches my hand tighter.

"What is it?" I whisper to him, although Etain is staring at both of us, listening easily.

He shakes his head.

Etain lets go of his hand, glides to the table and pours the tea, three cups.

"Dad," I whisper. "When was Joyce here?"

"Yesterday afternoon. She sat with me like you now. She's a strong girl, you know."

"Did she say where she's staying?"

"I don't know, love."

"Here." Etain gives me a cup. "Sit and drink it, you need the strength." She is nothing like Aislinn. She puts one on a little stool next to Dad and guides his hand towards it. He smiles gently.

"You were with Enda, love, weren't you?" His grip on my hand is nearly breaking my fingers.

"I was, Dad."

"Was he happy?"

"He enjoyed his life. He had a lot of friends. Enda was loved."

"I don't think he knew I loved him, Oona."

"He knew, Dad."

"I'll always regret I never said it to his face."

His hands are fumbling up my arms. I understand and bend my head close to his.

"Dad?"

"I'm glad you got away and had a good life. You take care of yourself and that girl."

"I will." I kiss his cheek and he claps his hand to it, smiling briefly.

Etain perches against the table, watching me, winding an escaped strand of whitish hair around her finger.

"Will you join us?" I say, and nod at the third cup on the table behind her.

"Oh, no. This is not for me." She drops a drip of milk into it, picks it up and treads into the small room. I strain to hear voices but there isn't a sound from inside.

The kitchen is the same: turf puffing; oil lamp on the

sideboard; the dresser with the Virgin Mary watching over; the picture of the Sacred Heart with the red candle lit in front of it, bad luck to let the flame go out; the milk and water cans beside the back door. All that is new is a cooker, ugly and out of place among these old familiars. My mother lingers here like a ghost.

"I'm sorry, love," Dad whispers.

"She's ready to see you," Etain says.

Tea scalds my hand. I swallow a cry.

"Oona." His head is darting about, searching for me. I reach for his cheek. There's only a day's stubble. Etain or someone else must be shaving him. Someone has been caring for him and it's not been me. The years I've missed rush back to drown me. There's too much. Too much has happened to him and yet I know at the same time it's been so little. An island life is a hard one, but unchanging in its hardness.

"It wasn't your fault," I say, bringing myself back to the man in front of me.

He shakes his head. "I never should've told her. I told your mam and I knew, I knew how she'd see God's work in it. But she's not well now. You understand what I'm saying, don't you?"

"It was never your fault," I say.

I kiss Dad and he's smiling and I feel a smile answering.

"I'll be back to you," I whisper to him and step into the dark of the little room.

"So you're back," a voice says from the depths.

"Mam?" I say.

She is sitting upright. A cup steams in her hand. Her face is just the same and wholly different. She is old. Her face is frozen in a stony hardness, carved-out eyes, a gouge of mouth.

I'm pegged to the floor.

"Well?" Her voice is smaller than I remember, but it still cuts through me. "What are you doing here?"

"How do you feel?" I ask.

She says nothing, just watches me, her hand clawing the blankets at her throat.

"I saw Kate," I say. "She told me you were sick."

She blinks rapidly but still says nothing.

"I'm sorry I left without saying goodbye," I say. "I married Michael."

"Him?" She laughs like I'd taken up with a tinker.

"And I have my own business. I make clothes like I used to with you. And I have a daughter. She's strong-willed and kind and a storyteller. She's studying at university. She's nineteen . . ."

I want to sit down but there's no chair. The room is stuffy and my breath catches in me. My mother's lips are tight together. Her wet black eyes are fixed on the dirty dot on the wall where Kieran threw a sod at Enda.

I need to go outside. The air is loud with the past, with our unspoken memories. I go to the pint-sized window, pull back the curtain and peer out. The wall is deep, the view green grass and grey rock. As a child I would stare out this window at the freedom beyond it; all it held seemed full of possibilities. Now I see it's so small. What I imagined for myself could only ever be small because I had so little to compare this view to.

Behind me, Etain coughs and I try not to jump. I didn't realise she was in the room.

"What's she doing here?" my mother says in Irish to Etain, not me. I don't turn, or show any sign I remember my mother tongue. I am still me. I am still Oona.

I hear Etain's light step and the creak of the bed as she sits down. This is it. My mother never lost a daughter. She just replaced a sinful girl with an angel.

"She's here to speak with you, Mary," Etain says.

"She can speak all she wants but I won't talk with her. Dirty Devil's child."

I don't turn. "I didn't come to speak to you," I say in Irish. The wind waves the grass outside, beckoning. "I thought you were dead. I'm here for *my* daughter."

A gentle, indrawn breath: Etain.

"I met her," my mother says.

I turn to face her. She is shrivelled and angry in the bed.

"Where is Joyce?"

Etain takes my mother's teacup and places it on the floor. She strokes a wrinkled hand. A part of me wants to touch my mother too, to rid myself of the memory of her always flinching away from me. A part of me wants her to forgive me but I see now she never can.

"She was asking questions," my mother says. "She was thinking she'd find her father here."

"What did you tell her?"

"I told her she might well meet him but who was to know who he was? There were a lot of men. She asked about you too."

"Mam, where is she?"

"I sent her to Éag." She clutches her chest, her eyes watering. She's in pain.

"You sent my daughter to the dead island."

"Where you lost your decency."

I want to spit on her but I sit on the bed. She flinches.

"I do think I forgive you for my childhood, but I don't for sending my child to a dangerous place on her own."

Her hands flutter about the blanket, her eyes darting anywhere but at me.

"I never wanted you to go there," she says to her chest.

"No, but you never wanted me to go anywhere." I stand up. "I won't be staying. You're welcome to her," I say to Etain.

In the kitchen, I kneel beside Dad. "I'll be back to you when I find Joyce."

"Where will you sleep, littlie?"

All I can do is squeeze his hand.

New Beginning

When I went into her room Joyce was playing alone. She was two years old, hair neatly brushed by Mrs. Lightly, and face spotless. Children were never meant to be so clean. She glanced up at me hovering in the doorway, rubbed her eye and turned back to her wooden blocks. I was a tolerated stranger.

I knelt down on the floor beside her and she nodded and handed me a brick. I placed it on the messy pile she had built and she nodded again and I couldn't stop myself from reaching out and pulling her onto my lap. She squealed, but didn't cry. I pressed my nose against her head. She smelled of tea tree oil.

"Will you be all right on your own?" Mrs. Lightly asked. I lifted my face from Joyce's warm curls. I hadn't seen my mother-in-law come in. She was frowning.

"Yes, I'll be all right by myself," I said.

"I meant with Joyce."

"I know what you meant."

Mrs. Lightly's cheeks reddened a little. "I'll just give her a cuddle before you go." She held out her arms and reluctantly I handed Joyce over.

She kissed Joyce's soft cheek, smoothed the child's hair and dress.

I could think of nothing to say. Mrs. Lightly had so easily seen into me and seen my struggles. I was glad Joyce was still so small and wouldn't know how some days I'd found it so hard to love her.

Mrs. Lightly watched us from a window as we climbed into the car. I waved, but I couldn't see if she waved back.

Joyce sat on my lap sucking a piece of cheese and humming to herself. We sped down the highway and onto smaller and smaller roads. Pat was strangely hopeful, and I caught the smiles from him. It would be better away from his mother. Every now and then he reached out to touch one of us.

The new house was wooden, and if it had stood next to Mrs. Lightly's it would've looked like a child's, but I still felt like a pebble rattling around inside it. I was used to just three rooms and this had eight: four on the bottom and four on top. There was what Pat called a porch at the front. He painted it blue. We were far from the noise of the local town, a good hour's walk, and the house was so surrounded by trees a person walking along the road wouldn't know we were there. I loved the rush of wind through thousands of leaves, the rattle of branches and thuds of the forest. It reminded me of the never-ending sighs and breath of the sea, the grating suck and slosh of stones along a shore.

There was no wall or fence to make a boundary between the wild and our house, so the trees invaded the garden with brambles and shade. Pat hacked at the thorny bushes, tearing his skin, but no matter how much he cut it just grew back thicker. Wilting leaves were walked into the kitchen and we burned fallen branches on the fire.

When Joyce saw the place, she squealed and bounced in my lap until I let her out to totter after a butterfly. I smiled at Pat.

"It's better than I hoped," I told him.

He grinned and I saw in his tired, happy blue eyes how difficult it'd been to find it. He found himself an office job and arranged for all the furniture to arrive before us. He had smoothed our road into the future to make life easy for us.

I made the garden thick with herbs: rosemary, green lace and mint, just like Aislinn's had been. I stole bushes from the roadside or the edge of the woods to begin my little patch: a sturdy thyme, a blackish parsley. I kept them in pots in the kitchen through the winter, pouring lukewarm water on them to keep them alive.

Joyce toddled about helping me, carrying weeds to the weed pile and bringing me my trowel. Sometimes I would set her digging her own patch too, where we planted primroses, purple clover and white flowers that burst open one day with a heady sweet scent. They were gone a week later. Just a memory.

In the warmer months Pat and I sat out on the porch and drank tea and talked. He told me all about his life before. His father whom he almost never saw but who smelled like soap and sweat and Marlboro cigarettes. His schoolfriends and the ball games he played. How he clung to his friends because he had no brothers and sisters. It hit me then just how far apart our lives were, but I had entered his and I would try to fit in. Late one evening, when I was thinking about turning in, he told me about her, the beautiful woman from the photograph, Sally. She was a smart one. They had been together since school. He stopped, and couldn't go on.

I told him stories too, but mostly I listened, wanting to soak in everything about him, about our new life.

Our first summer in the new house came to an end but we clung to the edges of it, wrapped in a blanket on the garden seat.

"Do you think she's like me?" he asked.

"What?"

"Joyce. Is she like me?" He was gazing up at the stars. How could he just look up at the stars?

"I don't know," I said. "You don't look that similar."

"I think she has the pointed Lightly nose, don't you?"

I stood, the blanket crumpling to the ground.

"I'm going to bed."

"All right," he said.

In the bathroom I poured a bath and lay under the cold surface. I wanted the cold to numb me but it was like knives. I still missed the raging sea and the high open sky. I was hemmed in by treetops and ice and mountains.

I had planted potatoes along with some other seeds a man in the town sold me: carrots, cabbage, beans. Beans were the hardest. If the frost did not get them the wind did, snapping them so often that in the end I gave up.

"You could just buy them at the shop," Pat said.

"I need to do something," I told him.

He built himself a shed where he made chairs, a table and Joyce's bed. He made me a carved chestnut box for my sewing.

It was rare to get fish and fish was what I knew. I could gut and fillet a mackerel in seconds. String it, salt it, dry it and a hundred others in a morning. In the town there was meat: thick and red and bloody. The first slab Pat brought home sat on the table while I walked around it, taking in its different angles. I salted it and fried it with onions and boiled some potatoes. Pat's chin ducked down to his neck at his first bite, which told me it was bad.

Every morning I worried about the mail. I hadn't put my new address on the letter I'd sent to Enda, so Mrs. Lightly would have to send anything on to me; but every morning there was only mail for Pat.

The working-Pat spent most of his time at the office, only coming home to eat and play with Joyce. To him she jabbered, but with me she was silent, thoughtful. She dashed about, demanding of him "Watch me roll" or "Food. Cake. Sweetie." Somehow she must have sensed I watched her. She still ran to me and wrapped her arms around my legs, clinging on as if afraid I'd vanish if she let go. Sometimes when she climbed into my lap I wept into her bright hair and she would whisper that she loved me.

As Joyce grew, I was afraid to look too closely at her face. Afraid of whose nose, whose island smile, whose wrinkled brow would show there.

At night, Pat and I slept without touching. He wasn't angry. He somehow knew I was afraid of his touch, of any touch, and some days he stayed later at the office and I guessed there was someone there who was able to touch him. Sometimes I woke screaming with the ocean blocking my throat. Sometimes I woke aching down below and I'd run from the house and stand in the cold night until it stopped, until the sickening feeling of the longing and the need was gone.

The Cold Bed

"We have to talk about this," Pat said.

We were finishing a lunch of egg sandwiches and potato soup. He often drove back from work to eat with us.

"What is it? Why?" I said, grabbing a plate.

"I'm not done," Joyce cried.

I dropped it back in front of her and he lifted her onto his lap.

There were no more late evenings on the porch. He worked. I sewed rainbows of little dresses, tended the garden and scrubbed the house from top to bottom. I still dreamed of getting a job in the town but the years had rolled on, and although I walked into a few shops I never knew what to say or how to behave. I couldn't shake the memory of the woman in the clothes store in the city who had mocked me. When Joyce was still small she needed me, but now she had started school and my days were often empty. I tried not to understand my mam but I did. A part of myself was missing whenever Joyce was gone. The girl who sat staring out the window of the cottage imagining her life across the sea would have been ashamed I hadn't made more of reaching the New

World. My recent freedom felt like a burden, the days stretching out ahead of me with nothing to fill them.

"There's something I need to tell you," Pat said.

"I don't want to talk about it. I'm busy." I snatched a basket by the back door and marched out and stood without knowing what I was going to do. If he had fallen in love with some woman, I didn't want to hear about it. I didn't know what Joyce and I would do without him, but I couldn't stop him. He might be happier with her. Weeds. That was what I needed to do. I tugged them from the ground, uprooting even the most stubborn.

A few minutes later the car groaned away and Joyce came snuffling outside.

"What is it, Joyce?"

"Nothing." She hopped from foot to foot. "My shoulders hurt."

*

In the kitchen I peeled the dead skin off her sunburned shoulders.

"Mommy," she said. "Why do you talk different than everyone else? You sound funny."

"It's my accent. I'm not from Canada."

"Where are you from?"

"Ireland."

"Where's that?"

"Far away."

"People at school say you're a witch and kill dogs."

"Huh. When I was a girl I knew a woman who everyone said was a bit of a witch, although I don't think that word was ever used."

"You knew a witch? A real one?"

"She did give my mother a potion once."

"What was your mom like?"

"She was the real witch. Now, how are your shoulders feeling?"

She peered at each one. "A bit better."

"Have you been liking school?" I said.

Joyce shrugged and I realised I'd never asked her this before. A whole year gone by and I never asked.

"I like it," she said in her adult way. "Did you like school when you were my age?"

"When I was your age I didn't go to school. Now that's enough questions. Let's go outside."

She slid off the chair and faced me, blue eyes wide. "You don't love Daddy, do you?"

"Why would you say that?"

"Some nights, you don't sleep in the same bed. Most parents sleep in the same bed."

"How do you know that?"

"My friends at school said."

"What did they tell you?"

Like a bird she tilted her straw head to one side, a lopsided child scarecrow with flaking radish shoulders.

"What else did they tell you . . . about parents?"

She nibbled her lip. "Oh, nothing much. Is that why Daddy was angry with you?"

"No," I said.

She peered up at me, blue eyes seeing too much.

She spun on her heel and ran outside, hair streaming, shoulders blazing.

When she'd disappeared into the trees, I yelled after her to come back but I didn't really want her to. I didn't want to see myself reflected so clearly.

*

At dinner Pat asked after our day. Joyce prodded her potato and said it was fine. He asked how her shoulders had got burned, why wasn't she wearing a t-shirt and hat? He didn't need to look at me.

I left as he was washing up and went up to the bathroom, where I filled the entire bath.

I lay there steaming, but my mind wouldn't stop; like the sun, Joyce had got under my skin, stopping me from floating through our life without feeling, without changing. The heat wasn't enough.

When I came out with soggy feet Pat stopped me in the hall.

"What?" I asked, dizzy from the scalding water. "You look like you're angry with me."

His forehead was creased up like a newly ploughed field. For the first time in our marriage he looked old.

"Can we talk?" he said.

"All right."

*

In the garden, I knelt in a patch of mint and listened. Joyce's bedroom window was open and her light, Canadian voice floated down to me. She was telling Pat a story about a wolf who nursed two boys.

I knelt there until I heard his tread on the back of the porch. I stood up and wiped my cheeks.

"I'm sorry, Pat," I said. "I know I'm hard to be around but, please, don't leave Joyce. She needs you."

"I wasn't going to leave," he said.

"If you are staying, there's nothing more we need to talk about."

"Oona, please."

"No. It's all right. I don't blame you. I don't." I strode towards the woods, briars dragging at my jeans.

"Wait, Oona. I haven't done anything." He caught up to me. "If you would just talk to me."

"I don't want to talk." I dodged a bush and stepped under the cover of the trees. "Just leave me alone, Pat."

And he did. He walked back to the house, and we were quiet for days, but he stayed.

The girl woke in her husband's arms and saw a sun rise over the horizon of the underworld. For the first time since she left her mother, she had slept. She felt rejuvenated, and starving.

She sat with her husband and watched the bony karst landscape painted gold. In the distance trees grew, and so they packed rucksacks and put on their shoes and walked towards the forest. Soon they reached grassy meadows bobbing with flowers and humming with bees. The air was sweet and warm and moist. The first trees they reached were weighed down with so much fruit, blushing in the dappled morning light. She reached up and brushed a heavy plum with her fingertips. Her mouth watered.

There was a rustle in the grass, the flick of a black tail.

"Just an adder," her husband said, smiling his long white teeth. "Eat."

She plucked the fruit and burst it with her bite.

———————————

The Fisherman

"Oona?"

I turn and Etain is jogging up the road towards me; the thatch of the house blazes gold behind her, a reminder that she is my parents' daughter now.

"You can stay at my mother's old place," she pants. "I still have a bit of straw in the hearth and I'll bring you blankets."

"I'm going to Éag," I say.

She looks up at the sky and shakes her head. "No one will row over now. A storm's coming."

A snappy wind has blown most of the clouds away and the sea is shimmering blue.

"It looks fine to me."

"You really have been gone a long time." She smiles and I want to hit her. "Don't be angry at your mam," she continues. "I know she seems bitter, but the years have been hard on her, and with your brother Enda. Well, it nearly killed her when we heard the news of him."

"What news do you mean?" I ask. "That he was a homosexual?"

She has the decency to blush. "No," she says. "When he died.

Your mam was afraid of you coming. She worried about you over the years."

"I'm sure she did."

"She loves you. She just doesn't know how to show it."

"Why do you put up with her, Etain? Your mother was so free. She always said the truth."

"Aislinn was a coward and selfish. Her own children weren't good enough to live for."

I moan, and the fierce, motherless girl doesn't seem to hear.

"She didn't stay for me," Etain continues. "Mary has been good to me since I was a little girl."

She is so sure and certain, sturdier in herself than I ever saw Aislinn.

"What about your brother?" I say.

"Hah." She bounces up on her toes, nods at me. "He left too."

I watch her leave, someone I will never know, walking back along the road.

She turns once to shout, "I'll leave you blankets at my mother's, just in case."

I race to the pier. A man with a cap pulled low on his head is stacking lobster pots and I call to him and he waves.

"I need to get to Éag," I gasp as I get close to him. "Is there a boat? Do you know someone who can take me?"

"You won't go today." He pulls his grey hat off and his hair is light. "There's a storm on her way. Stick out your tongue and you'll taste her."

"Please. Take me over quickly now, before it comes."

"You're the second person in two days who wanted to go there. But no one will bring you, Oona. Any boat will be wrecked."

Fresh green eyes in a round but now lined face.

"Jonjoe!"

He laughs. "You got there in the end."

"Is there really no way you can take me?"

"I'd like to for you, I really would, but it's not worth my life. There's the family to think of and I always fancied being buried on Éag, not under the waves. Come to me early in the morning, and if the storm's blown herself out I'll get a few lads to row you."

"Thank you, Jonjoe." I grasp his hand and he blushes.

"Better not." He smiles and gently pulls his hand away. "The wife's got eyes in the back of her head."

*

I walk the north of the island where there are no villages or cottages, not even a shelter for the cows. My path is along the cliffs. The sky is heavy with cloud and dark with wind and rain, and no matter how closely I look out across the waves I can't see Éag.

I think of Enda and the lake. I went to the cabin to wipe it all away, to sink and forget, but I couldn't. I thought I wasn't as brave as Aislinn. I told myself Pat would be happier with someone else; Joyce was grown and didn't need me. I had betrayed them both and it would be better for them if I was gone, but I couldn't. I needed, need them too much.

Aislinn's cottage is just ahead of me, clutching close to the cliff. Tears roll off me. The rocks are uneven beneath my thick hiking boots and when I fall it's because I've not been looking where I'm going. I focus on the pain of my bleeding hands and watch my feet as the rain cuts in from the waves and drenches me.

Inside Aislinn's old cottage the fire has been lit and there's a stack of blankets. The roof is still there, despite its blackened state from the fire all those years back, but it sags and drips and there are countless holes. I wrap the blankets around me and sit close to the flames, watching. The storm lashes through the holes in the roof. There are so few roofs on Éag to shelter Joyce and the only person who lives there is a fairy's son.

*

I wake and my child's father is looking down at me.

In the Forest

Joyce and I sat on the back porch that summer. I sewed clothes and cushion covers with the off-cuts.

I watched her lying in the grass, waving her legs that had grown so long. She was shooting away from me like a sapling reaching up for the sky.

It was hot and she dozed off on the porch after dinner. I carried her into the house. I was small but so was she for a six-year-old.

"Where've you been?" Pat hissed from the shadows of the hall.

"Quiet," I said. "Joyce is sleeping."

When he was asleep beside me I remembered the meadow, pressing my fingers across my breasts and stomach, tending and smoothing the thrum between my legs, stopping in shame, only to begin again until I shook and wept in relief.

*

I walked through the trees to watch the first green buds sprout on a branch and unfurl into the sunny green of summer, then catch

fire while the nuts dropped from their shells and all became blan-
keted in the pure softness of winter. Sometimes I would sit Joyce
on my coat and escape up a tree. It was a new thing, tree climbing.
Hand over hand, up and up, until I could go no higher. I perched
on the edge of the world, between rippling leaves and heaven. I
pulled cold air into me and let it expand out inside my body that
bent with the springy green of the saplings, my belly hollowed out
with the height, with the sky, with the corners of freedom. I was
back on the cliffs of home. And I forgot.

When I climbed down from my tree Joyce was curled up on
my coat with a book.

"Joyce."

"Mmm." She didn't look up.

"Will you go and get your dad?"

"Why?"

"Just get him. I need to talk to him and you stay at the house.
We won't be long."

She pursed her lips and snapped the book shut.

"Okay."

I stood bare-armed, bare-legged and barefoot in my light cotton dress. His face reflected green, sky, the edge of the world I had
just, almost, touched.

"Oona?" His voice was heavy with the pain I'd caused, my
years of distance. Questions hung from him like overripe fruit.

"I'm sorry," I said.

"It's all right."

I pulled him to me and kissed him on the mouth to try to
vanish the pain, swallow it. He kissed me back, uncertain, gentle.
Something inside me opened and I gave a small cry into his open
mouth. He stepped away and looked down at me and pulled me
against him, where I sobbed into his chest.

*

Some days when we were chopping vegetables together he'd run a hand against my forearm and ask me if it was okay. Sometimes it was.

Once, when we were out in the garden pulling weeds and Joyce was tugging the heads off the daisies, he worked close beside me and I let my head fall onto his shoulder, and we stayed that way for a long time.

The first time I turned to him in bed my body was stiff and I didn't know where to touch him. He lay still and I took my clothes off and lay against his pyjamas. I was drifting asleep when he placed a light kiss on my forehead. It fluttered through me. Another time, I put my lips on his and slowly moved his hands across my back and down. I showed him. After, we slept close together and one morning I woke and turned to him again. I peeled off his pyjama shirt with fumbling fingers.

"It's all right," he whispered. "We don't have to."

"I'm just nervous and I don't know what I'm doing."

He kissed me softly. "Okay," he said, and touched me the way I'd shown him.

When we came into the kitchen Joyce was eating a piece of bread and gave me a curious look, her head to one side, and I was glad I was taller than her so I didn't have to meet her eye.

In the evenings, when dinner was finished and Joyce was asleep, Pat and I found each other under the trees. We grasped and pulled at clothes and limbs, not knowing whose was whose. The leaves were in their autumn fire. When the frost crept back we continued meeting but at home, in the artificial warmth of the bedroom with the buzz of the fridge downstairs.

*

I knew from the first moment my son began to grow. I felt him unfurling, new and so green inside me.

I found Pat in his shed, bent over a half-made chair, forehead grooved, making a gentle thwacking noise as he hammered a chisel into the wood. I breathed in the usual smell of shavings and varnish, enjoyed the ordered mess.

He put down his tools and opened his arms.

"Wait," I said. "I need to tell you something."

Fear worried the crow's feet at his eyes. "What is it?"

"I'm pregnant."

"Oh."

"Are you surprised?"

"I didn't think." There was dust in his hair. He stayed where he was.

"You don't seem happy."

"I just want you to be . . . Aren't you afraid it'll be like last time?"

The draught from the open door made me shiver.

"I will manage. I'm stronger now. We're stronger, aren't we?"

He crossed the room and placed his hands on my arms. "Whatever happens," he said, "we'll be fine."

Adair

The winter came again and snow pressed against the shell of the house, piling in walls along the edges of the forest, sealing us in. Pat had to dig his way out in the mornings. That winter he was often away working in the city and Joyce was often sick.

My belly expanded like a swollen moon beneath my dress. This pregnancy was different. He was larger, realer. I could feel him, gentle, but full of life. Ready to be free.

He would look like Pat. A child of the forest.

"I don't want to leave you."

I was in the kitchen, darkened by the snow in the windows. Pat's pale face hovered above mine.

"Will you be all right?" he asked.

"We'll be fine," I said, stroking the mound of our baby.

He kissed my cheek, prickling it with his fuzzy jaw, and squeezed my hand.

"I'll phone if anything happens," I said.

Nothing was going to happen. It was two weeks before he was due. We would be gone to the city in a week to wait for his arrival there.

Pat smiled and stood a moment more watching me. I wanted to run to him so his arms could wrap around the hugeness that was now me, but I was too slow. He was gone.

It was dark for many hours. I cooked a stew, kept the fire alight and read a book. Joyce coughed and snuffled and kept asking for tea.

In the late afternoon we were sat in the kitchen, where it was warmest, and Joyce began weeping again. She hadn't learned to hide her feelings yet.

"What?" I asked.

"Nothing. I wish Dad was here."

"So do I."

We liked each other more when Pat was with us. He had a gift for loving us with blindness. But now she was off school with a cold we had to spend time alone together.

I gave her a tea towel to wipe her face. She sat on the floor with the wooden ark and all its tiny twin animals Pat made scattered around her.

"Why don't you tidy them up?" I asked.

"I don't want to."

"When I was your age, I was already mending clothes and collecting cockles on the shore."

She threw a sheep across the room and it clunked against the wall.

"Fair enough," I said.

My mind transformed from irritation to peace. It was happening more and more; one moment I was angry, the next blissful. I floated out to the other room to watch the snow fall through the big window, resting one hand on my belly. I'd been feeling low aches all afternoon, but pain was separate from my baby and me; like the snow all around, it couldn't hurt us.

Joyce coughed behind me.

"Mom." Her voice was soft and grating like sandpaper over wood. Her hands twisted together and apart. Snot dripped from her nose. I watched, waiting for her to tell me why I'd been disturbed. She looked at her feet in their knitted socks, bottom lip quivering, and turned and padded out again.

In the kitchen she was sat close to the stove. I picked up a horse, polished to a dark sheen, the grains of wood forming a rough pony's coat. I ran the smooth neck up and down my nose, humming.

From somewhere outside I heard bird song, lilting, sad notes. Why was it out in the dark and ice? Why wasn't it tucked up in its nest?

"Do you hear that bird?" I asked.

Joyce shook her head.

"You must. It's so clear."

"I don't hear it."

"It's beautiful . . . and sad. Come on. Let's go outside to listen. Come on."

I held out my hand but she looked at it and her face was full of fear.

"Let's go together."

Her blue eyes ignited and I reached out to take her hand. Water splashed out of me and spilled across the floor, drowning the shiny animals two-by-two and splashing Joyce's socks with damp flecks. She stared at me in horror.

"Joyce," I said. "Get a clean sheet from the cupboard."

She scrambled away from me, slipping on the wet floor.

"I need to phone Daddy," she said.

"Did you hear what I said? A towel. Now."

"You said sheet."

"Get me something. Your brother's coming."

She ran out of the room.

I should phone Pat, I thought, as I shuffled towards the door, but a pain pinned me where I squatted, ripping up my spine.

A stack of sheets appeared before me, Joyce's hands grasping them.

"Spread one on the floor, between my legs," I screamed, and the sheets tumbled onto the tiles. She ran from the room. I heard the front door open and slam.

"Joyce," I shouted.

I went slowly into the hall and wrenched the front door open. "Joyce?"

The snow whipped in white spirals but the black behind it and the ice stung my eyes. I turned to go back inside and saw her crouched under the window.

"Joyce, get inside now. You'll die of cold."

She shoved her hands under her armpits.

"Joyce, I'm about to push out a baby. Get in here now and help me."

"I hate you," she whispered.

I shut the door.

I tottered around the kitchen, panting and waiting for her to come back. The pains were chasing each other, faster and faster.

After forty minutes on the kitchen clock, the door creaked and a little white face lit up like a flame in the darkness.

"I'm afraid," she said.

"Joyce, I need you to telephone Daddy at work. I don't know the number."

"I know it."

The pains swelled and collapsed. The petal of a face was still there, dewdrop eyes wide.

If Mam could birth me all alone, I would meet my son without any guiding hands. But Mam had the Virgin come to her and cut me out and sing sweet songs to guide me. My boy had only me.

"I told Daddy. He's coming."

Feathers stroking my hand.

Pains billowed downwards. I screamed and squatted and pushed and pushed and on it went.

And then he was coming, a baby dropping into the cradle of my hands. He was bright white. Dead still.

"Baby? Baby!" My voice shouting.

I rubbed his back and he coughed and cried. Tears dropped onto his tiny body.

With the sheet, I wiped away the blood and water. He was awake. My baby. He waved strong arms and legs. I crouched on the floor, laughing. He was warm against me, the soft round head smooth against my skin. I wrapped him in a giant towel to keep away the cold.

I waited for the rest to fall out of me. The cord tied us together. I panted and shook but he was quiet as the snowflakes falling outside.

There was a click of light that exposed a child with yellow hair in a white nightdress and the horror of my blood and waters on the floor.

"Mom? Can you see me now?"

The baby mewled and I kissed his head. It was slick with something. With me.

"He's dirty," she said. "Should I pour a basin?"

Small, bare feet slapped by. The sound of water splashing. I jumped when a sponge touched his head, and took it to wipe him down. Small hands ran a cloth over my legs. A sniffle.

"Joyce, you're sick. Go back to bed. He can't catch it."

"He's a boy?" she whispered. "What's his name?"

"Adair."

"Oh."

"It means from the oak tree ford. Go to bed now."

She dropped a shawl over my shoulders and creaked up the stairs.

I used a chair to help me stand and padded slowly to the hall, warming him close against me. Through the window the moon was full and milky. The snow had stopped falling. Lights were out. I sat in Pat's big wooden chair and watched the bright night.

Adair's breath was gentle against my breast. He slept. His eyelashes were white, his downy hair conker-brown. My heart was near breaking with the love for him.

Yellow lights blazed. A car. He woke at the roar of the engine and began to cry.

"Oona." Pat's arms were around us.

"We've a son," I said.

He kissed my cheek, his beard wet with snow or tears.

"Oona, you've done it." He was crying. "The doctor isn't coming."

"It's all right. We're all right."

He laughed into my neck. I felt his smile. "What happened?" he whispered. "Where's Joyce?"

"I don't know."

"It's all right. Sit back down."

"I want to sleep now."

"I'll take you both upstairs."

"But the kitchen."

"It's all right," he said. "We need to cut the cord."

I nodded.

With a thumb, he stroked Adair's head. In bed, I kept one hand curled around his little foot.

When I came down in the morning, Adair held to my chest, all signs of the birth had been scrubbed away and a nurse was waiting to check we were healthy; but I didn't need her to tell us, I knew we were.

The plum did not quench the girl's hunger. She made her husband build them a little house close enough to the orchard so she could wander out every morning to eat. She sliced them into fruit salads and served them in a big blue bowl. Her husband made their home entirely of wood, carving flowers and birds into the beams.

The nights in her new house were too short. Sometimes when her husband climbed in beside her his eyes were lit like coal and he would burn her with his touch. At other times he kissed her breasts with petal-soft lips and after they made love she fell asleep like a child in his warm embrace.

Often he was both men, fierce and gentle, and it was both who fathered their children.

The girl's belly grew quickly, bulging into being almost overnight like the fruit that hung in the orchard, and soon she gave birth to twins, the daughter pale and quiet, the son pink-cheeked and laughing.

For a time they were happy playing and growing in the garden.

For a time.

———————————

A Father

Pat's face swims above me. He is lit up by the fire in Aislinn's hearth. His beard is soft with rainwater. I reach up to him but he straightens and steps away.

I'm lying on the floor in front of the spitting turf.

"Are you really here?" I say, pushing myself up. "Is Joyce with you?"

"No."

No, no, because she is far away on Éag with Felim and the dead and I drove her to them.

The room is dark, the shadows crowding in towards the fire, and he has pulled back into them, hidden.

"What are you doing here?" I ask.

"Joyce asked me to come here," he says. "She phoned my mom's two days ago." He's looking at me, at every sorry bedraggled bit. "Why didn't you wait for me?"

"I didn't know how to tell you," I say.

"I was so worried. You should have told me the truth."

"It's over now, isn't it?" The children who tied us together are gone now. "I'm sorry."

He crosses the room again, and for a moment I am hopeful, but he prods the fire with his foot. The damp turf is already hissing out.

I have never seen him worn so thin.

"Have you been eating?"

"Have you?"

"I can't remember."

"I brought food," he says.

"How did you know I was in here?" I ask.

"A fisherman told me."

I rub my cheeks to bring some feeling back and nudge myself closer to the warmth. He is here beside me and I still can't find a way to say anything true. He strides to the opposite side of the room, tapping the ground with his thick shoes, and I remember him wandering Inis with his camera, talking to everyone he met, the same as all the other tourists but special too because we had saved him from the storm, from death.

"What did Joyce tell you on the phone?" I say.

"Joyce just said she was safe."

"But she's on Éag."

"I know."

There's almost no shelter on Éag and cold kills.

I leap up, crossing the room in three strides, and fling the door open. A wall of water hits me. The black blinds me. I can see nothing, no lump of a rocky island out at sea, no sea at all, only the rain. There is nothing I can do, no way to help her, so I send out a silent prayer just like I used to do when I was little.

"Please God or Mary, keep her safe."

The sky howls at me like it's laughing. "Aislinn?" I say. "Aislinn, help me. Please."

He shuts the door. His hands on my shoulders steer me back

to the hearth, his lips say words in my ear and I want to scream at him and shatter his calmness. I spin away from him, turn to look back, but he just bends to tend the fire. There's a thunk as a sod hits the embers. The thatch drips; the roar of the ocean is so close.

"We left them to struggle and survive on their own," I say. "There was nothing kind or God-fearing about how people treated them."

He turns to me. "Who do you mean?"

"Aislinn and Felim. We were all terrible to them. We ignored them and burned their home. And I never tried to help them, not really. I didn't think to bring them food. I didn't talk to Felim about what was going on with him. I don't know when I stopped talking."

I walk to the window that now, without shutters, is just a gaping hole where the rain cuts in.

"It's all been a lie," I say.

Water pricks my face and I keep my eyes shut so I won't see him. I listen to the whoops of the storm.

"Pat, you're not Joyce's father."

"Will you not look at me?" he says.

I can't move and he doesn't touch me to guide me back to him.

I turn and he's breathing through his fingers, taking in sharp gusts of air.

"Why didn't you tell me before?" he says.

"I was afraid you'd leave us."

"How could you think I would leave you?"

"I couldn't do it without you. I was no good at mothering her, but you always found it so easy and she loved you. We wouldn't have survived if you went."

"That wasn't the reason you never told me, but I always knew I wasn't her father."

He is far away from me on the other side of the room, his back pressed to the wall, looking right at me.

"I was there that night," he says. "When it . . . when he did it to you . . . I was so angry for you, and the way people talked about you after."

"You knew."

I open the door again and step outside into the blast of water.

Brothers

I loved Adair more than anyone in the world.

I fed him from my breast even though it hurt and made me bleed. I wanted this closeness for Adair and me. This life and heat that passed between us.

The nurse who had come the morning after Adair was born kept returning. She was beautiful, with eyes like cut glass. Her name was Rose and for some reason she liked me. When Adair and I were well, he was big and I was still big, she would sit on a Sunday on our porch drinking tea with me while I bounced Adair on my lap. She never asked to hold him and I hardly ever offered. She seemed to understand we were tied to each other and breaking us apart caused us great pain.

Instead she spoke to Joyce, who nattered away, her tongue loosened and sweetened in a way it never was with me.

"Did my husband ask you to be friends with me?" I asked Rose one Sunday.

"You don't trust people much, do you, Oona?"

I laughed. "No."

Once Rose told me about her family and the terrible Catholic school where the nuns beat her and cut off all her hair. She didn't cry when she spoke about these trespasses but she spat when she spoke about the nuns. I told her about Father Finnegan striking the island children, but it could never be as bad as being locked up with twenty bitter nuns. Women can be just as violent as men, and those with religion are even more resentful, because religion tells us we are evil and if we believe it we become it.

*

When I told Pat what Adair's name meant, he said it fit. He knew. He didn't try to take Adair away from me the way Joyce had been stolen. He knew Adair and I were one.

Joyce didn't understand. She was too like me, but worse, quietly demanding. Always asking to hold Adair. I knew she was afraid, afraid I'd say no. So I let her, I did, watching closely, waiting to see if he cried, but he hardly ever did. She'd peer at him like he was a wild animal I'd found in the forest, brought home and asked her to accept as human.

Every now and then I left him to sleep in the ironing basket, and sometimes I found Joyce leaning over her brother, her face torn with pain and love. The struggle in her was beautiful to watch as she hung over him, frizzy yellow curls bouncing like a mobile he would reach up to touch. It was like she was trying to link his bloody arrival with the gentle lamb now sleeping in the linen. She didn't know it wasn't his fault. He was not the terror she had felt, but the life after the wounds. He was the daylight that heals.

This time, she straightened, saw me, pinked and ran out the back door, even as I laughed and called after her, a flash of sun on green. I stepped out. We could play hide and seek in the trees, I almost called, but then Adair woke and I was torn away.

These were the happiest days, the easiest. I rose early and tied Adair to me with a long piece of cloth and went about the house doing my tasks. Later I walked to town and met up with Rose. We drank tea or coffee and she chatted about the people from her past, but I never spoke much about the island. It was finished. It had to be.

Rose became more distant from me. I'd catch her staring at me, a look of irritation on her lips, but she washed it away as soon as she caught me looking.

"What is it?" I said. "What's the matter?"

"Nothing." She exhaled a long stream of smoke towards the trees behind the house.

"You've been a wet rag for weeks. What's bothering you? What've I done?"

"Leave it, Oona."

"What?"

"I know you're a new mom, but you never ask about me. You don't care. That's what friends do. They care about each other."

"I do. I ask you all the time."

"No. You don't."

She flicked her cigarette into the rosemary bush, where it hissed. "I'm going."

"No, don't."

"I'll see you in a few weeks. I'm going for a training course in the city. I won't be back for a while."

"You never said."

She shrugged. "You never asked."

She left and the guilt dragged on for days; no, to tell the truth it was only a day. I had Adair to care for.

*

One May day, I was preparing a chicken salad I'd found the recipe for in a magazine. My Canadian cooking skills had improved over the years. Adair was asleep in the basket. He was beginning to get heavy and I put him down more and more. I was less afraid of him vanishing.

Pat came in from the shed and I brushed the sawdust out of his hair and he kissed me behind my ear and a hum started in my pelvis. I ran my hands across his chest and up, inside his shirt, and breathed in the smell of new wood.

The telephone shrilled and broke us apart.

He groaned, squeezed my hips and went into the hall.

I whistled and picked up the chicken carcass.

His voice was a mumble, a note of surprise, but I couldn't make out the words. I got the mayonnaise from the fridge, levelled a teaspoon of mustard, a splash of vinegar, oil of choice. I rooted in a cupboard for my large bowl.

"Oona," Pat called.

"What is it?"

"There's someone on the phone for you."

No one ever phoned me. "Who?"

I was in the kitchen, then I was in the hall and Pat passed me the receiver.

"Hello?"

"Oona."

I sank to the floor. "Enda? Is that you?"

"It's me." There was a tremble in his voice, but it was his voice. Deeper and softer, but still his. "How are you?" he said.

"Enda. I worried you were dead. You never wrote back to me."

"Don't cry, Oona. It's all right. I'm all right. I'm sorry; I only just got it."

"Where are you, Enda?"

"New York. Can you believe it?"

"No. What are you doing there?"

"Working. I'm in the theatre sometimes. I can do a good New York accent. One day it could be the telly," he drawled.

"That's brilliant, Enda."

"How are you, Oona?"

"I have another baby. He's called Adair. You'd love him."

"I would and I will. I've got time off, so I'm coming up to visit you."

"When?"

"Next week. Are you free?"

"Of course I'm free."

"Listen, I'm using up my cents. How do I get to you? And can I bring a friend?"

I gave him all the instructions, then passed him to Pat to give the instructions better.

Pat hung up. "He ran out of change."

I nodded. My hands still shook. I stared at them, but they kept vibrating.

Enda was alive. Enda was in New York. Enda was visiting next week.

Pat's arms wrapped around me and I sank into him.

"Did you hear us?" I laughed. "We were speaking Irish."

*

The car pulled up. A slice of red. I'd never noticed Pat's Ford was like the heart of a flame.

I stood on the porch with Adair in my arms. The sun was dipping behind the line of trees beyond the road. My heart felt like it was leaping upwards, into the sky.

The back door of the car opened and a man climbed out of the backseat. He was tall, a cap shielding his face from the shafts of evening light.

"Enda!" I stepped into the long grass and stopped.

He lifted his head. "No." A sunlight-pale face. Aislinn's lips, nose and eyes.

The trees seemed entirely still and I couldn't breathe. I knew this face better than almost anyone's.

"Felim?"

He treaded toward me, quick as a fish through water, and I stepped away and pain splintered in the back of my head; stars burst in my eyes. I'd hit the porch trellis. He hung unmoving before me and roved my body and the house behind, instead of my face. His eyes, brilliant blue, were cold.

"It's good to see you, Oona," he said and climbed onto the porch.

The breath trapped in my chest rushed out of me.

Another man jumped out, tall too but with ink-pot black hair and eyes. The branches waved a little in the breeze.

Enda ran across the grass and, laughing, enclosed Adair and me.

"Is this Adair?" He touched Adair's black fluffy head. "He's one of us for sure. Look at the dark eyes on him. A Coughlan baby if ever I saw one."

I could only smile and the smile hurt my face, it was so big. I kept looking up at him, drinking him in, storing him up.

Enda glanced over his shoulder. "But will you look who I brought?"

And I did look, at Pat shaking Felim's hand and clapping him on the shoulder, and nothing was right about it. My two worlds colliding.

Enda left my side and draped his arm over Felim's shoulders and I saw just how my brother loved him. He had forgotten Liam, or he knew somehow that Felim hadn't hurt him. I pushed my lips into a smile and held Adair tighter. "You better come in."

In the hallway Enda announced, "This place is fine, Oona."

"I painted it."

"Yellow. Bold choice. I love it. Wouldn't Mam be green if she saw it? You should send her a picture."

"No. I won't do that. We're not in touch."

I saw the opinion in his eyes saying I should forgive Mam, but he didn't say a word. That was different.

In the kitchen, I put Adair in his washing basket, pulling at strands of thoughts. How long had it been since I'd slept a full night? Six months. I tried to push the thoughts away, but even so I couldn't look at Felim.

Enda was down on his hands and knees beside the table. "And who's this?"

"Joyce," said a small voice.

My fingers gripped the sideboard. I felt Felim watching me.

"Happy to meet you." Enda stuck his hand under the table-cloth. "I'm your uncle, Enda."

"Enda?" Joyce said.

"I know. It's a woman's name in this country, but where I'm from it's a name for men . . . and women too sometimes. Depends on what comes into your parents' heads when they decide to name you."

"Daddy named me. He named me after Grandma."

"You see what I mean, Joyce?" Enda said. "You're lucky your grandma had a good name. What would you've done if she was called Kitty?"

"Kitty isn't a name."

"It is. Swear to God. It's a terrible name I heard in New York and many a little girl's stuck with it now. I'm happy to be called Enda, and what about you, Joyce?"

Pat put a hand on my shoulder, beaming.

"Are you all right?" he whispered.

"What?"

Felim was stood in the doorway, hands twisting his hat, watching my brother, his mouth moving like he wanted to speak.

"You seem tired," Pat said.

"I'll get a bed made," I said to Felim. "In the sitting room. We only have the one spare room for Enda and I forgot you were coming. I mean, you can share."

He kept his gaze on the table. Enda had vanished beneath it. "Sitting room is fine," he said.

"Good."

I put the kettle on the stove. Pat sat down, smiled at me and coaxed Joyce onto his lap. Enda crawled out grinning, his hair stuck on end, and collapsed next to a now seated Felim, who was fascinated by my tablecloth. I'd done the embroidery myself. Meadow flowers.

"Biscuits?" I grabbed the cups and filled the teapot.

"You're so like Mam," Enda said. "You love to host."

"I'm nothing like her."

Pat raised an eyebrow at my brother.

"I'll not have the two of you in cahoots against me already," I said.

Felim was hovering behind me. I hadn't seen him move. "Can I help you with anything?"

"No, no, sit yourself down."

"I'd like to help."

"Put these on the table." I handed him a plate of chocolate biscuits. He clutched it and crossed the kitchen slowly. Joyce was chattering away to Enda about school, telling him she liked geography best and that she knew the names of all the countries in the world. Like me, she was prone to exaggeration. Pat blew Joyce's hair away from his chin. She laughed.

"You've not changed a bit, Oona," Enda said. "You're watching us quietly from the corner, taking it all in like you always did."

"Leave me alone and drink your tea." I slammed the teapot down in front of them and sank into the chair next to Enda. "I've missed having someone to argue with. Pat's no skill for rowing at all."

Pat pushed at the corner of his lip. "You'll have to tell me the best way to handle a Coughlan, Enda, or Felim, you must know? You've been dealing with them the longest."

"There's no right way," Enda answered for Felim. "Whatever you do is wrong."

Enda and Pat laughed. I couldn't take my eyes off Felim. Aislinn was there in the strong lines of his jaw, the fuller lips but not the mellowing of his skin or the close cut of his hair. He was changed and yet his silence and separateness from us was the same.

"Let's go outside," I blurted. "Have our tea in the warm. No, I'll grab us all a beer? I got some yesterday."

"She's been filling the fridge since last week for you," Pat said. "If you open it, you'll be crushed by jars of pickles."

"That's enough from you," I said.

They traipsed onto the porch laden with cups, Joyce trailing them, already pulled to her uncle. In a hurry I gathered the beers and went out, sitting opposite the three men on our long bench. One was bearded, two shaven.

"It was my time to be leaving the island," Enda was saying. I passed them each a beer and cracked open my own. Since Rose had been dropping over I'd started to drink a little with her, nervous and only a sip or two at first, but it was not so strong as whiskey. One can, and I still knew who I was.

"I tried at being a priest," Enda said.

"What?" I cried, dragged back.

"Got as far as Rome and realised it wasn't for me."

"Jesus," Pat said.

"Aye, I always thought the church was where my heart lay, but I was wrong."

Felim was covering his mouth with his hands and examining the garden, the hundreds of trees, uninterested in us.

"What about you, Felim?" I said. "What went on with you and Finnegan?"

Felim didn't look back at me, but said, "When I was young he convinced me."

Enda's neck pinked slightly. "It was Finnegan who separated us. Found out somehow and planted shame, especially in me. Took me a good few years in New York to get over it, and I still don't think I have fully."

"Tell us about New York," I said.

"Oona and I were there when we first married," Pat added.

"Were you?" Enda said. "I know all of nothing about you two."

"Ah, it's not interesting," I said.

"Ten years ago," Pat chimed.

"How old is she?" Felim nodded at the garden where Joyce was running with a yellow ribbon streaming behind her.

I swigged beer and the cold of it shivered through me.

"She's just eight," Pat said smoothly, but she was already ten; we'd taken her on a picnic two weeks before to celebrate. For sure it was just a mistake. A slip of the tongue. We were both so used to telling people she was eight.

"So how did you come to be in the US?" Pat asked Felim.

"Enda wrote to me and invited me over." He blushed and an inexplicable anger rose in me. "I delivered your letter to him in person."

I went into the kitchen and lifted Adair from the basket. He sleepily blinked at me and scrunched his face to cry. I shushed him.

Enda was still talking on the porch and Joyce's laughter rose above it.

I balanced myself against the doorframe.

"Let's go to the lake tomorrow," Pat called to me. "We have a cabin there we can all stay in. I'll bring the tent as well. We can cook food on the fire."

"Sounds like a dream," Enda sighed.

*

Adair cried most of the night, and as it was warm I walked him around the garden so we wouldn't wake everyone inside.

His sobbing lodged deep in me. I couldn't stop remembering and I couldn't stop feeling afraid. I held Adair tightly and continued to pace around my house, wetting my pyjamas with dew. When he eventually wore himself out and fell asleep, I slipped into the hall. From the living room, hushed voices filtered out to me followed by a stifled laugh. I laid Adair down in his crib and crept into Joyce's room. Her hair was fanned out across the pillow.

I fell asleep with my head resting by her feet.

*

We lay on the grass with the sky stretched over us. Enda reached out and took my hand, and for a moment we floated.

"Oona?"

"Yes."

"I want to tell you something."

There were no clouds.

"You can tell me anything."

"Thanks, littlie."

The sky stretching, stretching.

"So, about Felim."

"You've forgiven him for what he did to Liam?"

He was silent and I thought he'd never answer. I sat up and watched Pat lifting bags out of the trunk. Felim began to put up the poles for the tent he was going to share with Enda. Joyce ran about fetching him pegs.

"I have forgiven Felim. I had to."

"Why did you have to?" The words rammed out of me, surprising me with their force.

"I love him."

I lay back down and we were both quiet as the clouds drifted away and new ones replaced them. Joyce poked her head into the blue above us.

"Well, hello there, other littlie," Enda said and sat up, patting the grass beside him for Joyce to sit. "I know it's a terrible thing, but we don't know he did it."

"Have you asked him?" I said.

"No, and I won't. He'd think I don't trust him."

"But you can't trust someone who would do something so terrible, Enda."

"Who are you talking about?" Joyce said.

"No one at all." Enda plucked a daisy and presented it to her.

"I'm lonely, Oona. I don't have a family." He gave me a look, like he was waiting for me to say poison, like he knew it was there in me.

"You didn't write to me or call me when you first found out where I lived, did you?" I said.

"I was ashamed."

"But, Enda, I knew about you when I was fourteen. I saw you kissing Felim."

"Jesus."

Joyce giggled and Enda blushed.

We ate sandwiches and fruit salad on tin plates. When we were done, Pat suggested a swim. Enda whooped in answer, tearing off his shorts and t-shirt and racing into the water. Joyce laughed at him. His life and vibrancy was catching. Felim and Pat strode in more slowly, ducking under and shaking off their hair. Joyce unclasped her sandals and paddled. I curled around the sleeping Adair and watched, my mouth full of words I didn't know how to say. I knew for sure Felim was not good enough for my brother and yet still uncertainty raged through me like blood.

Joyce splashed wildly, making her way through the short drift of water between them and landing with a hoot of laughter in her father's arms. Her little dress hung limp on a branch. I couldn't speak with her here. Everything was so breakable, so fragile. Silence would protect her.

I took off my shoes, fetched Adair's cloth, tied him to me and slipped into the trees. Adair cooed but I didn't coo back. Hard earth and crushed leaves slapped my feet. I sang an old song of Mam's, but my voice broke on the high notes and the low ones. I tried not to think. I tried not to.

*

The fire burned on the lake. I watched the reflection dance, my feet bouncing up and down. I was trying not to run. Adair was asleep in my arms, because he couldn't sleep unless he was held. Enda and Felim sat either side of me, Felim smoking and Enda with his head thrown back marvelling at the stars.

"Just like home," he murmured.

I reached out and squeezed his hand.

"Do you two ever think of having children?" Pat asked. He was drunk. He'd only had three beers and they had spun him into the giddiness of a teenager.

"Adoption, I mean," he said, when no one answered.

Enda laughed. "It's a bit soon for that. And it's not legal for people like us to adopt."

"That's not right," Pat said. "I'm sorry. If Oona and I both die, you can have our kids. Take one now, if you like. They're a lot of trouble."

"No. They can't."

Pat gaped at me and Enda stared at the fire. A hand flattened against my leg and I darted up and strode away. Adair began to cry. Someone was following close behind me. I spun back to face him, but it was only Pat. I began to cry, and Adair roared at me. Pat stroked my back.

"It's just the way they are, Oona," he said. "There's nothing wrong with them."

"I know that. It's not . . . well, it's not that."

"What is it then?"

"Leave me alone, Pat. Please. I'm going to check on Joyce."

I went back to the cabin but Adair's cries woke Joyce.

"What's going on?" she mumbled.

"Nothing."

She sat up. "I like Enda."

I bounced Adair and waited for her to mention Felim, but she snuggled back under the blankets. I couldn't sleep so went out again to find Felim. I needed to look at his face and see if she was in it.

The sky was turning as pale as an oyster. Enda sat on a rock, shoes half-submerged by lake water.

"Felim's left," he said.

The water was cold. Stones cut up into my feet. I took deep breaths.

"Why did he leave?" I asked.

"I don't know."

Enda watched me, and I knew he thought I was to blame. I opened my mouth to say sorry, or say something about Felim, but I never spoke. Our life was so fragile and Felim was gone.

The Forest Child

Enda left later that day and I tried to forget. Over the next weeks I stopped picking up the phone in case it was him.

I stopped touching Pat and he took a promotion in the city. It was too far to drive every day so he stayed with his mother during the week and in September Joyce went with him for the better school, which meant I only had to see their faces at the weekends. I phoned Pat and he told me Enda had rung Mrs. Lightly's and spoken to Joyce, inviting her to go and stay with him.

"No," I yelled down the phone.

"What?" Pat said.

"Find a way to get her out of it. Tell her she has to stay for school or something. Please, Pat."

There was a long silence at the other end, and then, "Okay."

He hung up.

*

It was a time for just Adair and me. He was growing, crawling, finding the beginnings of his freedom. I brought him into the woods and showed him my favourite trees. The oak with the thickest trunk. The tallest pine. The birch with the family of beetles living in the bark. And of course the on-fire red maple.

His little face turned up to the roof of leaves, and sun and shadows played on his skin like flames. He lifted his long baby fingers to grab the light. I kissed his warm cheek and we kept walking.

I tried to focus on him but I was becoming distracted. The past and the island dragged me back. When I walked in the woods, I was walking on Éag, and when I held Adair I couldn't help thinking of Joyce but I would push the thoughts away again, distract myself with having Rose and her friends over in the evenings and scrubbing the house down every day.

Deep winter came again and Adair got a cough. I drove him to the doctor in town, who told me I was being "over-anxious" and prescribed a syrup, and soon my boy was chirpy and giggly again, although the rasp in his voice didn't completely disappear. I kept him by the hearth and knitted him hats and jumpers, but often when I picked him up his fingers were icy.

It became a rattle in his chest and his coughs became harsher again. I went and got more syrup, and it worked. Next, he got really hot. I pressed cold cloths to his head and chest but he was still burning. I rang for the doctor and he wasn't there. I rang again and he told me to come in, but the snow was thick and I couldn't put the chains on the tyres. I phoned him again and he said he would stop over on his way home. I phoned Pat and he said he would be with us soon. I dragged off my jumper and t-shirt, letting myself get cold, and pressed Adair's roasting little body to my cool chest. He shook with every cough and I wanted more than anything for me to be the one who was sick. I tried not to cry. I sang to him.

When his eyes were glazed open and his skin was so cold I couldn't bear to hold him any more, I shut his eyelids and placed him back in the crib for the last time. When I looked up, searching for the angel of death in the doorway, there was only Joyce.

Pat was gone when Adair arrived and Pat was gone when he left.

Pneumonia. The word was said over and over. I didn't understand what anyone meant. I couldn't understand.

*

Pieces of my past kept appearing in the snowy garden. I hated to look out at it, and kept the curtains shut, but Pat would open them. Shawls of snow were draped on the bushes and branches.

It was Enda who first took Joyce away for a holiday.

"Felim?" I said into the phone.

"He's gone now."

It was enough. I let him take my other child, because I was not fit to be with her.

The first time I scalded my tongue with whiskey I was eight. Most little ones had tried it younger but Mam watched me like my lips remaining dry was her ticket into heaven. Dad had fallen asleep and I lifted his fist, clenched around his cup, to my open mouth and poured the lot of it in. It burned like the devil and I wanted more. It sang in my bones and I didn't know I was singing too until Mam began to spank me with the spoon.

The bottle in the garden was laid out in the snow like a gift from the forest fairies. I finished it, of course I did, and sat on the kitchen floor nursing the feel of it in my belly. But it wasn't enough to wipe away the pain and emptiness.

When the green bloomed on the trees in the spring, it was

wrong. Nature couldn't keep moving when he was gone. To stop it, I didn't move. Most days Rose came and talked to me for hours. She'd kiss my cheeks and hug me before she left but the prickles of fire she'd once sparked in me had turned to dust.

Pat drank coffee and worked and cooked dinners and got thin.

When Joyce came back from her time in New York she was always standing in a doorway, watching, eyes so big and blue like water.

Enda visited again and talked and talked to me like Rose did. Once he asked me if I'd like to go home. I laughed at him for that one. Would you? I slurred. He spoke to Pat, and after that it was hard to get a bottle; there was never any drink money lying about and I had to go back to making clothes. I gave them to Rose to sell, but when she did she kept the money, saying I'd need it for a rainy day.

I was singing an old lament when I looked up and saw Joyce, pale as a petal.

"I miss him too, you know," she whispered.

"Wait, Joyce."

But she was already running to her little room.

Pat came back later and took me upstairs. I couldn't sleep because the bed was far too soft. It was like lying in a sinking currach. The memories kept appearing. Whiskey numbed them but the morning always came. When I opened the curtains they'd all be lined up in the grass, and I remembered, so I shut them. My herbs and vegetables and flowers were all dead.

The girl mother loved her children more than the breath that kept her with them. She let them explore their world, knowing freedom helps a child to grow and become strong. The twins began to stray further and further, tottering through the fields after butterflies when their girl mother was distracted with her thoughts, staring into the distance, her sewing abandoned on her lap.

One day, the little boy was playing by the river when he heard voices calling to him. The daughter searched the banks for her brother but couldn't find him. She ran to her girl mother, shedding a stream of tears behind her. He is lost. He is lost. He is lost, she chanted over and over but her girl mother blocked her ears. When the girl mother reached the riverbank, there was no sign of her tiny son. The poisonous waters had taken his body and, without a word to her daughter, the girl mother leapt in after him, sinking into the mists of dead memories.

The Father

I wake to the rushing sound of the sea in my ears and I am a child again, ready to be scolded by my mam and pushed down onto my knees. I open my eyes and a grey light is seeping through the open door where Pat is standing. He is so beautiful.

"Is the storm finished?" I ask.

"Yes. Listen, Oona."

I sit up. "We have to go."

"The sun hasn't risen yet."

All the blankets are piled around me. He must have put them on me. I can't remember falling asleep. We were talking about our children and now my arms feel empty.

"I hope she found somewhere. Somewhere safe." I wipe the grains of sleep from my eyes.

My jumper is unravelling in my fingers. His hand is cold against my wrist, pulling me against him. I cling to his shoulders, hold him like I never did when Adair died.

"Joyce will be fine," he says.

"If we don't find her—if something's happened . . ."

He pulls away from me. "No. In spite of everything you've

done and everything you kept hidden from me, I need you. I always did."

"You're a fool to have married me."

"I knew what I was doing." He laughs and kisses me lightly on the mouth. "I'm just going out to get some air."

"I'll come with you."

"No. I just need a few minutes."

"All right."

From the door I watch him stroll along the cliffs and head towards the horizon. When he is just a smudge I run to the pier and sit waiting for Jonjoe. The sky whitens fast. It's close to sunrise. When he appears, he waves and says his boys are on the way and ready to row me over.

I run along the sharp, rocky path towards the beach. I can't see Pat. I wish I dreamed all of this so I could do it all again, make it better. But there's no way to unpick time, like stitches on a dress, because it would happen again. I will always be me and the men in my life will never be different.

"Pat," I yell.

He's just there, naked except for his briefs, on the beach below me, the beach where Aislinn and her whale died. He strides through the waves like he was born from them, and like he's returning. I scramble down the broken cliff and race along the rocks, slipping, sliding, slicing my knee open.

"Pat!"

The Empty House

I was a terrible mother. Joyce stayed out of the house, away from me. The years shaved away, nailed in by visits from Enda and us to him. In the Big Apple, we looked like a family again. He took Joyce to the museums and Pat and I would lunch with Pat's old schoolfriends and check out our competitors in the furniture and clothes businesses. Sometimes Joyce and I went to the library and she would pore over illustrated books about ancient Rome or the Aztecs and I read Westerns. Those were the times that warmed me, just the two of us sat in the comfortable, musty air in a place where you are told to be silent, so it doesn't seem strange.

We stayed in cheap but cheerful hotels, shopped for second-hand books. Enda was waiting tables, as all his acting work had dried up, but he said he didn't care and from what I could see his life looked good. He shared a small apartment with two girls who adored Joyce, taking her to the cinema and record store, but were wary and distant with me. We drove across the border again and again, and Joyce was suddenly a teenager and wore makeup and smoked. Her indifference and grasping at maturity saddened Pat.

I tried to encourage him: "She'll be back to us soon. It's just her age." Or, "It's me she's mad at, not you."

At home, I saw her less and less. I tried to care but often forgot. I searched the house for the shadows of Adair, the memories, and slept in the kitchen on the rocking chair. Sometimes I woke in strange places: at the top of the stairs, my toes caressing the abyss; in the garden, the frost on my feet jolting me awake; standing over Joyce's bed sure she was missing, only to open my eyes and find her curled up asleep.

*

I woke in my kitchen chair and sighed with relief. I leant back again, but there were scuffles above, a laugh.

I ran upstairs, paused outside Joyce's room and pressed my ear to the door. A muffled cry and I pushed the door open. Limbs and clothes were tangled on the bed. I stood a breath too long on the threshold and hurried downstairs. There was the tramp of feet and the front door opening, closing. I waited. Heavier footsteps. I waited.

Joyce stood in the middle of the kitchen, arms crossed, blue eyes sparking.

"What did you think you were doing?" It was like she was talking to a fool child.

"Joyce, I . . . Did you want that boy in your room?"

"Want him? Of course I wanted him. I invited him."

"But were you careful?"

"Don't try to get involved in my life now. You're too late. Why don't you fix your own?"

"I'm sorry for walking in," I said. "But don't speak to me like that."

"Have you spoken to Dad lately? You just eat his food and let him clean up after you but you never even talk to him."

"Joyce, I—"

"You don't care about him and you definitely never cared about me. Just stay out of my life."

She spun out the door. I should have gone after her. I should have sat with her every night and talked to her, but I was sure I'd left it too late.

I stopped going to New York. Joyce went alone, and when I asked how Enda was she just shrugged and said, The same as always. I didn't know what always meant.

*

Priests wash every mother's sinful blood from their babies, but children are still punished for their mothers' crimes.

There was a small hole at the bottom of my baby's window. I noticed it after he was gone. I imagined the ice wind cutting through it and getting beneath his blankets. I saw the snow slicing in on the wind and settling on his cold cheeks.

No sea-fairy stole away my baby. If they had, I could make a deal. I could get him back. Cold and blue-veined, a water creature, but still mine. No, he was really gone, like the dead we sent to Éag.

I hurt everywhere and yet I didn't feel like I was attached to my body at all. I felt like I was lying dead in the snow beside him, except I had to get up and pretend it wasn't my fault, that I didn't kill him.

Fire in the Dark

"I'm going to tell you a story," Rose said. "And you need to listen to me."

I escaped often to Rose's home. It was small, on the outskirts of town, full of rugs and cushions and wooden furniture she'd convinced Pat to give her. There were always people coming and going. It reminded me of the cottages on Inis, always full gossip and laughter too.

I'd dropped in to tell Rose I wasn't coming to the party her friends were holding later.

"You're coming," she said. "You need to talk to people who aren't me. I need it."

It was late afternoon and I was sat at her table, nursing a coffee. The house was unusually empty, the only sound the crackle and chatter of the radio. Rose crossed to the windowsill and switched it off.

"Listen," she said. "A boy grew up always hearing the voice of the sea calling him. One day, he followed the music of the waves. He rowed his canoe across the water and he got colder and colder inside his fur coat. It got so cold the sea began to freeze, but the boy cracked the ice and kept on rowing. He kept rowing, until he rowed into the mouth of a whale."

My legs shook. Her hands were on my shoulders, pressing me down into the chair.

"Inside the whale was the whole ocean," she said. "The boy made friends with the seals and the salmon and the clams. He was happy and played with them all day. At night, he slept on the smooth tongue of the whale and he had only good dreams there. He didn't weep for his lost family. He'd forgotten them. But all that time his father was rowing his canoe on the waves above, searching for his lost boy. The father's mittens froze to his oars but he kept rowing. Ice got in his eyes and he couldn't see but he kept searching. In the dark of blindness, he lost his belief that he would ever find his son. He's still rowing the ocean, searching."

My chair clattered behind me.

"I don't want your stories."

"It's hard"—she grabbed my face and stared at me—"but you've got to let him go. If you don't, you'll disappear. You'll never find him and you'll be blind to what you still have."

"I don't care."

"But you do. I know you do. Cry. Tear your clothes, if you have to. After, you stop. Keep living. Don't let your missing him consume you. That's the easy way. Joyce needs you and so does Pat. If you're not careful, you'll lose them."

The slap rang out across the kitchen. Rose clutched her face. She should have slapped me back, roared at me, shaken me.

"I'm sorry," I said.

"I know you are. I just wish you'd listen."

She drove fast and said nothing to me the whole way to her friends' party.

*

The party was at an abandoned house outside the town. Someone had lit a fire in the backyard. I found myself a bottle of gin in the cupboard and filled my flask.

Sparks from the fire hissed in the grass and flecked my bare arms and knees. A boy watched me with black marks like fingerprints under his eyes and a white face that stood out in the darkness.

Rose sang a beautiful, trembling melody and I followed her inside and leant in and kissed her lips. It was still. For some sweet moments, I forgot.

She shoved me away. "What's wrong with you?"

"I thought . . . I'm sorry."

"Do you only think about yourself?"

The pale boy laughed and led me outside again, dragging deeply on a rancid-smelling cigarette.

"You want some?" he said, passing it to me.

I inhaled and the smoke seared inside me. I spluttered it out, my eyes streaming.

"Have some more," he said. "It takes a while to get used to it."

"What does it do?" I asked.

"Numbs you."

I took a long pull on it again, and it uncoiled inside me, fanning out.

"Make another," I told him.

"Mom!"

For a blissful moment I thought it was my Adair, but I looked up and saw the face of Aislinn.

"Are you mad?" she said.

I stumbled up, grasping her dress, using her as a post like

Mam had used me when I was too little to be given so much responsibility. I started to cry and one lone hand gently touched my arm.

"No," I said. "I don't want you."

"Mom."

"Get away."

The sound of someone sobbing.

"Go," I yelled.

Whoever was playing guitar stopped and all conversation fell away. The image of her wavered, and for a moment I put out my arms to catch her but she was already backing away from me.

I blocked out all thoughts and I sank into the night.

The boy kissed me, cold against a naked mattress in an empty bedroom. Outside I could still hear the party shouts, someone singing. I stayed awake to soak it in, but hope is a new-hatched bird rejected by its mother, sure to die.

I buried my face in the boy's neck and breathed in his smell of smoke and old sweat, and he woke and we had sex again like strands of smoke coiling together, only to be obliterated by the cold autumn air.

Curls pressed to the boy's forehead like a picture of a cherub I once saw on a postcard in the city. Asleep he was like a child, with the gentle breathing of innocent dreams. I unpeeled his body from me, stood at the window and waited.

Pat's car sprayed pebbles on the lawn. He kept his gaze ahead when I got in, and before I shut the door he jerked the car forward. I embraced it, his hatred. I wanted him to hit me but he just drove and drove, eating up ground. I didn't need to ask who told him where to find me. It could only have been Joyce.

The sun rose high in front of us and then began to fall behind. I didn't look back. I looked for the first time in years at the older man, clefts on either side of his grinding mouth and hair cut now with silver.

I couldn't speak but with the last dregs of my willpower I wished for him to stop driving this long dark road, turn on the light and remake me with his gaze.

The sky had turned black.

My eyes were dry.

The car halted, engine silenced, and all that was left was his breathing. Neither of us moved. Frozen both in hatred for me. I slid the handle down, the door popped open and I stepped out, into the night, into the dark. And he drove away, the small beams of light vanishing.

*

I walked the roads with only the voice in my head for company.

Night stretched like a black ocean. Dust rose into my mouth and cold entered my bones. There was no moon, but I kept walking, feeling my way step by step.

The lights of a car shone out. Small at first, far off and growing, growing, into a sound. I stepped off the tarmac and the bushes scraped my legs but the car roared past, headlights waving along the fir trees. It wasn't Pat.

I walked until dawn spilled white across the black outlines of the trees.

My mind brought me back to Éag, to Felim in the dark up near the cliff in the fairy hut. He pushed me down and pushed his way inside me, pushed Joyce inside me. The choice was stolen from me.

Everything swooped in, then burst out, fluttering away, and I wept.

A grey fox stood in the middle of the highway; its silver back shone and black eyes flicked over me and on, beyond me, back into the wild.

*

Much later, Pat picked me up. He told me he'd rung Enda and I could go to the house, pick up my things and take the bus to New York.

His hand rested on the gear stick. I reached out and he retracted it.

I cleared my throat. My mouth was parched.

"How is Joyce?" I asked.

"Talk to her. She deserves the truth."

He pulled up at the house.

"She was here when I left," he said.

I dragged myself out of the car and went inside. I poured a glass of water in the kitchen. My hands shook. They were covered in dust. I scrubbed them with the nail brush. In the bathroom, I splashed my face. I packed my bag with everything. I wasn't going to New York. I didn't deserve the kindness Enda would give me.

Outside Joyce's room I paused, and heard her muffled sobs, but I didn't go to her. I was too afraid.

The mother climbed out of the river with empty arms. Her son was gone, lost in the memories of the dead.

The daughter watched her girl mother and knew that although her body was no longer in the river, her mind still waded through its mists.

The daughter watched and waited for the joy and youth of her girl mother to return. She watched as her girl mother's hair turned silver and tears dropped, pooling around the wooden throne she would no longer leave. She watched her beloved father deliver fruit and leave it as an offering at her mother's feet, where it withered, uneaten.

———————————

The Men

Pat stands in the shallows, the waves crashing in to meet him. He ducks and the white vanishes him. I'm breathless, watching from the low cliff, but his head appears again and he whoops and trudges out of the sea to his pile of clothes.

Éag hangs on the horizon, a shadow, not far away.

I wave to him and he dresses quickly, jogs up the beach and climbs up the cliff.

"Good swim?"

"I've not washed in a few days."

I sniff myself and I'm sour as vinegar, but there's no time for me to dip in the ocean.

"The men should be ready to row us now," I say.

It takes only a few moments to pack up our bags and leave Aislinn's cottage. Jonjoe is waiting on the pier.

"Is this how you get the tourists to Éag?" I ask.

He grins, dragging his hand through his faded thatch of hair. "Not many people want to go to Éag, Oona."

Soon we are out in the open water, and the shoal of Jonjoe's sons row us hard. The sky is pink and thick with cloud but the sea is only lightly ruffled.

I turn my face towards Éag and clutch Pat's hand.

They drop us on the only shore. Ahead the island rises, so much smaller than the last time I was here. Jonjoe shouts that he'll send some lads back in the afternoon to fetch us. If the weather's bad, they won't come.

"Oona?" Pat says as they row away. "I recognise that guy. He was the one giving you drink the night we were here, wasn't he? Did he hurt you?"

"No. It wasn't him." The pain in my throat is worse. I swallow it back. I will tell him. "It was Felim."

I wish I had told Enda the truth.

Enda

The stillness of the lake calmed me.

I stayed out there for three months, walking and thinking about Adair. In my dreams he played in the garden, a little boy as high as my hip, throwing a ball. I caught it and ran to give it to him. I got close and the sunlight caught in my boy's hair and turned it gold. I pulled away, horror in my mouth as the child Felim reached up to me and laughed at my fear.

I searched the island for Adair. Every field, every cottage, every beach. Over the roar of the waves came a cry, and I ran towards it, into the cave. Dead babies crawled and wriggled over each other, screams from their hollow mouths. Tiny skeletal hands clawed at my clothes. I woke tangled in the branches of a holly tree.

Sometimes I considered ending it all, but Pat would come out and talk to me about himself and Joyce. We'd sit together saying little as the long evenings stretched out before us, and some nights he stayed over, his age-softened body curved against mine, holding me in place while I slept. He had, at least partly, forgiven me for what I did. Every time I heard the car I hoped Joyce would be sat beside him, and every time he pulled onto the dirt track I saw she wasn't. She hadn't forgiven me at all.

I became good at surviving with just the camp stove. I drank endless tea, and to entertain myself went to the library in town. I sewed and knitted and Rose collected and sold the clothes I made to her colleagues, friends and patients. She joked that I had finally become the hermit witch, only she told me she would be much better suited to it as she at least could heal people. I couldn't even heal myself but she had let herself forget how I had treated her. She is good like that.

Joyce went to university and Pat asked me to come home. I waited a week, but the weather was turning again, the winds were back, the lake calling me. I drove back myself.

Pat was sat on the porch and waved with a cigarette in his hand when he saw me walking up the path.

"What're you doing outside?" I said. "You'll freeze to death out here."

"I'll survive it. There are worse things than a little cold."

"When did you start smoking?"

"Oh, about three months ago."

My back and arms were stiff from the drive. He blew grey shavings of smoke into the night. The black trees pressed in closer to the house, reaching out their bony fingers. I took a cigarette from the packet and sat beside him on the bench.

*

For the fall break, Joyce came home. I made sure I was out at Rose's when Pat drove her back to the house.

"Joyce is upstairs," he said as soon as I came into the hall. It was late evening and the place smelled like a roast dinner.

"I won't wake her."

He said nothing. Just stared at me. He knew. He knew I was afraid of her.

The door banged above.

I couldn't stop looking at her. Those eyes blazing down.

"I thought I might make cocoa," I said.

She climbed slowly down the stairs.

"All right," she said.

Her hair was tied in a rough ponytail that hardly controlled its wildness. We all sat, awkwardly sipping our hot chocolates. Pat was the first to talk, and he talked about Adair. Joyce and I listened all night. Sometimes I caught her looking at me and I couldn't tell what she was thinking.

*

We went on for five days, talking little but hiking with snacks.

Somehow she was eighteen and I'd missed it. She was taller than me, and frowned a lot and chewed her nails and watched.

Pat continued to talk to the both of us, and bridged sentences between us as we couldn't find a way to do it for ourselves. But we were moving closer with each hike. I felt it in the way we both laughed when Pat slipped and landed on his backside, scattering potato chips in a wild arc. She studied in the kitchen while Pat and I made dinner. I felt her opening, and I was too.

*

On Joyce's last morning there was a knock at the door. We were all in the kitchen, eating fresh scones. Joyce ran to get it. There was a hushed voice in the hall. I stood up as she came back.

"Enda's here." There was a strange ring to her voice, as if she wasn't really sure if what she said was true.

The heaviness that had been lifting from my bones settled back again. The last time I'd seen him was two years before. I'd gone down to New York alone and we visited the enormous public library, eaten slippery spaghetti in a restaurant with plastic table-cloths and strolled through Brooklyn arm in arm to see the Irish in their new native habitat. He was quieter than the Enda I knew before but I never questioned him, because the fear had got in me that we were strangers, as remote from each other as Éag and Inis.

I found a man in the sitting room.

"Hello, littlie," Enda said. "It's good to see you." His lilting, island tone was the only part of him left. He was grey as a beach rock, rain-pitted and worn thin. "Don't be giving me that look," he said.

"What's the matter with you?" I sat on the floor next to him and took the shrunken fingers in my hand.

"I'm a bit ill is all."

"I'll have to feed you up."

"I'd like that, littlie. I really would."

He leant back and shut his eyes. I gave him another cushion, even though he was surrounded by them, and spent the morning with him talking about the island and our parents and Kieran. At lunch he instructed me to make the best meal of our lives. Joyce sat with him while I hurried around the kitchen, trying to make food that would be easy to eat. Joyce was laughing, and then fell quiet. I hurried back to them with soft rolls and soup slopping on the floor.

Pat watched me from the hallway. I tried not to catch his eye but he beckoned me over.

"You have to convince him to go to a hospital," he whispered.

"He just needs to rest."

"I think it's AIDS, Oona."

"No," I said. "That's a lie."

Pat's eyes were wide. The tide had pulled away the rocks I perched on, clinging to the hope of Enda healing, but now there was only water to hold me. Pat's hand steadied my elbow.

"You two gossiping about me?" Enda's eyes were shut. "I won't go to the hospital, but they told me I wouldn't bother you for long."

Pat was hanging onto my shoulder. Somewhere behind us I heard Joyce start to cry.

"Oona," Enda said, "I want to see the lake again."

"We'll go when you're better."

"No. It has to be soon."

"Tomorrow," I said to Pat and he nodded.

Joyce and I sat with Enda in the front room, playing cards while he slept. She was more distracted than me. I easily won. In the morning Enda was too exhausted to leave bed so we played cards on his quilt and I sang the songs he asked for, the ones I learned at Mam's knee, and Joyce hummed along, somehow familiar with them just from hearing me sing these lullabies to Adair.

*

The lake was as smooth as a tideworn pebble. Stars pierced the blanket above.

Enda leant on Pat, his cane limp at his side, and I set up the fold-out chairs so we could look at the water. Joyce sat on the ground between Enda and me, clutching his knee.

After a while Enda said, "I'd like to just be here with my sister."

Joyce sobbed and he stroked her head. It was too painful to watch them so I walked along the shore and listened to the slap of the lake.

When I got back Pat and Joyce were gone. They had left us with blankets, a flask of coffee, a fire and ham sandwiches. It was cold out and I wrapped all the blankets around him, cocooning his fragile body. His face was all that was visible, grinning, too many teeth.

"I'm sorry it's not the ocean," I said.

He smiled. "It'll do."

In the thick of night air the water was the only sound shushing gently against the muddy shore. If we forgot, it was almost like home.

"I'm sorry too, Oona," Enda said.

"What do you have to be sorry for?"

"That night on Éag. I was afraid to talk to you about it. I never told you I loved you and that I was there for you."

"That's just how we were. We never talked about what mattered."

"Now I don't see why. I wish I'd told you about myself too."

"But I could have told you I knew about you. I could have told you many things."

"You can tell me now."

I thought about telling him but I would ruin this night and many more. I would ruin all his memories of Felim.

"You tell me things, Enda. That's more important now."

We held hands, sitting at the edge of the water with the fire at our backs, his head on my shoulder, and he rasped out his stories, full of people I didn't know, places I'd never been. When he fell silent we both remembered the same man, but we were looking through different windows, on different pasts.

It was a long time before we went inside to lie down. I took the floor and he had the bed.

"Oona," he croaked. "Help me."

I climbed into the bed with him. He was so thin I was afraid to hold him.

His tears wet my shoulder. "Will you take me for a swim?"

"It's too cold, Enda."

"You sound like Mam," he said with a smile in his voice. "Take me for a swim, Oona."

*

We stood tall, side by side on the shore. The moon sent down her milk to light the water for us.

Enda smiled at me and he was beautiful. My tears fell into the water around our feet.

We wove our fingers and walked into the lake, his light frame leaning against mine. The water was an ice clasp. Our toes slipped away from the rough bottom and the chill rocked us, cradled us.

I still gripped his arm. He grew heavier and I held him to me. The moon began to fade and I walked us out again and laid him on the shore.

The sun rose, spilling across the skeleton treeline.

"Look," I said.

But he was gone.

*

Pat found us there and took us home.

It was Pat who got in touch with his friends and arranged everything.

At the crematorium Joyce, without a glance, told me, "You didn't really know Enda."

Pat hushed her, but she was right. The Enda I had known was the boy.

We all drove his ashes down to the sea. On a beach, an hour from New York, everyone took a handful and threw it into the waves. There were whispers about how Felim was afraid to come, rumours. I knew from Joyce that these people had lost friends already. Lots of them spoke about how shining Enda was, how he was the soul of the party, how he shouldn't have been taken young. I couldn't speak; all words had gone from me.

As we were walking back to the car, I heard Joyce give a strangled cry. She had sunk to the sand and was sobbing into her fists. I approached her, opening my arms, but Pat reached her first and she clung to him.

I was too late.

The girl mother was lost, the mist surrounding her, blinding her. She knew she was searching but she had forgotten what she had lost. She floundered in the dark, stretched her arms out in front of her, feeling her way. Her ears rang with the voices of the dead, their torn and anguished cries. All around her there was sobbing. She took a step and the world fell away. She smashed against a rock, her head cut open, and blood poured into her cupped hands. Blood everywhere, bright in the dark stone landscape.

She looked up and there above her in the cloudy black sky a light was shining. It was beckoning her.

———————————

The Sea-Fairy's Son

My fist shakes with fingers tight and ready. We are stood on the edge of Éag's abandoned village, outside the only cottage with a thatch shining yellow with its newness.

Pat is just behind me.

I knock. We wait.

Silence.

I step in and it's a dark cave of nothing. The place is empty. Only a scrubbed wooden table, the brush abandoned on the floor as if the owner just popped out to get a fresh bucket of water, back any moment.

"He's not here," I say as I come out.

From the night Felim and I were born, there was no escape. The island made us. It made us love and it made us hate. But in the end the people we hated most were our mams. His because Aislinn was too free and shamed him and mine because Mary was too imprisoned and ashamed of me. But a mother can never be what her child wants, she can only try to be what her child needs, and both our mothers did that at least.

"I know where he is," I say. "But I need to see him alone."

The wind whips at us, pushing me backwards and him after me. He raises his arm as if to grab me, save me.

"Are you sure?" he shouts. The sky howls.

"I'm sure."

"I'll look for Joyce," he calls. "Meet me up there." He points to the top of the island, to the fairy huts where years ago I told him I loved him, even though I didn't, and I was still that old Oona.

"I'll meet you there," I yell.

My teeth are chattering and it's not from the cold. I'm afraid. Afraid we are too late, that the island has stolen our daughter. I thought I would know if she was gone from us, dead, but now I can't sense her. I can only sense Felim. The knot that tied us when we were babies still holds me to him. Somehow I know him better than the child we share. I know he is close to the sea.

When she was born, Joyce's hair was bright and her eyes were blue.

Her laugh, the way she slurred her words. I listened. I knew and knew and knew she was herself but still, I watched, I waited for him to appear.

I walk down to the small strip of beach and at the end he stands with his back to me, his face hidden under a cap. I meet him halfway along the shore, on the seaweed line.

"You're back." His old smile lights his face, startling as always, as if from nowhere, and I have to take a breath because he is just the same. A boy.

There's a good gap between us. He takes a step towards me and I don't step back. We're the same height still. The same age.

"Are you going to run away again?" I ask.

"There's nowhere to go here but into the sea."

"How can you live here all alone?"

"I'm better on my own. Just me and the sea and the dead."

I can't see his face, only the grey roof of his cap.

"No one can survive alone," I say. "I know. I tried it."

"You're still the same, Oona." His gaze floods into me, into all the corners I don't want to be seen or touched, not by him.

"Were you happy with him?" I ask. "Before you two visited us, were you happy?"

He is lit up again by his sudden smile. "Those years, they were the best of my life. I forgot everything from before and he did too."

"Do you know he's dead?"

"I know. Your daughter told me."

"So he didn't write to you."

"No."

Felim lowers himself to the rocks and rests his arms on his knees.

"That first time, did you know she was yours?"

"I got a fright. I thought it'd kill Enda to know. It was rough enough with him thinking I killed Liam. I never did kill him, you know. He just fell and I found him. Everyone thought I did it, even my own mother, but it was worst with Enda."

His arms shake, and when I find strength to look at his face I see he is crying. I have never seen him cry before. Not when the priest beat him, or when Aislinn was carried up from the shore.

"Do you hate me?" he asks. "For what I did to you?"

There is a pain in my throat. Stopping the words. I press it, trying to force up all that is still unsaid, the tears. In silence, we watch the waves crash in. I think of all those who were lost to the sea. Felim's dad, Aislinn, my sister, hundreds, thousands more. People vanish so quickly from us. There is no time. I begin to talk.

"It was easier to hate you when I didn't know it was you. I did know somewhere, but I hid it, because hating the man I didn't know was easier. What you did, I never could get past it. It was stuck in me. I let it stop me from being there for Joyce. I let it but why did you do it, Felim?"

He rubs his eyes with his fist. "I was so angry all the time and you were right there. I knew you'd be leaving, off to someplace where you'd forget everything, and I don't know why but I needed you to stay with me. I thought you would."

I don't know what I wanted him to say, but it wasn't those meaningless words.

"Did you decide what you were going to say to me before you saw me?" I ask.

"Yes."

"But rape has no explanation."

He watches the sea, and the tears roll down his raincoat. I still can't cry.

"Your daughter is like Enda," he says. "She's not like us."

"Did you tell her who you are?" I ask.

"She already knew. She said Enda told her."

The waves crash up, close to our feet. All that time with Enda and he had guessed. All the words I could have said to him. And he must have filled Joyce up with the stories of our past. That's why she's here, to put faces to the names she already knew, to see the island with her own eyes, and hear the shush of the sea.

"I sent her up to the cliffs," he says. "To the place."

I stand, the stones clacking under me, and I hurry up the beach towards the path that winds up to the top.

I stop. "Will you still be here, Felim? When I bring her back?"

He stands and gives me one last smile.

Joyce

It was almost a month after her birthday when she appeared while I was asleep on the porch. Sleep was difficult at night and often I collapsed in the evenings on one of Pat's handmade chairs and fell into unconsciousness, only to wake cold and alone.

Joyce's face was a blurry light against the waving trees, the vanishing dusk.

"Are you a dream, Joyce?"

"No, I'm here, Mom." She smiled that smile that dazzled, the one just like her father's when he was a boy, wild, and I was a girl caged.

After Enda died, Joyce was the only light. I waited in the dark for her to come home from university so I could soak up those brief flashes of her. I would cook for her and Pat and we would talk about the surfaces of things and once a day dive deeper and those were the flaming moments that made me think perhaps, one day, we would understand each other. She told me she liked a boy and I said I love you and trust you. She said, I know. And we were silent again.

She sat beside me on the bench. We were so close. I wanted to cry. I wanted to tell her so much of what I'd always held down, and I wanted to stay silent. I wanted everything, all at once.

"I miss him," she said, and I knew she meant Enda and Adair.

She put her head on my shoulder. "Will you tell me now?" she asked.

There was no breath in me. I was cold except for the soft warmth of her body against mine.

"Please talk to me, Mom," she whispered. She touched my shoulder and I jumped away from her. I didn't mean to, I just did, my arms and legs moving without me.

"There's nothing to tell," my mouth said.

When I turned around she was still sitting, her head bowed, and then she looked up. "Just tell me. Please."

"He's not your dad."

"What else?"

Her eyes were bright, wet.

"There's nothing else."

She opened her mouth and I could see she was full of leaping, angry thoughts. You are not my mother, was what she meant to say, what she should have said, but didn't. Instead she nodded, stood slowly, lingering, waiting for me to change, but when I didn't, she strode past me away into the night.

I didn't follow.

The daughter of the girl mother, the twinless one, grew slowly, quietly alone. She spent days in the forest, talking to the ghosts she met there who told her all about herself and her mother. They told her of another world, the upperworld where they were from, and she became entranced by it, determined to go there.

She taught herself to touch that world through sleep, entering the dreams of the living, but when she stepped into her girl mother's dreams she found them dark with the mists of the dead river, the memories of the past. She lit a star in the sky of her girl mother's dreams and hoped her mother would follow its light.

————————————

The Girl

I'm bellowing her name.

The hill is steep and the path is narrow. I reach the ridge and hurtle along it. The way behind is empty. There's no sign of Pat ahead. It is as if the island has him somewhere hidden but safe. The cliffs are high and the rocks beneath are sharpened.

I can't breathe. I'm stood above the dead bed. Limestone graves huddle together, toppling into each other like drunks. I slip down the slope and arrive in the belly of the earth. No wind or rain here.

No Joyce.

My palms press to my face. I breathe in, out.

I climb up to where the path vanishes and falls over the edge of Éag.

Before me is the flat stretching out, no walls, no rocks, nothing breaking the line between earth and sea and sky. Across the water is Inis and Mam's cottage dropped onto the rocky land.

I follow the fall of the cliff, seagulls reeling below me. The sea is black and splashed with white. I search for Inis, but find now only empty, empty ocean reaching towards the New World. What remains of the ring of fairy huts now huddles in a half-moon. The others and the land beneath them have smashed into the hungry waves. One day the whole island will be swallowed. Everything vanishes into the sea.

She sits on a lip over the waves.

I wait.

I sit on a broken wall and watch the horizon; behind her small, hunched body the blue light of day shines on. She knows everything from Enda, from Felim, probably from Pat too.

I watch her. The sun sets the water on fire. The silence is an agony more painful than any words. When she turns, her face is open like a flower, beautiful, brief and already fading. There is little time for anything and we must grab it while it lasts. My mouth is so full I can't speak. I just sit beside her. We look at the gold-white where sea meets sky. The first pale star winks at us. The silence is breakable now.

"Tell me a story," she says. "Like you used to when I was little."

"Once upon a time, a woman gave birth to a daughter."

"That's the one."

Acknowledgements

Writing a book is an incredibly strange undertaking that requires a lot of lovely humans to pretend that it's normal. More people than I can count helped me.

To the following, I owe this novel:

My agent, Hellie Ogden, for her unquenchable enthusiasm even as the book laboured on long after we wanted it to be finished. And to everyone at Janklow and Nesbit for seeing something worth reading in an early draft. I will always be grateful to you all for your faith and support.

My editor Jo Dingley for loving Oona and knowing just how to make her shine. And to the whole powerhouse team at Canongate for getting behind this book. I don't think I'll ever get over my amazement and joy that I am one of your authors.

My over-the-pond editor, Diana Tejerina Miller, for incredible insight and an eye for detail when I could no longer see what needed work.

Fay Weldon for supplying wisdom with wit when I took this story down rambling paths and for being the best mentor any young author could dream of having. And all the staff during my

Bath Spa MA in Creative Writing for teaching me how to write better, particularly the wonderful Tricia Wastvedt.

My amazing first readers who gave me encouragement and great notes, especially Chrissy Jamieson, Susie Barnes, Clare Gallagher and Anna-Marie Crowhurst.

The gang at my Manchester writing group, you all made me a much better and braver writer, especially Stephen Clarkson and Sahil Gufar who read the whole beast when it was still rough and scaly. Also to Ian Peek and Rachel Rowlands for giving me such detailed and thoughtful feedback. I couldn't have wished for better early editors.

Mum, to whom this book is dedicated, for raising me to believe I should follow my dreams, no matter what. Rosie for your friendship and unflinching faith. You make me want to be my best self. Joanna and Alexa for your belief in my odd choice of profession and continued support, Helen Hughes for the publishing and life chats, all my aunties from Ireland and Scotland, Hazel and Rhian and other friends who've been there with coffee and conversations that have nothing to do with writing. You all kept me positive. Dad for reading to me when I couldn't read to myself. And Marta for all your support over the years.

Elza, Amanda, Dave and Robert for feeding me your incredible food, putting me up in London and welcoming me into your fold.

Always my thanks to my husband, Art, for your belief in me and for always supplying good food and jokes after I've spent long days at a desk. I'm so lucky to spend my life with you.

And most especially my gratitude to Oona, who made this writing journey magical.